Farewell the Stranger

Farewell the Stranger

SALIEE O'BRIEN

William Morrow & Company, New York

*With the exception of Colonel
Auguste Chouteau, none of the
characters in this book exist or
have existed in real life.*

To my Mother and Father, with love

Farewell the Stranger

ᴄᴡᴏ Chapter One ᴄᴡᴏ

INDIAN SUMMER lay golden upon all the valley. It dusted the forest sky, shimmered on the Mississippi, brightened the whitewashed log and stone houses of the village, and filled the air with a rested kind of waiting that was almost languor. It stroked the skin, warmed the hair, and tempted the mind into dreams.

Devora Griggs followed the path along the harnessmaker's stone building in a leisurely manner, her eyes searching gently ahead as they always did when she came to the shops. When they did not find what they sought, they were neither pleased nor saddened, but remained serene and hopeful for success another day or season or even in another year.

She stepped up onto the fine plank walkway, her shopping basket swinging easily on her arm. Her brother, Amos Griggs, had his Mercantile and Fur Trading Establishment in this block, and that was why the plank walk existed at all. Last spring, Amos had got the other shop owners on this side of Main Street to chip in with him, and he'd bought some old flatboats down at the Market Street landing, and had this laid. Hence it was the best walkway in the village, just as everything Amos possessed or planned or desired or tolerated, was the best to be had.

Devora liked to think of the walk as the meeting place for all the feet that came to St. Louis in this progressive year of 1808, and she slowed, her slippers clicking faintly on the wood, and dreamed about those that had trod it this summer.

There were big, thick, purposeful workmen feet in heavy Kentucky boots that scuffed it; shiny-booted feet of gamblers strolling into the taverns; modest, scurrying slippers of women feet, trailed by children; bare, calloused black feet thumped it on daily errands; moccasined feet of lordly Osage men padded it feather-soft, followed sometimes by squaw feet; patient, moccasined feet of hunters took great, reaching strides to shops, then back to the forests; moccasined feet of merry, dark-skinned French *coureurs* and *voyageurs*, wild as Pawnees; quick-moving feet of

[9]

bragging, fighting boatmen from Pittsburgh and Redstone; moccasined, sure feet of settlers moved steadily along it toward the land.

"Evenin', Miss Devorry," a man's voice said respectfully, and Devora glanced up, nodded to the group of men lounging in front of the Eagle Tavern, and hurried past. She could hear them murmur as she went, and knew quite well what they were saying, for Amos had repeated it to Reginal, his wife, who reminded Devora of it often enough.

"Handsomest woman in St. Louis, hitched or unhitched," was what the men were saying. And their women, at home in the whitewashed cabins: "Foolish, that's what she is—a very, very foolish old maid. Why, up to couple years ago, she could've had any Brummell in the village on his knees, and I mean with his heart out and marrying words on his tongue. Now . . ."

Devora had no fancy opinion as to her looks. She knew herself to be a tall, plain-featured woman with good, broad shoulders, handsome breasts, and square hands, which she used with pleasure. She had no particular regard for her build, except that it was strong and lithe and served her well. She had no vanity about her smoke gray eyes that were both quiet and quick, or her mouth, which was wide and the color of a dark rose, or her hair, which was brown and straight and so smooth it took naturally to braids.

Right now, as she walked, the first two fingers of her left hand were skipping and sort of prancing back and forth on the handle of the basket on her other arm, and she was half-smiling because she couldn't bring herself to be gloomy about either her age, which was twenty-nine, or her position, which was spinster sister in the home of Amos Griggs, leading citizen.

She turned into Amos's shop in the middle of the block, and moved through its dimness and tobacco and spice and fur smells, toward the rear. At the far counter, old Ned Pratt was finishing a dicker over some Pittsburgh pigtail with two tall Osage men, who were the only customers.

Ned glanced toward her and called, "Be with you in a shake, Devorry. There you be, my fine braves, there's your 'baccy, and thanks for the beaver. Come again. Bring all your peltries and trade for everything in the place, furs and all!"

He watched them out, chuckles running up and down his gray little body, then trotted over to Devora. "Evenin', Devorry," he said, looking up at her. "Good to see you . . . music to the eye, you be."

She smiled. "Good evening, Ned. Isn't Amos here?"

"No, he ain't, not him. Left a spell ago. Must've went the other way, if you missed him. He was all het up over getting hisself dressed for the Beauchamp party tonight."

"I know. And now it must be closing time; I shouldn't have come."

"Fiddle on that!" Ned snorted. "Give me your basket and tell me what you hanker for."

"I'd like a bit of black pepper, please. And some of those maple sugar squares, and raisins, and . . . oh, anything else you think of the children might enjoy."

He nodded his long little head. "You bet. Just you pleasure yourself now, and I'll see what I can find 'special for them two gals of Amos's. Won't take a shake."

He trotted off.

Devora could hear some kind of commotion outside while he was moving about, putting things into her basket, but she didn't go to the door to look. Instead, she let her eyes make friends with the gloom up and down the tunnel-like shop, and idly surveyed the goods in which her brother dealt, and from which he had already made a comfortable fortune.

All across the back of the store, which opened onto the river, and extending up the north side, were stacked the furs and other products which Amos accepted as currency from Indians, hunters, trappers and settlers when they bought their necessaries from him. At one end were the packs of shaved deerskins, weighing a hundred pounds, containing a hundred skins, worth forty dollars.

"That's here in St. Louis, before I pay a dollar and a half per hundred pounds keelboat freight to New Orleans," Amos would explain during his frequent, interminable dinner table exhortations. "Then I buy my merchandise in New Orleans and freight it upstream by keel at twice that per hundred pounds. Where the profit comes in, see, is I barter my stock at selling price, not what it cost me in New Orleans, and when my customer hands me over beaver worth two dollars a pound here, it'll bring me twice that in London, or even five times as much in Canton. That way I make two profits—one on my goods, and one on my peltries. Tell you, the way to get ahead in these parts is merchandise—furs and merchandise and brains!"

And Amos would lean back in his chair and beam, then scowl at Reginal, his flighty wife, who never listened to this talk, and who seemed, indeed, to sleep through it with her pretty eyes open. Then he would glance at Devora, who listened and understood and remained awake, but wasn't absorbed, and then he would scowl deeply and finish his eating in silent dignity.

Now, smiling about Amos, Devora looked at his shelves and counters.

Intrigued by this clutter and variety, she wandered over to the south wall where the merchandise in which she was interested was kept in stacks and piles.

She took a length of blue cloth between her fingers, breathing its dye-smell, testing its quality, planning dresses for Amos's little girls. She tried pearl buttons against the blue, and felt the texture of a hank of sewing thread. She stroked ribbons, and came to the Holland lace so dear it sold by the piece. This Devora touched only with her finger tips, thinking, as she had so often done, that if ever she did marry, she would wear Holland lace on her head.

She almost took one of the blue romal Canton silk handkerchiefs for Reginal, then laid it down. Reginal preferred to select her own finery. She passed on and stood before the table supplies, enjoying the mixed smells of coffee and cheese, and began to dream of how she would fill her kitchen shelves if she had a home of her own.

I'd want white flour and sugar and spices, she thought. Chocolate, and some of those sugar confections from New Orleans. Only, if I were wife to a poor man, I'd get along with corn meal and molasses . . . and maybe tea. She smiled at her own foolishness, and reminded herself to compliment Amos on how he kept anything a lady in St. Louis might fancy to serve her guests.

Gradually she became aware that Ned was standing beside her. He had her basket filled to the brim, and was saying, "I'll just lock up by your leave, Devorry, then I'll tote your basket as far as the blacksmith shop."

"Why, thank you, Ned," she said, and went out of the door and stood to one side while he secured it for the night.

When he had finished, she started walking, his head bobbing at her shoulder, his slight frame bent, his tongue going fast on this and that, none of it worth listening to, all of it pleasant for the passing of time.

At the end of the block, quite a few people had lined up at the edge of the plankway, and were looking down Market Street toward the river. Devora stepped over to the edge and looked too, and the first thing she saw was the rough-dressed man with the pack on his back and the rifle cradled on his arm, walking through the dust with a long, easy stride.

And the first thing she did was to draw in her breath and hold it. She felt her heart go warm and throbbing, and her eyes take on a shine and joy over what they had so often sought and rarely found—once, on a day five years ago, next, two years later, and finally now—this man.

He was the tallest man she had ever seen, with broadness to suit his height. He had sun-streaked hair and sun-dark face, wide at the brow, tight at the jaw, bleak at the mouth. As he came opposite Devora, he turned his head and looked directly at her.

His eyes were luminous black, and they behaved like his mouth by just being there in his face, grave and quiet and bitter. They remained on her while he halted from his walk, and she felt herself caught into a silent waiting. Slowly, those shining, bitter eyes read her from her braided crown of hair to the fall of her skirt, then his mouth went colder, he seemed to nod his head imperceptibly, his great hand clamped his rifle, and he went striding away.

Devora held her breath until her chest hurt, then breathed deeply to ease it, still watching him. He had measured her with his eyes for some purpose known only to himself, had estimated her, and taken his findings with him to ponder and consider. A tightness crept into her throat and she thought, How foolish. I'm a woman grown, not a flighty girl to spin fancies around a man.

Yet she felt disappointed and robbed because she had found him again, and he had walked on. While she watched, he disappeared into the shop that housed the post office.

"He ain't no newcomer, that big cuss," said Ned, at her shoulder.

Inwardly she started, for until he spoke there had existed only herself and the stranger in all the world. Now she stood again in reality, Ned beside her, the villagers along the plankway, the stone and log shops behind her.

"I've seen him before," Ned said. "Had dealings with him."

"I've seen him, too."

"He's traded with us off'n on four, five years. He ain't no new settler, like them."

Ned waved his free hand. Devora looked, and only then did she realize that the villagers hadn't been watching the big man at all, but something else. It was a caravan of settlers that had just crossed over on the ferry and was toiling up the rough limestone incline from the river.

Yonder came the lead wagon, and more were still coming over the cap of the slope. This first two span of oxen moved ponderously, eyes patient, muzzles moist and shiny in the evening light. They'd been white a long time ago, back during the spring rains, but now all of hot and dusty summer clung to them, and they seemed to moan a little, pulling their load. A lean, threadbare man walked beside them, occasionally popping his whip, the sound more a friendly nudge than a command.

· The Conestoga they pulled was a long, stout, fine-made wagon with strong wheels turned by a wheelwright. Its cloth cover must have been new and white once, with the oxen, but now it was the color of the sky on

[13]

a rainy day. Two children rode on the seat in front, and when the wagon had passed, Devora could see a woman at the puckered end opening. She waved to the woman and smiled, and the woman waved back and did not smile.

On they came, a straggle of wagons, carts, dogs, and cows. All down the line, trail-worn men in faded shirts and sag-brimmed hats trod beside their beasts, whips popping tiredly. Almost the only other sound was from the tall wheels of the carts, which were wooden hewn wheels on oak axles, that turned heavily, wailed from dryness, dragged up the dust, let it slide back again. The women and children had to walk with the carts. If they had a cow tied to the tailboard, someone stayed behind her to move her along with a stick at her heels.

Ned snorted. "Eastern deadbeats!"

"Ned, now," Devora said.

"Well, it's what Amos calls them."

"Amos!"

"He's a smart man, Devorry, he's a rich man. He wants the land left for trappers and hunters, and he ain't wrong. A merchant can make hisself a living bartering for peltries, but what can he make off of field rats?"

"Ned, Ned, they're people . . . like us!"

"Beggars."

"Dreamers and doers, that's what they are, going west, moving on and on, always on. They take the frontier with them, don't you see, Ned, and set it down a little farther than the ones before them."

Ned lost his seriousness and gave in to another attack of chuckles until he began to hiccup. "I swear, Devorry, how you rattle! You're a throwback, that's what you be! Best not let Amos hear you carry on—it'd disgrace him fierce. You must take after your paw, wanting to be a sodbuster."

"Father wasn't a real farmer. He was a villager, repaired clocks, trapped, read a lot. He was a quiet man, but he liked people."

"Then where'd you get this streak in you? This hanker for life where it's wild and dangerous? Here you live in one of the best houses in a fine, regular village of fourteen hundred souls, with parties and doodads . . . how come?"

Devora laughed, and the sound was like that of a deep-toned bell. "Now, who's carrying on?" she said. "I never told you I want to live where it's wild and dangerous. Gracious! I only—"

"Look at them poor cusses," Ned put in. "Dirty and tired and no roof to put their heads under—just look at them!"

Devora smiled at Ned, and still smiling, turned her attention to the slow-moving caravan. A cow at the back of a cart bawled, and that set others to bawling along the train. Folks on the plankway laughed, and one man shouted to one of the oxmen and asked if that was a Pennsylvaney cow, and did she give down Monongahela whiskey in place of milk. The oxman grinned and waved his whip.

Two brown little boys moved away from their cart and edged toward the plankway, staring at the shops. Devora got to looking at their bare feet, and that made her think of first frost that would be here any morning now.

"Here, you lads," she called, stepping down into the dust. "Come here."

They came shyly to her, and motioning Ned closer she reached into her basket and gave each of them a double handful of fine raisins, freighted up from New Orleans. The boys stared at them, big-eyed and wonder-mouthed, and she said, "Put them in your shirts, and I'll give you more."

When they went on, they were walking backwards, clutching their raisins, grinning at her. She accepted Ned's hand and stepped onto the plankway and resumed her watching.

A Kentucky hound trotted out from under his cart. He tucked his tongue into his mouth and went along with his nose high, trailing a scent in the air, so he didn't see the St. Louis dog coming until he jumped him. There was a short, loud skirmish, and the St. Louis dog skittered back through the crowd, sidled against a shop front, and sat down. The hound trotted on, ears slapping his jaws, nose up again after that same scent.

Devora wondered what all of these—men, women, children, oxen, cows and dogs—truly hoped to find at the end of their trail. Their dreams must get richer and grander and more beautiful the farther they went.

"Crazy, they're plumb crazy," Ned grumbled. "They've left farms and blacksmith shops and steady jobs and homes, and now look at them!"

"Before you know it," Devora said, "every family will have a cabin raised, fields of corn, and a winter hole filled with straw and potatoes."

"But what about this here winter coming on, and no crops made?"

"They'll manage," Devora said, the dream she had caught from the caravan deep in her. "Tonight, at the wagon grounds, they'll unhitch and picket the oxen and cows, and there'll be a cookfire at every wagon and cart. The woman will get out pots and spoons, and they'll make a home for a night."

"Fiddlesticks!"

"After they eat, they'll sit by their fires, the children will fall asleep,

[15]

and the grownups will talk of what they've seen on the backtrail and predict what lies ahead. Someone will bring out a violin, and it will speak up, and the young folks will swing into a heel-and-toe."

"I swan, I don't know," Ned said unhappily, "what Amos'd do if he was to hear you! You feeling dauncey?"

"I've even wished it was proper to go to the wagon grounds and get acquainted."

"You're coming down with some kind of sickness," Ned said. "I ain't never heard you talk so . . . so—"

" 'Fey,' " Devora said dreamily, turning her eyes on the shop that housed the post office, "That's the word, Ned—'fey.' "

"Not even when you was a young girl," he lamented. Then he said, "T't'ss, t't'ss," and kept saying it, clacking his tongue.

When the last of the caravan had gone toward the wagon grounds, people began to move along the plankway once more, speaking together. An excited bay cantered past, and the ruddy-faced man in the saddle lifted his beaver, bowed and called, "Good evening, Miss Devora. How-do, Ned."

"Good evening, Mr. Rankin," Devora said sedately, heard Ned grunt "How-do," then commence to mumble to himself.

After the bay was gone, and the dust his hooves had stirred waist-high had settled, Devora started homeward. Before she had gained two steps, a deep-throated woman's voice called, with considerable gush, "Why, Devora Griggs! Wait for us—I want to speak to you!"

Ned groaned. Reluctantly, Devora turned and smiled at a heavy-set woman who stood framed in the doorway of a shop, her arms and even her big, pouter-pigeon bosom, supporting a cluster of parcels.

"Good evening, Mrs. Dyer," Devora said. And to the doll-faced girl who appeared from inside the shop to stand beside her mother, "Hello, Phoebe. How sweet you look."

Phoebe cast her eyes downward, and permitted color to wash up her dimpled face.

Ned grunted at the newcomers, handed Devora her basket and said, "Excuse me, Devorry . . . Nettie . . . Phoebe . . ." and went quickly across the street and down the beaten path toward home.

Nettie Dyer swung her high-set nose toward Devora and advanced upon her, announcing, "Phoebe and Horace are invited to the Beauchamp dinner tonight."

"How nice," Devorra said.

"And they're going."

"I'm sure they are."

"Are you going?"

Devora smiled. "Why no, I'm not."

Nettie clicked her tongue.

"Your Horace is a fine young man," Devora said to Phoebe. "He's very handsome, too. Amos has a high opinion of him. I'm looking forward to your wedding in June."

Phoebe blushed deeper, and appeared to be trying to bore a hole in the plankway with her pale eyes.

Nettie said, "It's going to be a fine affair."

"The wedding?"

"No, Devora, the Beauchamp dinner. Every eligible man in the village will be there."

"That's what Reginal said."

"She and Amos are going, of course."

"Oh, yes."

"Weren't you invited?"

"I sent my regrets."

"Why?"

"I'm going to look after the children."

"Your brother's got blacks in the house, ain't he?"

"Yes, but Viney gets so sleepy, and the others are careless. And you know how Amos is about his little girls. He worries unless a member of the family is with them."

"Which means you."

Devora smiled again. "Tonight it does. But don't blame Amos. He wanted me to go. He's as interested in keeping me in society as a mother is for her daughters. Anyhow, I promised the girls we'll make candy."

Nettie's eyes snapped. "Devora Griggs," she said. "I've a mind to box your ears!"

"Why, Nettie."

"Well, I have! Here you are, as fine a woman and true a Christian as the Lord can look down on in this sinful day and age . . ."

"Nettie, Nettie!"

". . . spending yourself like money, doing for others, nursing the sick, running that big house for Amos and Reginal like you was their slave!"

"I like to do the things I do, Nettie."

"I told my mister. Just last night I told him. 'I'm going to speak plain to Devora next time I clap eyes on her, no matter where I am,' I says. 'I'm going to tell her to have a life of her own.' 'Better mind your own affairs,' my mister says to me. 'I've married off four girls of my own, and got the fifth spoke for,' I says to him. 'Now I'm going to tell Devora

Griggs, since she's too blind or too stubborn to see it for herself, that Will Rankin's crazy over her, and all she's got to do is bat one eyelash, and she'll be a married woman with her own slaves to wait on her, hand and foot!' "

Stabbing a look of pity at Devora, she came to a panting halt.

Devora said, "I know you mean well, Nettie. And perhaps you're right. Only, we all have to do what we think best for ourselves." She turned definitely to Phoebe. "What are you wearing tonight?"

Nettie cut in, with her initial gush. "A fine new Empire gown, with some body to it. Too bad you won't see her in it, Devora. It's pale blue . . . wonderful with her light hair. Not brazen, not in the least. And there's the set of cameos her papa gave her last month for her seventeenth birthday, that she'll wear, and—"

"And therpent brathleth," Phoebe put in breathlessly.

Nettie scolded her daughter with a smile, and said, "She means serpent bracelets. You know how she lisps when she's excited. As for you, think over what I said, Devora. I'm old enough to be your mother, and I've lived, and seen others live, and I've had experience. There's nice things you know nothing about you're missing without a man. Now, if you'll excuse us, we've got to get along home. We've a lot to do."

"Of course, Nettie. Good evening. Have a lovely time, Phoebe dear."

"Oh, I will, Mith Griggth," Phoebe blushed. " 'Bye."

Devora watched them go, the mother taking the plankway like a river ark, her slight daughter in her wake.

When they had rounded the corner, Devora looked toward the post office. As she was about to turn away, the big, strange man came out, stopped and stood looking across Main Street at her. She felt a quick impulse to hurry to him, speak and hear his voice reply, to learn all about him and tell of herself. She remained where she was, basket on her arm, head up and slightly back, waiting. For perhaps half a minute, across distance this time, he measured her again, and then he turned away, walked to the door of a tavern, and through it.

Devora lifted her skirt in her finger tips, stepped off the plankway and crossed Market Street, careful of the dust. When she reached the other side, she walked briskly along the beaten path.

She didn't look back.

ᥱᥱ᭙ *Chapter Two* ᥱᥱ᭙

By the time she turned west on Chestnut, Devora had pushed the big stranger to the back of her mind. The only difference between today and the other two widely spaced occasions when she'd seen him on Main Street, she told herself, was that this time he had stared at her. The quickest way to end her disturbing thoughts about him was to pay close attention to what was at hand, the streets and houses around her. This she proceeded to do with complete deliberation.

The ground on which St. Louis stood was not much higher than the river banks, but floods were repelled by a bold shore of limestone bluffs. The village was built between the river and a second bank, which stood some forty feet above the level of the plain. On this bank, was a line of works erected earlier for defense against Indians, consisting of several circular towers, a stone breastwork, and a small, stockaded fort. The fort had since been used briefly by United States soldiers, but now everything was deserted except the commandant's house, where courts were held, and the stone tower, which was used as a prison. Some distance past this line was a group of Indian mounds.

The village had three streets running parallel to the river for a distance of perhaps twenty squares, with a number of other streets crossing them at right angles. There was no promenade along the river, as the shops and dwellings that faced Main Street backed up to it.

The place was laid out in squares, each of which was divided into four lots, so that every owner had space for garden, fruit trees, and flowers. Some favored citizens, like Amos, had half a square, and a few, like Colonel Auguste Chouteau, who had helped found St. Louis as a trading post, occupied an entire square.

Many of the shops and houses were log, some built cabin fashion, others in French style, of large logs, dressed on both sides, set deep into the ground. Most of them had hand-hewn shingle roofs, the shingles hung across the rafters with pegs or straps. Some houses were made of stone, and a few of log and stone combined. All were one-storied, and all were brilliantly whitewashed. A number of householders had enclosed their grounds with stone walls.

It was four blocks from Amos's Mercantile and Fur Trading Establishment to his fine stone house on Barn Street. As Devora crossed diagonally from Chestnut, she studied the high stone wall around Amos's house, and thought how like her brother it was to protect his private world thus and plant flowers and trees in it that only he and his could enjoy.

Amos had patterned his house after one of the first stone residences built in the village. He had improved upon the original until his was even bigger and grander.

It had a very long front on Barn Street, and was unusually deep. It was divided off into more and larger rooms than any other house in the village. There were the central rooms, one for sitting, the other for eating, and each end of the house was divided into smaller sections which. Amos chose to call chambers. One of these, at the rear, was used as a kitchen.

Undoubtedly Amos's most satisfying moment was when, at table, he could relate some incident in which a local resident had pointed out his house to a newcomer just arrived by keel or even by Conestoga, and referred to it as "the Griggs mansion." For years, Reginal had been as pleased as Amos over this sort of prominence, but lately when he brought up such a happening, she would draw her pretty features into a charming pout, toss her curls and complain, "I'm sure that's lovely, Amos, that's wonderful, and it's true! But I want a brick house with an upstairs! When are you going to build me my brick house with an upstairs, darling?" Amos would clear his throat, scowl, and look around his fine dining room. Then he'd look at his pink and pouting wife, smile, and say, "Soon, Reginal, soon. You'll have the first brick house in St. Louis, the first upstairs." "With a central hall, and a mahogany staircase that curves?" Reginal would demand, her eyes sparkling. "Promise, darling, promise?" Amos would glance at Devora, smile indulgently, and then he would promise, and Reginal would likely spring up from her chair, run around the table, and kiss him on the bridge of his nose.

Devora walked slowly on the pathway outside Amos's stone wall. Truthfully, she liked to watch her brother enjoy his prosperity. He was a steady man, dependable and shrewd. He loved his family, and thought always of its welfare and comfort. Because of his goodness, Devora could only love and humor him, despite a deep-rooted difference between them in their sense of values.

At the time of their father's death, Amos had become father-brother to Devora. He was twenty-six, she fourteen. Their father had left sixty dollars in hard money to Devora, whom he loved, and fifteen hundred in money and property to Amos, because he was a man, and instructed him to look after his sister as long as she remained unmarried.

They were living in Ste. Genevieve at the time, and Amos was employed in a mercantile shop. As soon as he sold the property, he quit his job and brought Devora to St. Louis, which he considered a place of opportunity.

He rented a cabin and hired a teacher for Devora so she would be able to take her place in the village as a lady in the years to come. His money he invested in mercantile stock and rental on a shop. Within three months after their arrival in St. Louis, he opened his establishment and worked in it tirelessly, day and night. He grew worn and pale but never discouraged, and finally could afford to hire Ned Pratt to help him. From that point he prospered, until today he was one of the wealthiest men in the village.

At first, Devora kept the cabin for Amos. Then, ten years ago, when he married Reginal and built the big stone house, she kept it for him and his bride, who was as enchanting and irresponsible as a beautiful child and would always be, and who suited Amos admirably, for she was his reward, his luxury, his beloved, for whom he could do great things. When the little girls were born, Devora looked after them, along with the house.

She found time, too, to help neighbors bring their children through illnesses, and knew very well how fond they were of saying what a shame it was that a natural-born mother like her had no children of her own.

She loitered now on the path, looking at the vines that squirmed over the stone wall. They were tired and dry and brown from summer. She was thinking they were not as dead as they looked, and that they were determined things.

A vine would cling to what it had. You could chop it to bits, and it wouldn't cry out or make any kind of protest, but would just cling, as best it could, to the thing it had always clung to.

Like me, Devora thought, coming to a stop, one hand on the vine. Like me.

Her hand moved to where the vine went over the top of the wall and splayed inside. It won't stay like this, she thought. It's only waiting for spring, when it will bear leaves and blossoms and fragrance and beauty.

Her trailing hand stroked the vine, and her dreaming eyes lifted beyond the wall. Amos's house being situated on the westernmost street of the village, she could see the fenced miles of common fields to the north, where each family had a grant measured in arpens on which to grow food. To the south, she could see the grazing commons, where the villagers drove their cattle every morning. Beyond was timber, soon to be touched with color by frost, then stripped to winter bareness.

She looked at the western sky. The sun had gone, but overhead it was pouring its rich dregs on a tumbled cloud bank, and the colors were running down and thickening in the valleys of the cloud mountains.

Reluctantly, she began to move along the path once more. She knew she should go into the house, because Amos and Reginal would be in a flurry to get off to the dinner party, but she loitered, pulling one finger along the wall until it came to the top of the iron gate.

Here she lingered to smell of the evening. There's no supper smoke like October smoke, she thought. Or no time like when the geese come. If only they didn't sound so lonely, if they could travel their flyways with happy sounds. Or perhaps to them their sounds are happy, and they're really having a good journey as well as an urgent one.

The moment ended. She pushed the gate open, it gave its iron growl, and she stepped through, out of the world of herself and longings that nobody knew about, into Amos's gray stone world, where, outwardly at least, she was content. She went up the stone path, onto the gallery, across it, and put her hand on the door.

It was yanked inward so abruptly she stepped back. Amos stood there, shaved and bathed and already in his gray velveteen knee breeches, his white silk stockings, and his new lawn shirt with the jabot down the front. He was a little taller than Devora, yet gave the impression of being short, perhaps because of the portliness that had come upon him since his fortieth birthday.

His dark hair was rumpled on his egg-shaped head, and when he saw Devora his brows jumped into an impatient scowl. "Really, Devora," he said. "This isn't like you, not like you at all. Where have you been?"

"Just to the shop, Amos."

"For so long?"

"I got to chatting. And to dawdling. I'm sorry."

He pulled his eyebrows farther down his nose. "Reginal is in a real pet," he said. "Come in, come in. Do something with that basket. She won't let Viney touch her—hair, dress, anything. Won't let her in the chamber, and now Viney's talking to herself in the kitchen. I had to fasten her corset, and you know she claims I squeeze her breath out of her and make it pinch. Now she won't even let me in the chamber."

Devora laughed, patted her brother's quivering cheek, and went into the sitting room. The two little girls came running across the bare, polished floor and bounced up and down beside her, grabbing at the basket and shrilling. She moved toward the dining room, the children dancing along beside her.

Amos closed the front door with a thud. "Gentle down, girls, gentle down," he said. "Devora, wait." She stopped, and he came to her pushing his fists against his hips. "Will you girls be quiet?"

They kept right on with their noises, which sounded like a tree full of excited birds. Amos deepened his voice to penetrate their twittering.

"I've been wanting to speak seriously to you for some time," he said.

"Yes?"

"Why must you go off with a basket on your arm this particular afternoon?"

"I needed to get things for these wild ones."

"Viney could have gone, should have gone."

"Viney has a misery."

"Well, Myrtle then, or Rose."

"They were helping Viney."

"I could have sent Ned over with what you needed, if you'd told me."

"Yes, Amos."

"Devora, I don't understand you. I try, but I fail. You know I don't like for my sister or my wife to walk the streets carrying a basket."

"Dear Amos."

"I wanted you to attend the Beauchamp dinner."

"Yes, Amos."

"I wanted to buy you the finest gown to be had."

"I know you did, Amos."

"But what did you do? You refused to go."

"I sent my regrets."

"Same thing, same thing. You didn't want to go."

"No."

"Why not?"

"They're so much alike, those dinners."

"You could have gone to please me."

"I've gone to so many affairs for that reason."

"What ails you, Devora? Don't you know what they'll think, what they'll say?"

"Who?"

"Everybody! They'll say we make a servant of you. They'll say we want you with us, which is true, and that we don't care if you never have a life of your own so long as we can use you, which isn't true."

"Of course it isn't. You and Reginal know that, and I know it. The others don't matter. Now, hush your fretting, Amos. It'll bring on your indigestion." She turned, walked briskly through the dining room, into the kitchen, and set her basket on the table. "Here you are, Viney," she said.

The slave woman was bent over an iron cookpot hanging in the fireplace. She was stirring with a jerky motion, and now she whacked the wooden spoon on the rim of the pot. Tenderly, she put one hand to her hip and, without really straightening, walked her bony frame to the table, laid the spoon down, and began to unpack the basket, grumbling to herself, shaking her white head over each item. The little girls remained with her, snatching, getting their hands slapped.

When Devora came back into the sitting room, Amos was standing before the stone fireplace, his hands clutched behind his back. The silver buckles at his knees were reflecting light from the candles on a nearby table.

"This is an extremely important evening," he said. "Socially speaking, and from a business standpoint. That's why I'm upset. If you won't go yourself, it seems you could be here at the crucial moment . . ."

"Amos darling, is that Devora?"

Reginal's voice wafted into the sitting room in harried sweetness. Devora knew by the sound of it that her sister-in-law had been adjusting it for the evening ahead, but at the moment Reginal's patience was ragged, and the sweetness suffered a bit.

"I'm coming," Devora called.

Amos said, hushed, "You see what I mean."

Devora laughed. "Amos, your nerves! You're so sure of yourself at the shop and around the village, even at these parties, but so jumpy when it comes to woman fiddle-faddle. Go finish dressing. Are you going to powder your hair?"

"No, by God! There I draw the line. But my cravat. Devora, you—"

"No, Amos—you. Light those extra candles in your room and use the big mirror. And whatever you do, don't come poking into Reginal's quarters—we'll need every inch of space."

She was smiling as she went to her sister-in-law.

Reginal Griggs's natural voice was high-pitched and small. Her pretty blue eyes were baby-wide under deeply auburn curls, and her pouting mouth was plumply sweet and red, and now it said, "Oh, Devora, wherever have you been? I had to do my own hair, with you gone and Viney in one of her tantrums!"

"I'm sorry," Devora said, "but feedaddle, we've time. You're already half-dressed, and your hair is perfect."

Reginal, rosy-clean, powdered and perfumed, clad only in underwear, white silk stockings, and heelless, rosetted green slippers, turned to her full-length mirror and pouted at herself. When Amos had wifed her, she had been a tiny lilac breath of a girl with a gentle whisper of dimple in each cheek. Now her cheek dimples were deep and positive, and she had added one to each elbow. Her flesh had pinkened and softened, and she was at this moment a very exasperated bit of plumpness. All of it was showing through the sheer chemise that was sheathed over her long corset, merely touching her buxom breasts, short enough to show the dimples in her knees that had come with those of the elbows.

"Oh, Devora, do you s'pose I'll *do?*" she wailed.

"You'll be the prettiest woman there," Devora said, "and Amos will be the proudest man."

"Where's my new gray silk vest?" bellowed Amos from the next room.

"Please . . . ooh . . . please!" Reginal's voice broke completely. She pattered over to the connecting door and said firmly, against the wood, "Amos!"

In there a drawer banged.

Reginal ran back to her mirror, her slippers making a small patting on the waxed floor. "My gown, Devora . . . hurry, darling . . . careful . . . my hair . . ."

Devora lifted the dress from the bed and settled it over Reginal, not disturbing a hair of the carefully careless array of curls.

The gown was sleeveless, had just a scrap of bodice above its very high waistline, and a narrow, straight skirt to the floor, as narrow as Reginal's roundness would permit, and it was made of the thinnest apple green sarcenet and crepe. So sheer it was, that when Devora had got it properly hung and tidied and adjusted and pampered, there was still Reginal to be seen through it and the chemise. There was precisely the correctly fashionable amount of her on display to cause everyone at the dinner party to look at her by stealth to see how much of the woman was visible, and then comment on how lovely the gown was.

"Not even Mrs. LaFleur will do better than this," Reginal told her reflection.

"Or Josephine Belisle," Devora said.

"That one! She won't notice anything all the blessed, complete evening except Will Rankin!"

"I saw him awhile ago. Horseback."

"She'll get him, Devora, Josephine'll get him! You know she will!"

"I hope so. If she wants him."

Reginal gasped, made a small red circle with her mouth in the attractive way she had, caught a glimpse of it in her mirror, and said, "I'll never understand you, Devora! All the years and years you've smiled away every man who ventured near you, and now—"

"Here goes my last chance?" Devora smiled teasingly.

"Well, it could be—and it isn't funny! Will Rankin's a match for any woman, a splendid match! One of our wealthiest men, too. And important."

"Oh yes, he's important."

"And at your age, darling. After all, you're only three years younger than me. What's wrong with Will, anyhow?"

Devora thought of Will Rankin's ruddy, lusty face, with the combed, scented hair roached down over his forehead. She thought of the fifty years he had lived, and of the tight mouth and the tight fingers dealing out bottom pay to hunters for their peltries. She thought about his faded, harried little wife, dead a year, and abruptly her teasing smile was gone.

Then she found herself thinking about the big, strange man who had stared her over a while ago. She recalled the strength in every line of his body and face, and dreamed of the tenderness that must surely lie within that strength, and felt her mouth soften.

Reginal's voice pressed in on her. "What's wrong with him, tell me that."

"Well, he isn't Amos, for one thing."

"Devora!"

"Amos is kind . . ."

"Such indecent talk!"

". . . and he's honest . . ."

"It's positively nasty!"

". . . and he has lovable qualities that would appeal to any woman . . ."

"Talking like you want to marry your own brother!"

". . . and I prefer to live in his home rather than that of a man I can neither love nor respect. And I wouldn't marry him even if he weren't my brother, you silly goose, because what he wants from life isn't what I want."

"I never heard such silliness! It doesn't prove there's a thing wrong with Will!"

"If there is, let Josephine be the one to find it out."

Reginal gasped and flipped her curls. "Oh! I told Amos, I told him years ago, when I was a bride! I told you you'd get left! You're too choosy, you've always been too choosy! Oh, darling, we'd be lost without you, but just the same, you could make such wonderful connections for Amos, to say nothing of what you could do for yourself! And the prestige!"

"Reginal, you're getting too excited. Your nose will turn pink."

Reginal fled to her mirror, inspected her nose minutely, then whirled around. "Oh, why do you get me all upset at such a time? My cameos, I nearly forgot my cameos! No, darling, the new, big ones—the set! Oh, I do hope to impress the Beauchamps. He can do so much for Amos when that new fur company is organized."

She gave herself a farewell pat here and there, permitted Devora to drape the new white evening mantle over her shoulders, and trotted into the sitting room. Devora followed, carrying by its long ribbon the spangled green indispensable which held her sister-in-law's handkerchief and small silver comb.

Amos was waiting at the front door, square and dark and fashionable. His velveteen coat, of a darker gray than his breeches and vest, was cut in a long, slanting line from chest to tail, and embroidered with gold lace along the front edges. His lawn cravat was folded in many pleats, massed high about his chin, and tied in a small bow in front.

He looked Reginal over critically while Devora arranged the ribbon handle of the indispensable on her arm and said, "Beautiful, beautiful. Come, come."

Reginal filled her fingers with skirt as carefully as if she intended to lift herself through the front door, and went on to the gallery, instructions about the children floating back from her. Devora followed to the top of the steps, said her good-bys, and watched them disappear into the gray dusk.

She went inside and to the kitchen, where she found Viney crouched over her fireplace spooning corn mush into two identical bowls. The little girls were arguing over the sweetening, and Devora had to settle that.

Viney came hobbling to the table, favoring her right leg, carrying a bowl in each hand, mouthing complaints. "Ole Viney good nuff wax flo's . . . but not good nuff tech curls . . . no 'deedy! Old Viney, bawn fo' her curls evah was thought 'bout . . . old Viney bresh 'em curls since day she's bo'ned . . . on'y not today . . . today ole Viney get chase out! 'Go cook, Viney,' she say, 'go cook pot-likker . . . go cook cornpone . . . do dis, do dat . . . don' put yo' ole black han's on mah haih . . . don' tech mah dress . . . go wax yo' flo's . . .'" She thumped the bowls on to the table, one in front of each little girl, making two separate thumps.

"You know you don't wax floors," Devora said. "Myrtle and Rose do that."

"Ah got to stan' right ovah 'em . . . wheah dey now, ole Viney ask you dat . . . ah tell you . . . dey in the cabin, dat wheah, lazin' 'roun' . . . ain' no 'count, dey!"

"Why Viney, your own granddaughters!"

"Take aftah dey mammy . . . bof dey mammies. Ah tol' dat Rafe boy . . . ah tol' him not be no stud-nigger, but he jus' would . . . den Mistah Amos, he go buy 'em, an' now ole Viney got mis'ry in her laig . . . an' she got Myrtle an' Rose . . . Dem younguns ain' holdin' dey spoon right, Miss Devorry, look 'em!"

Devora dealt with the spoons, then sat down at the table with the little girls, thinking how much like their mother they were. They were like Amos too, with solid shoulders and backs, but their auburn flutters of curls, eyes of glittering blue, and pouting mouths were Reginal, certainly.

They are so sweet, Devora thought. But not even for children of my own, could I take a man another woman had possessed. Then, deliberately, she challenged herself. Or could I? Am I wrong, and the others right—Nettie, Amos, Reginal, our friends—in saying I should be sensible? No. I'd be forever remembering her—poor little Mary Rankin, worn and forlorn and wistful—starved. And when he put his arms around me, and his mouth on mine, I'd—and I'd think how it might be if he were another man, one like the big stranger, and my soul would die. Oh, for pity sakes, Devora Griggs, live your own life the way you want it! Will Rankin has a dreadful way of combing his hair down and making a squirrel's tail out of it.

She got up from the table abruptly. "Hurry, you little wild flowers," she said. "How about that candy?"

"Candy! Now hit candy," wailed Viney, raising her voice in lament. "Me an' mis'ry an' candy an' not put mah ole black foot in dat room!"

"Go to your cabin, Viney," Devora said. "I'll wash the dishes. Go to bed. Put your mis'ry medicine on your leg."

After that there was no chance for thinking, not in the bedlam of melting sugar, burned fingers and tongues, and the eagerness of the little girls, that constituted the next two hours. It was considerably after their rightful bedtime before Devora had heard their prayers and left them asleep in their own room, which was next to hers.

At the sitting room mirror, she tidied her braided hair and straightened the set of her long-sleeved dark dress. She put a new candle in the peak of the candelabrum on the table near the fireplace, pulled the short-armed rocker close to it, took up her knitting, and sat down.

She was nearing the end of her winter knitting, and when she finished this pair of long white stockings for Mable, the younger of the little girls, she would be through except for one last pair for Frances, the elder.

She worked for a while, absorbed. At last she got up and poked at the fire one of the slave girls always started at nightfall this time of year, added a small log and sat down again, holding her work so the candle-light shone on it.

Darkness had brought a lively wind from the river, and by the way it whistled she knew it was a cold wind. She listened to it hurrying around the corner of the house. At the front, it was rubbing a limb of the walnut tree against the roof, making a scratching sound.

Now it was beginning to find its way down the chimney, teasing the flames. She let her knitting drop to her lap and watched. The wind would catch at the flame, and when the flame jumped for it, would be gone. Then, just as the flame settled down, the wind would pounce again, flatten it, and shake sparks out of the burning wood.

Watching the wind at the flame, Devora thought about the settlers' caravan. They'd have fires going within their wagon circle, and an outside fire on a nippy autumn night is a pleasant thing. It had always been a delight to Devora to see the wind snatch the smoke from such a fire, twist it into a silver veil, and puff it away.

When she was a little girl, she'd beg her father to make a yard fire outside their cabin, and sometimes he would. He'd roast slices of venison and bury hickory nuts to bake in the ashes. While they cooked, he'd crouch at the fire, and she would stand beside his knee, in the circle of his arm, and wish that they could remain so forever.

She thought again about the settlers. She wasn't thinking any particular thing, except that maybe they'd be in their wagons by now, wrapped in their blankets, trying to get to sleep. She didn't know that she herself was about to doze.

At first she thought the knocking was the wind thumping the house. Then she knew it was at the front door, and wondered if it were already time for Amos and Reginal to be getting home. She laid her knitting aside and glanced at the tall wooden clock, which said fifteen minutes past ten. The knocking came again, deliberate and loud and determined in the silence of night.

She took up a short candle and held it to one burning in the candela-brum. As the new flame coned into blue and yellow, she remembered that she had neglected to bolt the door after Amos closed it. Her pulses jumped in her wrists, and she took two running steps with the intention of dropping the bolt, then slowed to a walk, impatient with herself.

It's because the hour is late, and I was sleeping, and the knocking startled me, she thought.

It came again, steady and firm.

She put her hand on the latch, and swung open the door. The cold wind hit her, and snuffed out her candle.

A man stood before her, a blurred hulk against outdoor blackness. She could make out a pack he carried on his back, and the lay of his rifle along his arm.

She said, with a catch in her voice, "Step up, so I may see you."

He filled the doorway.

She backed off, holding her useless candle, and stared up into his face. He was holding his coonskin hat in his hand, and his hair was unkempt. His eyes were black and luminous and waiting.

Her breath caught, and she stared at him. She knew him. He was the big man who twice today had stopped in his tracks and measured her with those dark eyes. He was the disturbing man she'd remembered for five years, whom she'd had to push out of her mind only a few hours ago.

Now he had brought himself to her door.

⸙ *Chapter Three* ⸙

THE WIND kept curling past him, flickering the candles across the room. His voice came out of him heavily, like it wasn't his natural tone, but a part of the wind and the night.

"Devora Griggs?" he asked, pronouncing her name more deliberately than most. "De-vo-ra," in three separate syllables.

She nodded.

"Spinster?"

Warmth sprang up her neck and into her chin. The wind hit the warmth, and she shivered. Again she nodded. She wanted to tell him that Amos didn't talk trade in his home, that Amos would be perturbed to learn that he had come here.

Instead, she retreated farther into the room. She felt her hand lift, gesture him inside. He was not the kind of man, either in appearance or calling, that Amos would invite or even tolerate inside the house that sheltered his womenkind.

Yet he was inside. He had already closed the door.

The hollow at her throat was beating, beating.

Never before had she behaved in such a brainless fashion. It was stupid, the whole affair. Twice today on a public street, for all to see, this man had looked her over. Now he had come uninvited to her brother's home to ask her bluntly if she were an old maid, and she had not only told him she was, but had also admitted him into the house late at night, when she was alone.

She felt her hand motion again, felt herself walk to the fireplace and turn, still holding the dead candle. He came as far as the center of the room, where he stopped.

He was tremendously tall and broad and clean in buckskin trousers and horn-buttoned coat. Around his neck he wore a bandana neckcloth, wrapped in numerous folds. There were deerskin moccasins on his feet, the pack on his back, a small axe strapped to it, the rifle on his arm.

He was handsome in a completely homely manner. He was too big;

everything about him was too big—nose, shoulders, bones, feet. The lines in his face were much too deep for a man not beyond his midthirties. His hair was too long, and it was an ugly brown on top, weathered and sunned around his big ears and down his neck to a faded tan.

He was looking at her in his measuring way, and close up like this, she could see that it was also a hungry look, as if he were searching for qualities he yearned to see, but she couldn't tell, either from his motionless face or his black, shining eyes, whether he was finding them or not.

Imperceptibly his eyes changed, until they were studying her with fierceness, as if they could read, if they were fierce enough, what she was thinking, and what she was likely to do at any time in her life. Now she, in her turn, examined him as he was examining her, tried to find what it was that had persuaded her to endure his presence and his scrutiny.

The fire log broke, sparks sprayed out from it, the fire blazed, fell. These things she heard, sensed, even saw, in her memory. Apprehension began in her, crept up her, pumped on her blood, throbbed in her temples, but it was no part of fear.

No, she thought clearly, I'm not afraid of him.

She thought she must tell him to put down his rifle and pack, but did not. While she was thinking that, he shifted his firing piece so it lay entirely along his arm, and that hand came up to help the other one hold his hat. His hands were big, the fingers long, large, with squared ends and broad nails.

The wind whined at the corner of the house. The tree limb began to scratch the roof again. She'd have to tell Amos about it tomorrow.

Only he'll hear it tonight, when he's in bed. He'll have it cut off. In the morning, at breakfast, he'll say it's bad for the shingles. But I'm glad it's there. I need it; the sound helps me. I wouldn't want to wait here, like this, unable to talk or move or think, him looking at me, me looking at him, battling with our eyes, and not have the limb, which is a thing that is a part of home, and thus familiar.

The clock was tocking loudly and slowly. She heard a voice that might be her own, because something stirred her lips, and they tickled with a tiny outrush of air. His mouth was motionless and stern, maybe more sad than stern. Actually, the only way she could be sure it was her own voice was that she knew it wasn't his. It was a tired, small sound feeling its way through the silence, and it said, "What do you want with me?"

The clock told off fifteen seconds. She counted them. One . . . two . . . nine . . . fourteen . . . fifteen. He had heard her, for his eyes changed. She couldn't tell what had happened to them exactly, but they were different. Maybe they shone more and were darker.

His voice started deep in him and came out slowly, as if he were measuring every word. The words said, "I want you to marry me."

They fell into the quiet pool of her private self, circles of unquiet that grew into wild, round mountains of waves. Six words, six waves, six mounting torrents battering her for understanding. She couldn't move or speak or even breathe. She must wait. The waves would subside into circles, and the circles would quiet, and the pool would be still again. If only she kept waiting.

Nothing was wrong. She was here, he was there, half across the room, yet close, closer than her skin or hair or lips. The fire was behind her, and would be needing another log directly. The tree limb was stroking the roof.

She could smell the liquid tallow of the burning candles, the odor of the burning log, even the hotness of the red ashes. Her thoughts stirred, awakening lazily. This man had said what he had come here to say. He'd been on the road a long time, on his way to tell her that. If he'd been walking for days with his pack on his back, he must be tired.

She said, in a whisper, "Won't you . . . sit down?"

There was a fireplace chair opposite hers. He reached it in one long stride, lowered his pack to the floor beside it, leaned his rifle against his pack, and sat down.

She backed to her rocker and sank into it, holding the unlighted candle, both hands cupped around it. She couldn't quit staring at him. Her breathing was shallow and painful, but she scarcely noticed.

He sat with his legs spraddled, forearms resting on his legs, his hands hanging between them, holding his hat.

"My name is Jerd Warner," he said.

She inclined her head as she would have done had he been introduced to her in public.

He took one hand from his hat, reached into his coat pocket, and took out a letter.

"This was at the post office today," he said.

She waited.

He extended it to her.

"I'd be obliged if you'd read it."

She had to leave her chair and go to him for it. On her way back, she put the candle on the fireside table, and when she sat down in her rocker he had both hands on his hat again.

The letter was addressed to him in a thin, looped script. The ink was

[33]

pale, and when she moved the paper, the scent of lavender drifted up from it. Quickly she unfolded it, and there was a smaller sheet inside. The script on this was bold and heavy, written with a square stroke, the letters formed with conviction and decision.

She read the words almost at a glance, then sat staring at them before their meaning penetrated. Deliberately, she reread them.

Saint Louis

Miss Sudie Williams
Wilmington, N.C.
Dear Sister In Law,

Seeing I hardely know you this is not easy to rite. You know of my Wifes and your Sisters passing from Mister Doerflinger my nabor who rote. And that the babes are looked after by another nabor, a kind Woman. I have studied what to do, and the best is if you would come to Saint Louis and stand up with me before a Preacher and be a Mother to the motherless babes of your twin sister. It apears you are the closest to a Mother they can ever have. You would be my respected Wife like your Sister. Waiting respectfully for your pleasure and hopeing to hear from you before winter I remain

Jerd Warner.

"She wrote her answer on that outside sheet," he said now.

Devora turned to the sheet of paper, and the inner side was filled with the same spidery, pale script as that on the address. She read swiftly.

Dear Jerd.

No we are strangers, me barely seeing you when you married Sarie. I onley got there in time to stand up at your wedding, and even the way I cried saying goodbye to my twin, I was thinking if I could onley of seen you first, I would of got you for myself, twins or no twins. You were so big and wonderfull. I was married some time ago to Captain Zebediah Bennett and he is in the Army, and not home much. That is why I am sending your letter back, as he is very jelous and I would not like him to see it, and this way I know is safer than even teareing it up. Your everloveing

Sudie.

Thoughtfully, Devora refolded the letters, and took them back to him. He returned them to his pocket, and she sat down in her rocker and carefully fixed her dress skirt. The first two fingers of her left hand went prancing along a soft fold and got it arranged. By the time that was done, she had decided this was probably the most uncomfortable moment of Jerd Warner's life.

She looked at him, and he was watching her.

"It wasn't necessary to show me those," she said.

"I want everything out in the open."

"Yes. I'm like that myself."

"Are you willing to hear me out?"

She nodded.

"I've got two hundred arpens of river bottom land some days walk from here, mostly west. Bought it outen a land grant with my savings. Built strong outhouses and barn, and dug a cellar. Never felt able to buy a horse. I keep twenty dollars hard money on hand ag'in trouble. I've got corn in the ground, grub put by for winter, span of oxen and a cow. Just picked her today, she's a good milker. I've got two young babes that need a mother. I'm going to take my cow and my wife back with me, starting at sunup tomorrow."

He came to a stop, and Devora met his eyes. They were still and waiting and she thought dazedly that perhaps this was the longest speech he had ever made.

For the first time now he took his eyes from her, turned them slowly about the room, missing nothing, brought them back. "I only got a cabin," he said.

She watched the fire, then said, "Two babies."

"Twins."

She kept watching the fire. From the corner of her eye, she could see him begin to swing the hat gently in his hands.

"How old are they?"

He quit swinging his hat. She looked in time to see his fingers crush the soft coonskin brim.

He said, "Born last winter. They ain't walking yet."

His voice had set, his eyes were unwavering, and there was hurt in them. His dead wife, she thought, he isn't over that.

She got up, took the fire iron and poked the log. The wind came down after the sparks. The flame stood up taller, hotter. She turned her back to it, still holding the fire iron.

He sat staring at his hat. She wished he would swing it again.

He said, "I've got to get back to my land. Got to butcher and get my corn in." He moved another disinterested look around the room. "I raised my own cabin. With the assist of neighbors."

His gaze came back to her and waited.

"I ain't a timid man."

"No."

"I need a woman. I want a good woman for my babes."

"Yes."

"I know this is hard for you to say yes or no to right off."

"It is—a shock. Such a proposal coming out of nowhere. I feel numb, the way you do right after you cut yourself, before the bleeding starts. I can't think."

"There's some time. Not much, but some."

He began to swing his hat. She'd wished he would do that, because it was a friendly thing, and now he was doing it.

She watched the swinging hat, and thought of some of the other men she might have married. Sid Cowan, his new young beard atremble, his fine, velvet knee square in the middle of his silk handkerchief when he proposed. The young French *voyageur* turned explorer, with his long white fingers and fiery tongue; solid Chester Gaines; Roger Belton, with lots of land, and lots of slaves. She thought of Will Rankin.

Then she looked at Jerd Warner.

"We both need time," she said. "I'll bring coffee."

"Thank you kindly," he said.

She went to the kitchen. She prodded at the smoldering fireplace ashes, fed fresh wood to the roused fire, set the coffee to make.

"You're too choosy," Reginal had said, only hours ago. She'd been saying that for years about boatowners, landowners, shopkeepers, fur traders. Always Reginal said, no matter who the man, "You're too choosy."

And never knew, or so much as suspected that Devora took the measure of each suitor, compared him to the big man she had seen twice on the streets, then rejected him. The man who was waiting in the sitting room. The man she had dreamed of, but now did not know what to do about.

She set out plates and cups, cut slices of Viney's wheat flour bread, spread them with butter, laid them on Jerd's plate and added thin, curled brown chips of hog rind and squares of the candy she had made for the little girls.

What can you say when people are so set on getting you married? How can you say to your sister-in-law, See here, I want more than just a man, any man. I want more than you got when you married my brother, dear as he is.

I want more than a house and food, more than children. I'm not looking for a doctor or a shopkeeper. I'm not waiting for an opportunity to become wife to a position or a fortune. I'm not even looking for a husband, if you come right down to it, but I want the right one, and if ever I meet him I'll marry him, not alone for what women call love and what men do not call by any name, but also for the most important thing of all to any human being.

If I marry, it will be for a way of life, out of which will come contentment. I will put all my moments, all my duties, all my deeds, all my smiles and tears and pains—all these things that are the fiber of family love—together and save them for my old age, so that it will not be barren, but filled with treasure.

And no amount of book study or Indian scouting or fur trading or money or religion or fine clothes or smooth manners or educated speech can put into a man the thing I must have. For he must be a man who has in him the same want I have in myself—a yearning for me as I will yearn for him, and a hunger for a way of life, and such a determination to attain it that out of this we can grow our man and woman love, our man and wife love, and from that love seed our children and nurture them, and bring them into adulthood with the same yearnings in themselves.

When she came back into the front room, she still had done none of the thinking that had to be done. She took Jerd's hat so he could steady his plate on his knee. She held it for a moment before she laid it on top of his pack.

She sat and sipped her coffee while he ate and drank. When he finished, he handed her the plate, said, "Thank you kindly. No more, thanks," and she took the dishes to the kitchen and returned, and still she had done none of her thinking.

She sat in her chair and studied him in the same manner in which he had studied her on the street today. She searched him for what must be part of him if he was for her, and she felt a stir of excitement and hope that in the bigness of him, in the marrow of his great, strong bones, in the brain hidden in that powerful head, might exist what she sought.

But how to recognize it, how to be sure, not of the certainty, but even of the possibility? Her chest warmed from the quickening of her heart, and she questioned herself silently, If I could be sure of the possibility, would it be enough, could I decide to choose him on that basis, as he has chosen me?

"I'd like for us to talk," she said. "To become acquainted a little, and exchange opinions. To learn more of each other than we can through our eyes alone."

"I'm notional," he said. "What do we take up first?"

Suddenly she smiled at him, felt her lips curl and quiver, felt her cheeks curve and her eyes narrow. For an instant amber specks flickered in the astonishing blackness of his eyes, or maybe it was candle glow, and then they were gone, and he continued to regard her with deep soberness.

"I did sound serious," she said. "But then, I am serious."

"We both are."

"Would you mind telling me how you came to . . . choose me?"

"I seen you on that walkway. First thing caught my eye was how you stood. Free and strong."

He paused, watching her.

"Go on."

"I looked you over, your face particular. It had good in it, and it was strong. It belonged to a lady."

"I saw you looking."

"And you didn't carry on like most women do when a man gawps. You knowed I had my reasons, respectful ones."

"I sensed it, perhaps."

"Then I went to a tavern. I ain't a drinking man, but I went, and I sat at a table and read the letter I got today, and I studied. You had sure looked fine."

"Then?"

"Some men was in the tavern. I knowed them as good as I know anybody here. I told them my need for a woman. At first they guyed me, but when they knowed I meant business, they told me about a widow lady lives other end of the village."

"Mrs. Fletcher—Annabelle Fletcher?"

"That's her."

"She's a nice person."

"I went to her door. She gave me a invite in."

"Annabelle never sees a stranger."

"I told her my need. She said she understood."

"Yes."

"But I didn't ask her. Couldn't somehow bring myself to do it, then and there. She acted friendly, even notional. But I kept remembering how fine you'd stood on that walkway."

"How did you explain to Annabelle?"

"Told her the truth. That I'd seen another woman, and felt obliged to find out about her, too."

"And?"

"She was agreeable. Wants to study on whether she hankers too much for village life to leave it. We've got our understanding. If I decide ag'in her, well and good; if she decides ag'in me, well and good."

Devora gazed at him, the beat of her heart quicker. Apparently deceit was not in him, or he would not have told the bald truth to two women under such circumstances. Of course, such frankness could, conceivably, stem from stupidity, but this possibility she discarded immediately. Jerd

Warner had been intelligent enough to study her for the qualities he sought in a wife and to recognize them.

She said, now, "What did you do after you left Annabelle?"

"Made my dicker for my cow."

"Oh, yes."

"Then I went back to the tavern. One of the men I'd talked to was still there."

"Oh."

"It stuck in my craw, bringing you into tavern talk."

"You had no choice."

"Still it wasn't fitting."

"It was all right."

"I couldn't hardly ask the widow."

"Of course not."

"Well, this man at the tavern. I told him how you look, and right off he come up with your name. I asked if you was married, and he said no. He told me what a rich man your brother is, and that he'd throw such as me off'n his place."

"Amos means well."

"I figure it's up to you to say yes or no. That you ain't one to let nobody run you."

Devora looked into his eyes, and they were steady and honest. Her heartbeat remained warm and quick. He had recognized her basic integrity, which was decision and determination.

"I was drawed to you because of yourself. Widow Fletcher is a nice little woman. She's decent, and she's neat. But if a man don't try for the best, he sure won't never get it. That's why I'm here."

"I see."

"It ain't flattering, none of it, but that's how it is."

"And if my answer should be no?"

"I'll go back to Widow Fletcher."

"And if she says no, too?"

"Then I'll have to stay until I find me a fit woman. But I need bad to start home tomorrow at sunup."

They were silent together.

"I know I speak rough," he said at last. "I'd be obliged, in case you see fit— If you'd smooth my talk, I'd be obliged."

"What do you want out of life?" she asked point-blank, and held her breath, waiting for him to answer.

"That all goes with a young feller, his wildness and his wants," he said heavily. "I'm thirty-six."

[39]

"I mean as a man grown, as you are today, at this moment. For instance, do you want money and thousands of arpens of land?"

He shook his head. "Money ain't important. I've got as much land as one man can farm."

"Position then, do you want position?"

"If you mean like your brother, here in the village, no. If you mean to be respected by my neighbors and homefolks, yes."

There was exultation in her; it was rising, rising, pulsing in her throat, but still the questions came off her not quite steady lips.

"Power, do you want power?"

"What real power can a man have excepting over himself and his own actions?"

"Do you want to rule, even in a small way, as in your own home?"

"If I did, it wouldn't be a home. It'd be a slavequarters. A home is . . . well, it's everybody pulling together."

"And children, do you look forward to having them?"

"I've got babes."

"I mean . . . more children."

Dull red stained his face, and she felt an answering warmth roll up her neck and touch her hair.

"I'll make out with what the Lord sends," he said.

"Then there's church . . . do you believe in that?"

"My mammy was a Baptist, back in North Car'liney. I've got nothing ag'in churching."

Her voice was shaking. "And when you are old, Jerd, what then?"

He looked at her for a long time, and did not reply.

"What do you want for when you are old?"

"I reckon," he said, speaking more slowly than she had yet heard him speak, tasting the words as if he must never forget them, "I want my cabin, snug like it is today, with my same land and trees there, and my babes growed fine and strong, fetching their babes to me. I want a fire to warm me in winter, garden mess to eat in summer, and my same neighbors to pass the time of day with."

"And your children, what do you want for them, when you are old?"

"I want them not afraid to work and sweat and speak out for the right as they see it, fight for it, if need be."

"Kill for it?"

"If killing's needful, yes, kill for it."

"What more?"

"I want them to rule their temper, not kill unless it's terrible needful."

"Yes, yes."

"I want them—"

Running feet hit the front steps, hammered across the gallery.

Devora rushed toward the door, but before she could get there it was flung open, and Amos burst in, shouting, "Devora . . . Devora . . . where are you?" He stopped just short of crashing into her, grabbed her shoulders. "The girls—are they all right?"

Reginal came trotting in, wailing, cape flying, hands fluttering. Devora freed herself from Amos, opened her arms, and Reginal fled into them, hid her face, and whimpered.

Over her sister-in-law's curls, Devora looked at her brother and said, "Of course they're all right, Amos."

He went right on shouting in his excitement. "Sam MacKay, that new fellow lives on Church Street, he happened to come past here, and he saw a man coming in this house, walking right in the front door! Trapper or Indian, he wasn't sure which. He came on the run to tell me—took a hell of a time. The servants wouldn't let him in, and when they finally did, couldn't decide whether to disturb me or not. My God . . . and it my house . . . at this hour! Thought he might be a rabble-rouser."

"It was me," Jerd Warner said from the fireplace. "I'm regretful if it made you trouble, but I'm pleasured you're here."

Amos wheeled, faced across the room to Jerd, who had risen from his chair and was standing motionless, huge, leather-brown, that faded hair hanging to his shoulders.

Chapter Four

Amos CHARGED across the room and surged to a halt. "*You're* glad?" he thundered. "What the devil do you mean?"

"I come here for a purpose. It ain't but right I should tell you my business."

Amos scowled. "Business? Why man, I don't talk trade in my home! Didn't my sister tell you that?"

"This ain't got to do with peltries."

"What, then?"

"It's got to do with your sister."

"My—" Amos wheeled his glare on Devora. He set himself solidly, legs well apart, and pushed his chin out. "Devora, be so good as to come here," he said.

She disengaged herself from Reginal and moved to his side.

"Did he molest you?" Amos demanded.

Devora's lips began to twitch, ever so slightly. She saw Amos noticing that, and tried to control it. She knew he hated that twitching private laugh of her mouh; it infuriated him, because it always meant he'd made a fool of himself in her eyes.

"I'm all right, Amos," she said. "I want you and Reginal to meet my guest. Mr. and Mr. Griggs, this is Mr. Jerd Warner."

Jerd started to extend his hand, then let it fall. "Howdy," he said. Amos scowled.

"Devora . . . oh, Devora!" Reginal gasped, and ran to Amos. "What a bold, brazen way to behave!"

Jerd said, his quiet voice dominating the room more than Amos's shouts had, "I reckon I'll speak for myself from now on out, Miss Devora."

Reginal wailed, "Oh . . . oh!" and edged toward the couch.

Jerd continued, "Mr. Griggs, I come here to ask your sister to marry me."

Reginal gave a tiny scream and collapsed full length on the couch, one white arm hanging. Amos glanced at her in absent-minded concern, then pushed his fists against his hips and stared at Jerd. Outrage reddened him, sparkled in his eyes, and compressed his lips.

Devora got a small china bowl off a table, went to the couch, and held it under her sister-in-law's nose. Reginal began to breathe hard, and opened her eyes. She sat up and looked Jerd over, rosy lips parted, blue eyes wide.

"She ain't give me my answer yet," Jerd said.

Amos turned, took a step to the fireplace, threw one arm up on the mantel, and looked at Jerd in absolute disbelief.

They all waited in the unfriendly silence, Reginal on the couch, Amos at the fireplace, Jerd in front of his chair, his pack to one side. Devora had returned the bowl to the table, and now she stood beside the pack too, with it between them. Reginal kept readjusting herself with slow, trembling breaths, never taking her eyes off Jerd.

"If it suits everybody's pleasure," Amos said finally, pushing himself away from the mantel, "I'm ready to hear your apology, Warner—for invading my home, throwing my wife into a swoon, and making outrageous statements concerning my sister. If you'll apologize properly, I'll dismiss the entire matter. Otherwise—"

"I'm real sorry about your missus. But if Miss Devora feels the need of me apologizing, that's for her to say."

"I want no such thing," Devora said.

"Well, I do, by God! And I intend—"

"I aim to tell you how it was."

"Well—talk. Go on."

"I come to St. Louis this trip to marry me a woman. If I could find one that was good enough."

Amos's jaws tightened and made plump little bunches of muscle at the hinges.

"I've purely got to have a woman help me raise my two babes. Being a man with a lack of proper time for sparking, I come straight to your sister, soon as I picked her."

Amos turned to the mantel again, breathing heavily, one hand raking through his hair. He gave his thigh a hard slap of finality.

"My great God," he moaned. "You'd think he came here to buy a cow!"

"He's already bought his cow," Devora said.

"Be quiet!" Amos shouted.

A trembling, "Oh . . . !" came from Reginal.

"Stop that!" Amos ordered.

She gasped, but she stopped.

Amos turned to Jerd. "Go on. Finish."

[43]

"I'm done."

"I want to know what you said to my sister."

"I figure that's her affair. She can study on it and tell you, if she wants."

"My sister is a woman, a lady. Ladies do not clutter their minds with thoughts and business matters and decisions. Their men do it for them."

"Amos," Devora said quietly, "he did me honor."

Amos stared at her, dumbfounded. Then he let out his breath and spoke to Jerd with savage, held-in patience. "I suppose, by your own lights, you meant well. You did ask my sister to bear your name. But let me point out certain facts to you so you won't make the same mistake with your next . . . er . . . candidate. Don't you realize that our civilization makes certain demands of a man when he asks for the hand of a woman in marriage?"

"I ain't asking civilization. I'm asking your sister."

"A proper courtship, time or no time, that's one requisite. A sense of fitness, with the man taking stock of himself as an individual, and as a provider."

"Your sister sees what I am. As for the other, I ain't a beggar."

"A consideration of whether, as in this case, you would be elevating a woman's station in life, or pulling her down to your own level."

A ripple of movement that was no more than a tightening of muscles all over his body fixed Devora's attention on Jerd. She put up her hand against the flutter in her throat and stared at him. Never before had she seen pure rage. His fists were tight; his mouth was clamped shut. His face was expressionless, but violence roiled in his eyes.

"Jerd," she said, softly, "Jerd."

Gradually, his long, hardened muscles relaxed; his fists became hands. His eyes quieted.

"Tell him, Devora," Amos said. "Tell him your answer is no."

"I'll tell you no such thing, Jerd Warner," she said. "Because I don't know yet."

Now she saw the amber in his eyes, saw it for sure, and the slight upward swag at the end of his mouth, which, under different circumstances, might have sprung into a smile, and she thought if ever he did smile, it would remake his face, lighten it, youthen it, take away that heavy homeliness.

"I ain't meaning to be no ways undecent," Jerd said.

He spoke wearily, with no trace of the wrath which had so recently taken him, as if he had fought the battle and determined its issue somewhere in the depths of his great body.

Reginal, who had been gasping aloud, now flew off the couch crying out, "Devora, how can you do this to us, how can you?" She flounced to a stop beside Devora, her shocked eyes on Jerd, her bosom swelling and falling.

For the first time, Jerd seemed to be aware of the low cut of her gown. His eyes lingered in disinterested appraisal, then swung to Amos.

Amos said, his voice shaking with impatience, "I've taken care of my sister for a good many years. I've seen to her education. She's had plenty of opportunities to marry that I would have sanctioned, but this is not one of them. I shall be blunt enough to ask you to leave my house."

Silently, Jerd picked up his hat and rifle, reached for his pack, slid the strap over his shoulder, and went to the door, where he turned to Devora, who had followed. She faced him, and their eyes held while she took the look he gave her, all of it, and then she smiled.

Our eyes can talk and understand, she thought.

"Likely you'd best study this over," he said.

She was still smiling, and she said softly to him, "There are some things a woman can't think her way through. Maybe you'd say she has to feel her way through them. And when she feels the rightness of what she is considering, then she knows and has no need for thinking."

"And if she don't feel the rightness?"

"Then she feels wrongness, or uncertainty, which is the same thing."

He said, "I aim to make a fire yonder for the night." He tipped his head, and his faded hair touched his shoulder. "Where the trail hits off towards the woods. Along about daylight, I'll be ready to move."

She looked full up into his eyes, earnestness making her mouth loose and soft and wide, and let her own eyes show her inmost warmth for him. And when he had seen, and she knew that he had, and that it was her promise of a promise, she said, "About daylight, I'll know for sure."

He opened the door. The wind hit them. He went into the wild blackness, and she stood in the doorway, the wind pressing her skirts against her, flying them behind her into the house, until she heard the sound of the closing gate. Then she shut the door and bolted it.

Amos advanced on her with a brutality she'd never known he possessed. "Why don't you go with him right now?" he shouted. "Roll up in his blanket with him on the trail!"

"Merciful Heaven, will the horror of this night never end?" Reginal cried, beseeching the ceiling.

"Don't talk that way, Amos," Devora said. "It will be just another thing between us."

"You crawled all over him at the door!"

[45]

"That's a lie."

"Why did you let him in? Why didn't you have him thrown out? Why didn't you call for help?"

"Because I wanted him to stay."

"Why? Tell me that—why?"

"I wanted to know what brought him here."

"Well, now you know."

"Now I know."

She smiled.

He stared at her. "You've lost your mind," he half-whispered. "My own sister—you've lost your reason—that's it, that's the only thing it could be!"

"Why?"

"Your attitude!"

"I'm as sane as you are, and you know it."

"The way you behaved—like he was your equal!"

"Isn't he?"

"The way you looked at him!"

"I find him attractive."

"God!"

"Well."

"If you're considering, even for a moment, the fellow's proposal—"

"You want me to be married."

"Only if you better yourself."

"Well."

"Good God, Devora, if you marry, when you marry, it must be a suitable match!"

"Yes."

"It must be a man of . . . of position, not this field rat!"

"Jerd Warner is no field rat; he's a settler."

"What's the difference?"

"Amos, Amos."

"Do you know what it would mean, married to him? Tell me, do you know?"

"Not exactly."

"I can tell you! Instead of a house like this—" He paused, lifted one arm and moved it in a slow, sweeping gesture that included every silver candlestick and every polished table. "Instead of a mansion like this—"

"A cabin."

"On a godforsaken prairie."

"On our own land, Amos, with our own trees and our own grapevines growing."

"With you behind a plow—a wooden plow, mind you—your skin like cowhide, hands red and rough and big—"

Devora lifted her hands and looked at them, turning them, a soberness on her mouth.

"You'll be like those women you see sidle into my shop on the rare occasions when they can get to the village at all—timid and out of place. Thin and scarred and tired, old before their time, old enough to be their own grandmothers, their wits dulled from work, work, nothing but work —woman's work, man's work, oxen work! Devora, I've prepared you for better, for the life I give Reginal, and you can live it here with us and welcome, or with a man of your own station, whichever you choose!"

"Thank you, Amos."

"Devora," Reginal said, "come to your senses. If you traipse off goodness knows where with that man, you'll never have decent clothes—"

"You won't have a darkey, you can depend on that," Amos said. "You'll slave for yourself and for him, too."

"You'll never be invited to a party."

"I suppose," Amos said, "it has not occurred to you, Devora, that when you admitted your woodsman to our home, you tore us away from a very important social event?"

"I'm sorry, Amos. Truly. Why don't you and Reginal go back to your party?"

"Where is your sense of propriety?" Amos shouted. "Picture the circumstances, the surroundings! Fine food, imported china, heavy linens, costly silver, cultured people, the best in the village if you please, in the Territory itself, and a common man, a good man but a laborer, comes bursting in—"

"Surely not into the very room?" Devora murmured.

"My embarrassment would not have been greater if he had. At any rate, they all know I was called away by an emergency. I left in haste, it is true, but in dignity. None of them knows the nature of the emergency. Now you would have me go back and explain it was only my sister, that we believed a man had broken into our house, and I rushed home to save my sister, but it proved to be her suitor, a backwoodsman, a—"

"Hush that name-calling, Amos."

"Hold your tongue!" he roared. "I've pampered you since you were born! My big mistake was having you educated! I should have let your studies drop when Father died. The little he taught you was plenty— by God, for you it was too much! Learning has gone to your head! I

[47]

should have known a woman's head couldn't hold it, couldn't manage it! Oh hell, go to your chamber, go to bed."

"It's not that simple."

"I've had my say. You'll not defy me."

"And if I do?"

He stared at her, speechless.

She sat down, picked up her knitting, and began to work.

He glowered into the dying fire.

Reginal sank miserably on to the couch, making damp sounds through her nose. "I can't believe it," she whimpered. "I simply just cannot believe it."

Devora said, busy with knitting, "This makes seven pair. You'll have only one more pair to make, if I leave."

"I simply will not accept it. It just can't be true. Why Devora, what would we do without you? What would the girls do? Think of them at least, Devora. Why, it's preposterous!"

"And you've tried so hard to marry me off." Devora was talking now with that little quiver to her mouth. "All the women I know have tried. Desperately."

"But not to this . . . this terrible . . . man-animal!"

Amos gave his thigh a terrific slap. "Shut up!" he yelled.

Reginal jumped up from the couch, assumed her best pout, and flounced out of the room.

Amos sat down on the couch.

"You're old enough to know what you want."

"Thank you."

"You've always been stubborn."

"I suppose."

"It seems you really intend to go tramping off into the woods."

"I'm considering it."

"With this plow-pusher, a pack on your back."

"Yes, I'd take a pack."

He dropped his head into his hands. Her eyes touched him with longing, and almost she went to him, but resisted the impulse and continued to knit.

"It isn't that I don't respect you, Amos," she said. "It's just that this is a thing I must decide my way, not yours."

When he looked up again he said, "You know you can never come back here."

"I know."

[48]

"If you go, after Reginal and I have lived this down—if we ever do—have the decency, Devora, never to come out of your woods again."

She kept knitting.

"I don't want you seen on the streets of this village."

"I know."

"I've supported you for fifteen years."

"Yes."

"It appears to me you've lived up any amount Father might have hoped I'd give you of my share."

"Father gave me what he wanted me to have."

"I've held it for you intact."

"Yes."

"I can give it to you now. In hard money."

"I can send for it if I want it."

"You'll want it."

"That's to be seen."

For a long time they sat, Devora knitting, Amos with his elbows on his knees, hands clasped, staring at his thumbs, working them aimlessly. At last he got up, banked the embers in the fireplace in a neat hump, and moved toward his chamber.

"Amos."

He stopped.

"If I go . . . I'd always planned, if I married, for you to be there."

He didn't answer.

He didn't say good-by.

He walked out of the room.

She finished the stockings, smoothed and rolled them, put them into her knitting basket. This she set on a table, and went on to the front gallery.

The air was so crisp it stung her nostrils and hurt her lips as she stood gazing out over the neighborhood. There was no candle gleam from any other house. They all stood black against the night, quieter than the night.

She moved to the end of the gallery and looked to the north and west, beyond the houses, across the common fields, her eyes sweeping the blackness in which lay the beginning of the timber. The trail ran to it, a double line of wheel ruts deep with mud when it rained, piled over with feathery dust in dry times. She traced through the darkness to where she thought the trail wiggled into the timber, but there was no winking point of campfire anywhere.

She stood holding to the gallery post until the wind stiffened her, then went inside, closed the door noiselessly, and bolted it. She darkened the sitting room, saving one candle to light her way. She could hear Amos and Reginal talking in their room, but when she pulled to the door of her own bedchamber at the far end of the house, she was enclosed in silence.

She lighted the ready-laid fire, put a shawl around her shoulders, snuffed the candle, and pulled her small rocker to the window. She sat, not rocking, with just the fireglow. The new flames nibbled and snapped at the kindling, crept upon the wood, gnawed, popped, flared, steadied.

It was very odd to be sitting here, preparing to think about whether she would marry the big, strange man who was somewhere in the darkness awaiting her decision. It didn't seem that any of this had really happened, that she had promised to consider marrying a man she had seen twice, dreamed of for five years, but never met until tonight.

She rocked gently. The firelight threw her shadow on the wall, and she watched it, not thinking or feeling, just rocking, her hands, palms up, lying in her lap. If she was doing anything at all, she was remembering her father, remembering with her heart, how lovely he had made her motherless childhood.

And then he went to sleep one night and did not wake up next morning, and her childhood was gone.

When, in her choking grief, Amos held her and tried to help, she slid her arms around his neck and whispered against his cheek, "I'll never leave you, never, never."

He hugged her and gave the half-laugh he used when he was embarrassed. "Not for a long time," he said, "for you're only a little girl. But someday, a fine young man will come along and steal you from me."

She shook her head. "I won't get married. Because there is no one who could possibly do. He wouldn't be Father, or you."

ᕫᴥᕷ *Chapter Five* ᕫᴥᕷ

TONIGHT, fifteen years later, Devora sat rocking before her bedroom fire in Amos's fine house, her hands, palms up, lying in her lap. She recalled her girlhood words to her brother, and now she smiled gently at them, sighed a little over her father, and grew thoughtful.

She leaned forward in her chair and looked through the window into black night. When the light at its bottom first sparked, she thought perhaps it was in a distant cabin, then rested her forehead against the pane and carefully measured the dark distance. The light was where the trail took to the woods.

It was his fire.

He was waiting, too.

She watched the spark grow to flame. If he had not come, there would be darkness on the slope tonight, with just the lonesome wind in it. She sat, the night pressed against the window, and suddenly and frantically was afraid. Somehow that flame tied her to the future, and only if it kept burning would she be able to find the way.

She could only wait, frightened.

She waited.

Her own fire made small sounds. A piece of wood broke and cast off its sparks, and she waited. The wind whined along the eaves, and the walnut limb scraped the roof, and she waited. Shadows marched out of the dark places and defeated the splashes of firelight on the walls, and she breathed very carefully.

His fire began to go. Devora lifted her hand to pull her shawl closer, but pushed it open, for she felt the flame come into herself, strengthen and glow, and knew it would never go out, and then, with its warmth in her, the feeling she had awaited stirred, unfolded, and was clear.

Now she knew.

She was a very fortunate woman. It was a very wonderful thing to have waited years for this man who had goodness and earthy ruggedness and honesty in him, this man who saw no breach of manners in walking

[51]

for days to where there were women and asking one of them to come and mother his children.

Her hands had been holding each other. Now her right forefinger touched the ring finger of her left hand.

I'd be pleased if he gave me a wedding ring, she thought, though I don't expect it, for he's not a wealthy man. Also, he is a man who thinks marriage is between two people, and a ring is unimportant, and so it is. But if he gives me one, I'll be happy. I'd like to glance down at it as I work and know what it represents. But then. And I don't care too much about wedding finery . . . even the Holland lace. I really don't. What good would it do me afterward? Well, there's my white shawl. That's plenty, my gracious. He certainly never would want a big wedding and a crowd and a lot of show. He'll like the white shawl. He'll think it's plenty of dressing up, and it really is.

She sat, not rocking, eyes dreaming, and lived through the dawn time of her wedding. She walked the glad miles home beside her husband, heard their voices friendly in talk and laughter and becoming acquainted, and when they got to their cabin, she hung all their clothes on wall pegs, hers beside his. And at night she set their shoes side by side under the bed.

Her mouth curved at the indecency Reginal would find in such thinking; it softened at how Jerd's arms would feel holding her.

Later, from the silence, she knew the wind had died.

Dawn was near.

She poked her fire, lighted a sperm lamp, and set about making ready. She spread two woolen blankets, one inside the other, on her bed, and in the center of them laid a careful selection of her father's books, consisting of the *Bible, Pilgrim's Progress, Poor Richard's Almanac, Robinson Crusoe*, a volume of *Shakespeare*, and the first books from which her father had taught her to read, and which she would use for teaching Jerd's children.

Next she packed her new green dress, her new slippers, all her other dresses, stockings, underthings, and nightwear. She added an assortment of fine handkerchiefs, and on top of everything she put her toilet articles, sewing equipment and writing materials, then folded the corners of the blanket in and tied them.

The gray dress she was wearing would do for the trip and must, therefore, serve for the wedding as well, for they would be leaving immediately, and she could not outrage Amos by returning here to change. She put on her stoutest pair of slippers and thrust those she had been wearing into her bundle. Then she took down her hair and combed it and wound it in braids around her head, slipped into her pelisse and knotted a dark shawl over its shoulders for extra warmth.

Last, she took up her white shawl and held it in her hands. She had made it herself, of the softest, thinnest wool, knit sheer in a pattern of open lace, and when she put it over her head and arranged the folds, it truly made her into a bride with rich, shining eyes and a young and happy mouth.

She had never worn it before, thinking it too youthful, and she would wear it only now, then put it away and keep it always. A daughter often wears a garment from her mother's wedding, and perhaps in the future, on a day that would be more lighthearted than today, her own daughter would make use of the bridal shawl.

Smiling, Devora lighted a candle, put out the lamp, and tiptoed from her room. She left her pack at the front door, the candle on a table, and went into the chamber where the little girls were sleeping. Softly she made her way to the bed, drew the covers up a little, and let her fingers kiss their cheeks. Frances stirred and whimpered, and Devora held her close as she had done so many times . . . lowered her and tucked up the covers again.

When she came back into the sitting room, the candle flame looked blurred, and she blinked her eyes until it cleared, and went briskly into the kitchen, where she set about making up a packet of food.

She was just finishing when Amos said, from the doorway, "So you're going."

She turned, and in the candlelight he looked crumpled and dear in his long night robe, hands at his sides. His face was weary and quiet.

"Yes, Amos," she said, "yes, Brother."

"You haven't called me that in years."

"I haven't felt so . . . young . . . in years."

"I've been awake all night."

"I'm sorry."

"I've turned this thing and twisted it, and I cannot see any logic to it."

"No, I'm sure you can't."

"I'm over my anger."

"Thank you."

"I could forbid you to go."

"Yes . . . you could."

"But it would mean nothing."

"It would mean something, but I'd still go."

"I can only ask you to stay, to give up this madness."

[53]

"That I cannot do."

"I didn't think you would."

They stood looking at each other through silence, across a distance far greater than that of the room, a distance that lengthened, with no turning back.

He held out a small pistol that had been hidden from her in the folds of his night robe. She took it.

"You'll need it to keep the Indians off in the woods," he said.

"Amos."

"Country's infested with them, you know it."

"I suppose."

"Bound to be, with the Osages at war with three tribes."

"Yes."

"I put shot in your bundle."

"Thank you, Amos."

"Have you taken enough food?"

"I think so."

"You're ready to leave?"

"Quite ready."

"This is good-by, then."

"Yes."

"I mean good-by."

"I know, Amos. As if I've died."

"You have died."

"There won't be a scandal. You're an important man, and you'll command respect, no matter what I do."

"I intend to."

"I won't come back to the village."

"Thank you."

He stepped aside, and she went through the door, her eyes gentle on his face.

"Tell Reginal good-by for me," she said, and he did not answer.

In the sitting room, she slipped the pistol into her belongings, waited until she heard Amos go into his bedchamber, then took up her pack and went into the brisk dark morning. The wind had cleaned and freshened the air, and it was sharp against her cheeks. High in the eastern slant of the overhead, a hint of light was coming into the blackness.

She went down the gallery steps, pausing on the bottom one. Her past was ending, to exist hereafter only in Amos's memory and her own. Thus, when she moved off the step, she would cut her life in two, and nothing she ever did in the future could join the parts again.

[54]

She stepped down, walked rapidly to the gate and through, opening it so swiftly it didn't have time to growl. She started along the path where she would meet her man coming out of the dawn, and where they would stand together for a moment while he smiled at her and took her hand.

Already morning light was definite along the tops of the trees, and now she sensed movement ahead. It was still dark there, and at first the movement was just a stirring of the darkness, then there seemed to be a form, and before she could really be certain, he was in front of her. She could make out the line of his hat brim, the breadth of his shoulders, and the hump of his pack.

He said, "You going with me?"

"Yes."

"Got your plunder?"

"Here."

He took her pack, hefted it and said, "I'll fix it so you can shoulder-pack it, come day."

She was able to see his face now, though indistinctly. He wasn't smiling. But of course not. He was a sober, sound, plain-thinking man, and he was deeply serious about the business of making his marriage and starting for home. The smiles and gladness would come later.

He said, "I spoke to a parson last night after I left your brother's house. Told him I might roust him out early."

He didn't take her hand, but then he couldn't, not with one arm holding her pack, his rifle in his other hand. He started toward the village, and she followed, walking behind him, which was the only possible way to walk, dark as it still was, loaded with gear as he was, and on such a narrow path.

When he stopped at the parson's gate on the far side of the village, neither of them had spoken again. There, in the dim morning light, he turned to her.

He noticed the shawl. He studied it, staring at the soft point it made at the top of her forehead, tracing it down along her shoulders, his face still, and gradually hard.

She couldn't help stroking the softness of the shawl and asking, "Do you like it?"

He started to speak, stopped, then pushed himself to words in such a reluctant manner she knew he didn't want to say what he was going to, but that he must.

"Would you . . . take it off."

Her stroking hand dropped; her searching eyes remained on his face.

"Of course," she said.

She put her food packet on the ground, and in silence lifted her wedding shawl off her head, folded it, and tucked it into her pack that he was still holding. Then she pulled her black, plain shawl up from her shoulders and looped it under her chin in everyday fashion.

"Much obliged," he said, and went through the gate.

There was a light in the house. He went up the steps, rapped at the door, and it came open a crack.

Parson Releford stood tall and thin and old in the yellow streak and asked, "Is it you, Mr. Warner?"

"Yes sir, it's me and my lady."

"Come in, both of you."

Jerd set the packs down, but kept his rifle in his hand and stepped inside, Devora following. This was a very small sitting room, and there was a new fire ablaze in the little white fireplace. There were two women in dark skirts standing at the fire, holding their hands out to it. One was the parson's wife, and the other was her sister, a neighbor to Nettie Dyer, mother of the lisping Phoebe.

Well, Devora thought, with Nettie's friend here, it may possibly take until noon for the entire village to hear that Devora Griggs is married at last, but I doubt it'll take that long. She stepped to where the light would reveal her face and said clearly, "Good morning, everybody."

The women pointed their faces at her, their lips fell apart, and their numb astonishment held them motionless. The parson blinked, his mouth moving silently. He glanced at the women, cleared his throat and said, "Good morning, Devora . . . good morning, my dear."

The women jerked their heads in a simultaneous nod.

Devora said, "Mrs. Releford and Mrs. Villette, I want you to know Jerd Warner."

He looked at them unsmilingly, said, "Pleased," and again they jerked their heads. He turned to the parson and asked, "You get us our paper fixed?"

The parson stepped over to a table and tapped a document spread on it. "If you'll both sign now," he said in obvious relief, "we can proceed with the—er—ceremony."

Devora put her packet of food on the floor under a chair, and followed Jerd to the table, the women moving in behind her. She watched the parson dip the quill into the inkhorn, hesitate, then hand it to Jerd, who leaned his rifle against the wall, set his name to the paper quickly and passed the quill to her. She could hear the shocked breathing of the women as she signed.

[56]

When she had finished, the parson said, "Har-u-m-ph . . . is every-body here that's coming?" and looked directly at Devora.

She smiled and inclined her head and Jerd said, "Yes sir, there'll be just those already present. Can we get on with it now, sir?"

The parson took up a small Bible, stepped out from the table and said dismally, "Stand before me."

Devora moved to face him, her hands holding to each other. Jerd stood beside her, and the women arranged themselves, one on his left, the other on Devora's right.

Silence took the room, broken only by the whispering fire and the tocking clock.

The parson opened his Book and inspected its pages bleakly. "Take her hand," he said.

Jerd extended his right hand to Devora, and she slid her left one into it. Her fingers went searching happily until they found the spaces be-tween his, and hurriedly snuggled in. His hand was hard and warm and firm, and her fingers tightened and clung with almost all the glad strength in them.

She watched the parson's old, spotted hands clutch his Book, and heard him say, in a singsong, "Do you, Jerd Warner, take this woman, Devora Griggs, to be your lawful wedded wife, do you promise, before God, to love her and cherish her, in sickness and in health, for better or for worse, until death do you part?"

Devora shut out the shocked disapproval and held to the parson's voice and herself and Jerd. He looked down at her, and the lines in his face deepened until he was like he had been last night.

"Do you?" the parson's voice prodded.

Jerd tightened. She could feel it in his hand, see it in his eyes, a tightening that grew into bitterness, then somberness closed over it, and he said, "I take her."

Her hand held to his, telling him this was right, right.

The parson's voice came at her.

"Do you, Devora Griggs, take this man, Jerd Warner, to be your lawful wedded husband, do you promise, before God, to love him and cherish him, to honor and obey him, in sickness and in health, for better or for worse, until death do you part?"

Her eyes still on Jerd's, she whispered, "I do."

Something like pity touched the old parson, and unaccountably his eyes watered, and he stood holding his Book and stared at Devora Griggs as if he had never seen her before. He understood, vaguely, from his lost boyhood among chattering sisters, the kind of rosy dreams a young girl fashions concerning the man she will some day marry, how many babies she'll have, whether boys or girls, and what she will name them. Looking at Devora's face lifted to her man, a half-smile holding her happy faith, the parson knew the vow she had just whispered was now her very life.

His voice rasped as he said, "The ring, please."

Still looking at Devora, Jerd shook his head in the negative.

The parson intoned, "By the right invested in me by the church of our Lord and Saviour, and by the law of the land, I declare you man and wife."

Devora waited.

Jerd dropped her hand, turned to the parson, who had closed his Book, said, "Just a minute," and went out the door.

She stood where she was while the two women, one after the other, bent over the table and scratched their signatures on the marriage paper. When they finished, they went back to the fireplace and stood regarding her.

Jerd returned, handed the parson two otter skins and said, "Thank you kindly, sir."

The parson glanced at the skins, at his wife, then laid them on the table. He picked up the marriage document and gave it to Devora.

She took it in both hands and, holding it carefully, said, "Thank you, Mr. Releford . . . Mrs. Releford . . . Mrs. Villette. And . . . well . . . good-by."

"Good-by," the three said in unison.

She got her food packet and walked out the door, Jerd behind her. He took up both packs and went down the steps, his rifle riding his forearm. With the barrel of it he held the gate open for her.

They went through the gray morning side by side, walking out in the street. She glanced back. There was a blur of faces at the parson's window.

"I suppose they're curious," she said.

"Who?"

"The parson and his ladies."

"Likely. Most ladies are curious, and someway a parson seems lady-like to me."

She looked up at him quickly, her eyes merry. "Why, Jerd!"

He returned her look, completely serious. "I don't mean they ain't manly. But they ain't supposed to have rough thoughts . . . all that. Yet I've knowed parsons to be as good in a rough-and-tumble as any man, but always on the side of what was right and proper."

When he turned his face ahead again, she was content. It didn't matter that he hadn't laughed with her. Nothing mattered, for today the world was new. She was this man's bride, and that was a beautiful thing. The glory of being bride, being woman, made her breath go uneven. She thought she could not possibly wait to experience what lay ahead, and then she began to smile at herself and to watch the side of Jerd's big, stern face as she walked with him.

Up the street a piece, he stopped at a cabin that had a pole stable in the rear. She waited at the gate while he went up and rapped on the cabin door.

A freckle-faced man opened it, spoke to Jerd, glanced at Devora, and stared.

"Good morning, Mr. Murray," she called.

He nodded, turned away, and took Jerd to the stable. When they came back, Jerd was leading a low-bellied cow, which he brought to Devora. He gave her the rope to hold, and went back to pay Murray, and she could hear the clink of silver as he counted out the price.

By the time he rejoined her, Devora had tucked her marriage paper into her pack and was petting the cow, rubbing her hand along the soft, light-colored jaw. The animal kept nudging her with her wet, friendly nose.

"She's due to freshen any day," Jerd said. "So we can't walk her too fast. It'll likely take us a number of days."

Devora stroked the soft, warm throat, and the cow tossed her head.

"What's her name, Jerd?"

"She ain't got any, far as I know. You give her one."

She looked away to where bright morning was swollen along the line of forest beyond the river, ready to burst and flood the earth.

" 'Dawn?' " she asked.

"If it pleasures you."

"And your babies—what are their names?"

He glanced at her sharply, then laid his hand on the cow and began rubbing her shoulder.

"Reckon you'll have to put names to them, too," he said at last.

"Thank you, Jerd. Jerd."

"Yes?"

"Are they both boys?"

"Boy and girl."

He went abruptly to a bush that was growing up around an old stump, broke off a small whip and brought it to her.

"You can walk behind Dawn and keep her moving along steady with this if she gets laggy on me," he said.

[59]

He shouldered his pack, caught hers under one arm, holding his rifle in that hand, and the cow's rope in the other.

"Let me carry my own pack," Devora said.

"Later. After we get out of the village, we'll stop to eat, and I'll fix it for you then."

Following the downhill slant of Main to Market, Devora watched how the sudden sun, red and enormous, pushed their shadows ahead of them —first Jerd's, knobby with packs, and Dawn's, low-slung and waddling, and last her own.

The village was coming awake. Smoke was standing up from every chimney. A few shops were opening, and clerks were rolling out kegs and tilting them on stobs so customers could see into them as they walked by.

Amos's shop was still closed, but Devora knew that Ned would come hurrying along at any moment, intent upon getting ready for the day's business. She hoped she would see him so she could tell him good-by and carry a final glimpse of his kind old face away with her.

Dawn began to pull over toward a watering trough, and Jerd gave her her head. While they waited for her to drink, there was the sound of wheels and hooves entering Main from Market. The cow lifted her dripping muzzle, swung her head in that direction, returned to her drinking.

The hauling cart, loaded with wood, and the team, came toward them. The horses were great, beautiful high-headed grays. Their owner, a man named LeFevre, hauled wood from Carondelet for a living, and Devora had seen him driving this team many times and had never failed to admire it, but she wasn't looking at the horses now. She was watching Jerd.

Never taking his eyes off the grays, he dropped the cow's rope and Devora's pack, stood until LeFevre pulled up at the trough, then started moving slowly, with a kind of reverence. LeFevre spoke from his cart seat, but Jerd did not notice.

He studied the horses, not touching them or speaking, changing his position to view them from every angle. He was a big man, and laden with his shoulder pack he appeared even bigger; they were big horses, and the way he was fairly humbling himself before them was not a common sight.

The nearest horse fluttered his nostrils in the trough, jerked his head up, tossed it and sent a spray of water into Jerd's face. It stood all over his sun-dark brow and cheeks in big, twinkling drops that began to make tiny paths toward his chin and the bottoms of his jaws. The horse whickered, thrust his muzzle into the water again, and Jerd gave his own big head a shake, throwing off the water drops, and smiled, his eyes tender upon the horse.

Devora saw the smile strip years from his face. It lifted the creases away, smoothed his cheeks, gentled his chin, and gave warmth to his mouth.

He stepped to the near horse, ran his hand along the back and over the hip, patted, and once he chuckled. LeFevre, taken with his absorption, lingered even after the team was through watering. When he did lift the reins, cluck to the horses and drive south, Jerd watched them go.

Devora led the cow over and stood with him. Her hand touched his, and he took her hand and held it, then slid his fingers up her arm to her shoulder and grasped it tightly, still looking after the horses.

Her breathing made a small sound.

He turned on her and stared down at her blankly. The smile dropped off him, and his hand fell from her shoulder. Dismay showed in his eyes, and there was a sudden whitening around his mouth.

At first she thought it was anger.

But it wasn't. It was live, torturing fear.

Bitterness clamped onto him. He took the cow's rope from her, strode over to her pack, lifted it and started north, leading the cow.

Devora walked behind the cow, her knees unsteady.

Something was wrong.

Something terrible was wrong with this man who was taking her into the wilderness.

He was in torment. It was her duty and desire to help him, and she did not know where to begin.

On the walkway in front of the shops was a lone woman, and at the next corner some men were standing. They were all staring.

Devora hardly saw them.

She saw only the hard, stern set to the back of her man, and the bitterness that showed in the squaring of his shoulders, and the way his head rode his neck.

So they walked, in the street, up Main, down Market to Church, out Vine, her thinking only of him, not caring if all St. Louis watched them go. And all the village did watch, from the pathways, from behind window curtains, from stables, and the villagers would remember.

They would never forget how the strange man came from the back country, his pack on his shoulder and his rifle on his arm. For many a year they'd tell of it: .

" 'Long in the evenin' he come . . . big, onfriendly lookin' cuss . . . come in off'n the nor'west trail. Left out with fust sun next mornin', leadin' his cow . . . a cow he'd paid fer with Mexican silver . . . an' the finest Christian woman as ever lived, that he'd paid fer with two otter skins . . . her trailin' the cow . . . jest like a squaw. La, this village'll never see sech another queer case. I can see 'em yet . . . headin' off yonder, makin' fer the timber, passin' along that ridge with the red sun showin' 'em off, makin' 'em look black an' queer an' onreal. Him . . . big, with his pack an' her pack an' his firin' piece, an' that old coonskin hat down on his head . . . the cow . . . bulged in the middle, an' workin' her head up an' down as she went . . . then . . . our Devorry . . . all woman . . . tall, an' her back straight as ary a rod, that stick in her hand, her chin up an' her head proud . . . lookin' straight ahead, an' the Lord's new day all around her."

ᴇᴤᴧ Chapter Six ᴤᴧᴧ

Aꜰᴛᴇʀ ᴛʜᴇʏ had ascended the second bank, they were some forty feet above the village. Here Jerd stopped, lowered Devora's pack to the ground, unshouldered his own, and leaned his rifle against it. The cow, rope dragging, began to graze.

"I reckon we'd best eat and be done with it," Jerd said.

Devora sat down on the grass and opened her food packet. She selected two slices of bread and butter, laid face to face, and two hard-cooked eggs, and held them up to him.

"I've got my own grub," he said.

"Will it keep?"

"I reckon."

"This won't."

"It don't matter. I can shoot us some birds."

"This isn't my brother's food."

"It's from his house."

"So are my clothes, but they're mine."

"He paid for the clothes. He paid for the grub."

"I earned them."

"I'm sure you did."

"So they're as much mine as what you have in your pack is yours."

"Yes."

"And it isn't right to waste food."

"You can eat it."

"Jerd, please. I fixed it especially for . . . well, for our wedding breakfast. Please eat it."

Again she offered the food, and gradually his obstinacy left him until he looked as he had last night, serious but friendly. He squatted, took the bread, laid it on the grass, and peeled his eggs. He ate them appreciatively, dipping them into the salt and pepper mixture she gave him, seeming to forget her presence.

What breeze remained from last night's wind was hitting them, but

[63]

coming through the warmth of the sun, it felt only pleasantly bracing. Devora took bread and an egg for herself and began to eat, letting her eyes wander, taking farewell of her surroundings.

The village lay beneath them, and the Mississippi, low at this season, flowed past it and disappeared into the southern curtain of woods. Back from the houses, among a few tall oaks, four or five springs arose and threw their waters together in a silver rivulet which, a short distance below the village, gave itself into the brown river. Chouteau's pond lay below too, a glittering, hundred acre sheet of water, its grassy banks set with trees, persimmon, hazel bushes and grapevines. To the west, the country spread itself charmingly, neither level nor hilly, its rolling surface rising almost imperceptibly for miles, and swelling into the horizon.

Her eyes on the beckoning distance, Devora asked, "What's it like, Jerd?"

He turned to her. "What's what like?"

"Out there . . . where we're going. Your country."

He waited a moment, thinking, then moved his great hands in a gesture that included the village and all its surroundings.

"There ain't no village, just a fellow I heard of trying to start one for the Osage River Indian trade. There's just my cabin and fields and woods . . . neighbors' cabins, not too many or too close. The country itself I'd say ain't so different than this, and yet it is. It's hilly in places. Here is all right . . . it's good country, but I figure mine's better—soil, climate —and it's prettier, too."

"You really like it."

"It suits me."

"Yes."

"Reckon you'll pine for this?" he asked.

"The village?"

"It or anything."

"No. I'm never coming back."

His eyes searched her.

"Amos," she explained.

"He throw you out?"

"No."

"You come to a split."

"I suppose you could call it that—or a parting of our ways."

"Over me."

"Amos has worked hard to build a certain kind of life for himself and his family. I've chosen a different kind. That's all there is to it."

"And he don't want you shaming him."

"He's my brother, and he's been good to me."

Jerd stood abruptly. "It's time we moved on."

She stood with him. "First, fix my pack so I can carry it," she said.

He reached into his own pack, brought out a stout band, ran it under the tied corners of her blankets, knotted it, and tied its ends, making a long loop. Leaving her pack on the ground, he hoisted his own smaller one, which was equipped in the same manner, lowered its loop over her head so it fell across her upper chest, then settled the burden on her shoulders.

She looked up at him in astonishment. "Why, it's so light!" she said.

"It'll take on weight," he told her.

For an instant she thought he was going to smile, and she waited, a half-smile on her own lips ready to spring into laughter, but he turned away, swung her larger, heavier pack to his shoulders, took up his rifle, and went after the cow.

Devora followed, her load riding easily, her switch ready for the cow's heels. Jerd started out, making his own short-cut trail, and she kept pace, holding to her rear position in their small caravan.

Watching his long, free-swinging stride, she duplicated it as best she could, learning quickly how to keep her skirts from wrapping around her legs. The sun lay the length of her back, striking at her right cheek. She breathed the clean, sweet scent of the cow, smelled the drying autumn grass, listened to her slippers tramping through it, and marveled at the silence in which Jerd's great, moccasined feet trod the earth.

Once he glanced back, never breaking his stride.

"Too fast?"

"No, it's fine."

"Fast as we can walk the cow," he said. "We go northwest till we hit the Missouri, then follow it home."

Not until the sun was directly overhead did he change his gait, and presently come to a stop in a walnut grove bordering the river. He dropped his pack, let go the cow's rope, and she wandered down to the water.

Devora had long since taken off her head shawl, and now, after lowering her pack to the ground, she slipped out of her pelisse and tucked it and the shawl away.

"Tired?" Jerd asked.

"Not really. I'm mostly warm and thirsty, and quite hungry."

"We've got to rest the cow and let her graze," he said, "so we can eat, too."

He took a wooden mug from his pack, went to the edge of the broad, dun-colored river and filled it. When he returned, Devora held the mug in both hands, stared at the mud swirling in the water, then lifted it and drank. It was unpalatable and medicinal, but she finished it all, handed Jerd the empty mug, and made a little face.

He said, "You'll get used to it. I've even met fellows that are so partial to it they swear Rocky Mountain water sickens them because it's so clear." She laughed.

He went back to the river's edge, and while he drank his fill and sloshed the dirty stuff over his face and hair, she opened the food and laid out another meal of bread and hard-cooked eggs. They ate in silence, and afterward, sitting together in the shade of the trees, she studied his face openly. It was as it had been last night, serious and friendly.

"I'm ready with more questions," she said, smiling.

"What do you want to know?"

"Tell me about our neighbors."

"Neighbors in my country ain't the same as in your village."

"People are people."

"It's mainly distance I'm speaking of."

"Oh, yes."

"I reckon our closest is the Pikes."

"How close?"

"I'd say seven, eight miles."

"Tell me about the Pikes."

"There ain't much to tell. They're just—well—folks."

"Old or young?"

"Not neither—just medium, yet they top me in years. Him, anyhow. It's hard to tell about her."

"Do they have children?"

"No. They're the ones that's keeping my babes."

"That's kind of them."

"Yes."

She watched his face, which didn't change, waited for him to say more about his twins, and when it was evident he had no such intention, longed to ask about them, but dared not lest it cause him to withdraw from her as he had earlier in the day.

She asked, instead, "And our other neighbors?"

"Well, there's the Doerflingers . . . they live farther off . . . no younguns. Some married children off some place. They could be your parents in age, and they're real good folks. There's a young, unmarried fellow named Piepmeier . . . he goes back and forth to St. Louis a good bit. Then there's the Weed family—they've got a whole passel of younguns, and I don't never see them except at a preaching, or a baptizing. Same way with the Mitchell outfit. I've heard about some new folks I ain't seen, and there's two families of Johnsons—brothers—that've got big broods and live away off, but I have met them from time to time. One thing, everybody in my country is friendly, and everybody's glad of any company whatsoever."

"They're lonely."

"I reckon."

"Do they all go to St. Louis to trade?"

"Not regular. But one time or another, they've been."

"Do they walk?"

"Them with horses ride. Some use the river."

"Do you ever go by boat?"

"No."

"Wouldn't it be quicker, at least on the way down? To build a raft, I mean, and ride the current. The water looks so swift."

Slowly his face darkened, its lines cutting deep. He got up abruptly, strode to the cow, and retrieved the end of her lead rope.

Forlornly, Devora turned her look away from him and studied the Missouri, the broad stream of fast-flowing mud studded with dead tree trunks, broken by islands of dreary sand; tried to read from its ugliness why it had been wrong for her to mention boat travel to Jerd Warner, and whether that was connected with the dark and mysterious thing that was bedeviling him.

He returned, leading the cow. He shouldered the larger pack and said, face like granite, voice grating, "Let's go. We've got miles to put behind us afore dark."

He started west, falling immediately into his long, free-swinging stride.

Devora struggled with her pack, got it in place, and hurried to overtake him.

It was cooler going through the forest, where only an occasional bright ribbon of sunshine hung between the big trees, and birds flickered and chirped, but the walking was harder and their progress somewhat slower. Even so, Jerd picked his way unhesitatingly and surely, detouring around brush growth and logs, avoiding depressions, keeping to solid ground. The river was off to their right, hidden by the forest.

At first Devora watched both Jerd and their surroundings, then just Jerd, and finally the path alone, her one thought to meet the pace he set. By the end of the first hour, she began to notice a sore place on her left heel. After another hour, her shoulders were distinctly weary, and her upper chest was heavy from the pack-weighted band across it.

By midafternoon she was so tired she wanted only to sink to the ground, but Jerd led endlessly on, never speaking or glancing back. Thus, when he did halt unexpectedly and drop his pack and the cow's lead rope, Devora simply came to a stop, switch in hand, and looked at him.

"We'll rest a spell," he said, and sat down under a tall cottonwood.

Gratefully she unshouldered her pack, moved heavily to a nearby cottonwood, and sank down. A strand of hair had escaped its braid and was hanging along her cheek, and she swept it up with the back of her hand, and leaned against the tree trunk.

Jerd was watching her, the bitterness gone from his face. "Thirsty?" he asked.

She nodded.

"Me, too. Afore we start, we'll mosey to the river with the cow and drink our fill."

She nodded again.

"We won't be stopping any more 'til we reach our campsite," he went on. "I don't figure to walk very late, though. Want to get settled afore dark."

She tried to smile, found it too much effort, and felt her eyes go shut. The silence of the woods closed in and pounded at her ears. The cow moved away, lay down, and began to chew her cud. Groggily, Devora identified the various homely noises she made, and they felt good to her ears.

She hadn't realized she was dozing off until Jerd spoke. She opened her eyes, and he was standing in front of her holding out the wooden mug, which was brimming with water.

"I've already watered the cow," he was saying, "so we'll have to get started."

She took the mug, drained it without breathing, and handed it back. "More?"

She shook her head and scrambled stiffly to her feet. "I'd have to be thirstier," she said cheerfully, "or fond of drinking mud, one or the other."

Again she thought he might smile, and she waited for the friendliness this would make between them, but he picked up the cow's rope and started walking. Wearily she shouldered her pack and trudged after him. Her heel, which she had neglected to examine, hurt with every step. The pack rode the tiredness of her shoulders, the band sawed at her chest, and she wondered, in sudden dismay, how it was possible to get so tired so soon, how she would feel tomorrow, and whether she was going to start marriage by being a burden rather than a help.

Deliberately she pulled her thoughts off her discomfort, set her chin, and settled into walking much as she had seen oxen bend their necks to the yoke and lean into the long pull.

The forest was silver with dusk, rich with greens, when at last Jerd threw down his pack. They were standing in a walnut ringed clearing, beyond which lay a tiny, grass-covered valley. At their feet a creek gurgled and threw its ripples along its stony bed, flinging itself toward the river.

The cow began to drink.

Devora and Jerd both drank deeply of the clear water, and when they had finished, he said, "You might graze the cow a spell while I get us some supper meat."

She picked up the lead rope.

"Tie a chunk of wood to that when you turn her loose, and she won't stray," he said. "And keep her at this edge of the valley so you can get her under cover in a hurry."

She looked at him questioningly.

"Indians," he said.

"Hostile Indians, this close to St. Louis?"

"There ain't but one thing you can count on about an Indian, and that is you can't count on nothing. If you don't figure to run into him this close to St. Louis, that's right where he'll be, hiding in the brush, his tomahawk in his hand. So take that pistol you spoke of with you."

"Yes," Devora said reflectively, "I will. I've heard plenty of stories, but somehow they never seemed quite real."

"I reckon they felt real enough to them concerned," Jerd said.

He took up his rifle, and in a few noiseless strides disappeared.

Silence closed in, as deep and impenetrable and threatening as the forest itself. Panic took Devora. Jerd had abandoned her. He was never coming back. She was alone in a world that was a ravening wilderness of trees, river, wild things, and Indians. Her skin prickled; her scalp crawled; her heart knocked, sweat sprang out of her armpits, and her breath stuck in her throat.

The cow lowed.

Devora focused her gaze on the animal and found the soft eyes regarding her. A shudder rolled down her body, and when it was gone her knees were unsteady, but she was able to breathe.

Weakly, she tugged at the rope and led Dawn over to her pack, got out her pistol. Holding it ready, she proceeded toward the valley, picking her way, placing each foot with the utmost care, literally tiptoeing through the forest, her eyes quick on every fallen log, treacherous bush and enemy tree.

At the valley's edge, she tied a piece of branch to the end of the rope and turned the cow loose, herself remaining well back in the trees. She stood there alert, holding her pistol, keeping out of view of any skulking Indian who might be watching from the forest beyond, her own eyes constantly searching for the first hint of bear, panther, or redskin.

When the shot sounded, she sucked in her breath, letting it out with relief when she realized it was Jerd, getting their supper meat. Another shot came and, at intervals, two more, then there was just the silence.

She waited, as carefully watchful as at the beginning, but her panic had drained away. Presently Jerd would return; he was her bulwark against danger. She would no longer be alone.

When she saw him re-enter the clearing, such relief came over her that she began to tremble. He motioned her to remain where she was and now, in the intervals of surveillance, she watched him gather wood, start a fire that gave off only a pale blue smoke barely visible from this distance in this light, then crouch beside the creek to dress his game.

In only a short time the first sweet smell of roasting meat lifted. A feeling of safety engulfed Devora, but her eyes were careful as she looked across the valley into the growth beyond. She knew suddenly that, though her fright was gone, out of it had been born a respect for the wilderness and a caution that was already as much a part of herself as it was of Jerd.

It was dark when he walked down into the valley and returned, leading the cow. Back at the little, bright-flamed fire, she saw he had split open four squirrels, roasted them on sticks, and had made tea. She got out more of the bread and butter and the last of the eggs, and they feasted in companionable silence.

The cow made moist, cud-chewing sounds, the fire snapped, and the forest held blackness around them like a great, soft blanket. It was too warm to sit by the fire. The day had grown hotter by the hour, and the night was sultry and uncomfortable, but the fire was a good thing, a home-spot, a hearth-spot in the wilderness, and they lingered beside it.

When they had finished eating, there were two squirrels left. These Devora packed with the last of the bread, and then she went to the creek, washed her face and hands and teeth, pulled off her slippers and stockings, and lowered her burning feet into the rush of water. It stung her heel, and she felt lightly with her finger tips and discovered a blister that had broken and worn into a sore. For a long time she sat with the cold water hitting her ankles, and listening to the sounds Jerd made as he came to the creek some distance away, washed, and returned to the fire.

His voice reached down to her, low and comfortable sounding, and said, "We'd best turn in now, if you're done washing up."

She arose stiffly, her slippers in her hand, a stocking stuffed into the toe of each, and moved toward the fire-spot, her wet feet tender and cold against the harshness of the unseen earth. She walked toward Jerd, her heart quicker, nostrils flared. She was his wife, but now that the time was here, she was not ready to receive him as husband.

He was feeding small pieces of wood to the fire and said, over his shoulder, "I've piled rocks around this to hide the flame from any stray Indian. I aim to keep it burning all night."

"Oh," she said, and added, out of need for impersonal talk, "to keep mosquitoes away?"

"Them and any wild critter that might take notions about our cow."

"I see. The smoke isn't bad."

"That's apple wood for you. It makes a thin smoke that ain't easy to spot from a distance. I always use it or hickory when I camp out, and for that reason."

His offhand tone eased her confusion somewhat, but she stood motionless, uncertain as to what to do.

"You'd best unfasten your pack," he said, doling more wood into the fire, "and spread yourself a blanket to lay on, and something to cover up with. It's liable to turn chilly along toward morning."

Relieved to have occupation, she set down her slippers and went to her pack. She removed the band, untied the knotted ends of the blankets, and laid them open. The firelight wavered on her belongings, which were topped by a small leather pucker-mouthed bag she had never seen before.

Experimentally, she lifted it. It was surprisingly heavy. She put the fingers of her other hand near the bottom, pressed, felt the hard outline of coins, and dropped the bag. The coins rattled as it landed on the pile of her clothing.

Tears stung her eyes. Amos. He had kept her inheritance in his bedchamber, then, and had slipped it into her waiting pack when he passed it on his way to the kitchen this morning. Was it only this morning? Already her brother and his fine house seemed a lifetime behind, a world-distance away.

She stood looking at the leather bag, her tears unshed and stinging, and such homesickness sliced through her that she winced. She felt a rush of pain over leaving everything she had known for the unknown, and then Jerd's voice came to her, low and warm, and it said, "Do you need help?"

She tossed her tears away with a fling of her head and answered him clearly, "No . . . I can do my part," and with steady hands lifted her worldly goods off her blankets, placed them in the shelter of a bush, covered them with her pelisse against dew, and turned to the fire with her blankets.

Jerd stood up, knocking wood particles off his hands. "You bed down on that side," he said, "and I'll take this side. I've already tied the cow over there, just beyond me."

He went to his pack.

Devora doubled one blanket, laid it on the ground, and arranged the other one for a cover to be pulled up. She rolled her shawl into a pillow, laid her pistol beside it, then sat down in the middle of her strange bed.

Jerd flung his blanket on the ground and stretched out on his back, his head pillowed on his arms.

"Did you ever camp out afore?" he asked.

"No."

"Likely it seems strange to you, then."

"Yes . . . yes, it does."

"Scarey, even. But there ain't nothing to be jumpy about."

"No."

"I'll keep watch."

"I'll take my turn," she said.

"That ain't needful, not tonight. I didn't find no Indian sign whatsoever. I'll doze along with one ear out. I'm used to it."

She kept staring into the fire.

He said, after a while, "You'd best go right to sleep, if you can. You've had a hard day."

Embarrassed, she lay down. She could see the swell of his chest in the firelight, but his head was in shadow. Her face began to burn over the thoughts she'd had about him earlier. Jerd Warner was no man to hurry his bride, to make his demands in the forest like a black bear or a panther. He was concerned now about getting safely to his cabin; only there would he establish his marriage, and in a proper manner.

Gradually the ground beneath her began to make itself known. It was hard and knotty, and she shifted position. The woolen shawl scratched her face. She lay motionless, her body aching, every pore sweating in the fire heat, her heel throbbing.

She closed her eyes, and immediately the forest began to crackle and pop, and she wondered why she had thought it was a silent place. Each new sound left her tense, waiting for the footfall of a sneaking Indian or the pad of a wolf or bear. An owl hooted, and she lifted her head and listened. She looked across at Jerd, but he was breathing steadily and did not move. She lowered her head, certain that between the hardness of the ground, her various discomforts and the dangers in the noisy forest, she would never sleep. Yet even as she thought this, the red of the fire blurred, the noises of the forest grew dim, and she slept.

⊶ *Chapter Seven* ⊶

SOMEONE NEEDED her and was calling her name. She was struggling to get up, but her bones were too heavy. She tossed to her other side and tried to sit, but the bones held her. She gasped for breath, but her chest would not move, and she moaned. She wanted to open her eyes, but the lids were locked, and she flung out her arms and moaned again.

Something firm took her shoulder and shook it. From hazy distance Jerd's voice kept saying, "Devora . . . Devora, wake up!"

Dazedly, she fought the rest of the way out of her uneasy sleep and pushed into a sitting position. She felt strips of hair hanging down her cheeks and neck. Her mouth was parched and bitter, and her whole body ached. It was hard to breathe, and she realized the air had grown oppressively close and hot.

She squinted to adjust her eyes, saw that it was still dark, the fire was even smaller than it had been, and Jerd was standing at the foot of her pallet looking down at her.

"Awake?" he asked.

She nodded.

"There's a storm coming up," he said, "and it acts like a bad one."

A backlash of lightning showed momentarily against the overhead blackness. Devora scrambled to her feet and stood looking helplessly around their small camp.

"Where can we go?" she asked.

"Nowheres. There's no cave hereabouts, big or little."

"What about our things?"

"We'll pile them together, grub and powder on the bottom. We ain't got much time."

Without warning, a dazzling flash lit the clearing, followed instantly by utter darkness and a tremendous clap of thunder that left Devora with her hands over her ears. A few big drops of rain hurtled down, plopping on her head, soaking through to her scalp.

In two jumps, Jerd was scooping up his belongings, was throwing

[74]

them on top of Devora's, stuffing his powder and the food in at the bottom, was racing for the cow, yelling, "Put the blankets over that . . . hurry!"

A blast of wind swept through the clearing, almost pushing Devora off balance. She snatched up her bedding and footgear and went in a stumbling run to the precious heap of clothing and supplies, her bare feet treading sticks and pebbles, hardly feeling them.

Lightning speared out, directly overhead this time. It made a sizzling noise, which was quenched immediately by the roaring thunder. The big raindrops came faster and thicker.

Devora dropped her shawl and slippers on the pile, flung one of the blankets over the whole thing, hurriedly made sure it covered every part and hung to the ground, added the second blanket. As she rushed back, she glimpsed Jerd tying a sizable rock to the end of the cow's lead rope.

The wind came blasting through the clearing again, and as she stooped for Jerd's blanket, it caught her skirts and whirled them to her waist. She knocked them down, clutched the blanket and ran back to the pile, where she spread it over the others and tucked them all in securely around the bottom.

Her breath sobbing, she stumbled back to the fire for her pistol. The lightning came again, followed by thunder, and then rain was falling fast onto the remaining flame, hissing on the coals, sending up fragments of smoke and steam. She bent to pick up her pistol, and rain dotted the back of her dress, sinking coolly through to her skin. After she straightened, she thrust her pistol securely inside of her dress.

Jerd was shouting at her, but she could neither locate him nor distinguish his words. A blaze of lightning showed him on the creek bank, his hair standing out in the wind, and the simultaneous explosion of thunder sent her catapulting to him. The instantly heavier rain pressed her hair to her head and streamed down her face.

As she reached Jerd, he thrust something at her. Involuntarily, she put out both arms to receive it, and it was a rock. She staggered under its weight, and Jerd shouted again, but now thunder and lightning stood down together in the clearing, illuminating the wild scene and thrashing it with noise, and she could not even hear his voice. Wind hurtled through the din, snapping branches off trees, and the thunder exploded time after time and extinguished both light and sound, and the rain came dumping in floods, soaking them.

"Put the rock on top of our stuff . . . to hold it down!" Jerd yelled hoarsely.

Devora half-ran, half-fell up the incline and across the clearing, her wet skirts tangling around her ankles. She aimed blindly for their blanket-covered mass of goods, guided by the lightning stabs that both bewildered and helped her, and when she got there, dumped the rock on it, only to have it fall off onto the ground.

She fumbled for the rock, lifted it, and placed it carefully in the center of the pile, feeling the goods sag under its weight. Jerd came slogging up, a rock under each arm, and added them to hers. When he was finished, he grabbed her hand, pulled her to the middle of the clearing and to the ground at the spot where once their fire had burned. The cow was tethered there, and now she edged closer to them.

Devora sank back on her heels, crossing her arms over her chest in an effort to keep the pistol in her dress dry. Lightning sprayed the sky, forked downward, struck, sang and burned, sprayed again. Flash followed flash, and thunder crashed upon itself continuously. The wind tore at Devora's hair, slapped it back with rain, poured rain into her eyes and mouth, pounded her sodden dress with driving, icy water. Sometimes she was aware of the breaking of a tree or branch, and once, as the clearing stood out in a bright crackle of lightning, she could see fallen trees, standing trees that had split, others with limbs stripped from them, and behind them all the writhing blackness of the tortured forest.

"We're safest here," Jerd shouted.

"Why?" she screamed back.

"Not so apt to be hit by a tree . . . or lightning!"

She nodded in the pouring, crashing dark and endured. Moments passed, and still the storm raged without pause, whipping its tireless violence over the land.

Steadily, Devora grew colder. The black, flashing sky kept deluging her, its water running down her body into a raw, cold puddle that rippled against her thighs, and in spite of her determination not to do so, she began to shiver. Her teeth chattered, and her hands went numb.

Jerd had been sitting with his shoulder touching hers, and now his arms came around her, and she leaned in sweet, glad comfort against him. In silence they watched the falling darkness, and the rain wedded and blended them, bestowed upon Devora her first real sense of closeness, and enriched her faith in the man she had chosen.

The storm itself abated, but the rain poured as fast as ever. They moved to the half-shelter of a tree. Hours passed, and still the rain fell. Even after grayness had crept into the clearing and established itself as daylight, the rain dropped in an unbroken silver wall into the beaten forest, hammered the puddled ground, streamed over the miserable cow, and shot off Jerd's hat brim and shoulders. It covered Devora like a garment, seeped into her pores, choked her when she pulled in a sudden breath, and set her to coughing.

Watching how the rain enveloped the blanket-covered pile of their belongings, Devora thought of the food packed away near the bottom, and her stomach hurt with hunger. She stared at the rain hitting the soggy blankets, wondered almost indifferently what condition her clothes were in beneath them, and waited.

When she first thought she detected a lessening in the downpour, she wouldn't let herself believe it. She closed her eyes, counted deliberately to fifty, opened them, and the rain had definitely thinned. She glanced into Jerd's face, and he nodded.

"Looks like it's sure letting up," he said.

She looked at the rain again, too sodden to speak, newly aware of a chilled, sore ache throughout her body, in addition to yesterday's stiff weariness.

Quickly, once it had begun to slacken, the rain spattered into nothing, and the sun broke through. Jerd got to his feet and pressed water out of his clothes, and Devora did the same, first laying her pistol to dry on a rock. Already the sky above the clearing was cloudless, and the sun was shining brightly.

Jerd gave the cow a friendly pat on the rump, walked over to their belongings, and dumped off the rocks. He lifted the blankets, wrung the water out of them, and handed them to Devora, who spread them on the ground in the sun.

All her packed clothes were dripping, so while Jerd put the damp food to dry and led the cow to the creek, she wrung them out and draped them on bushes. She laid everything else on rocks, took her hair down, pressed the water out, shook it loose as best she could, and left it hanging in strings on her shoulders.

Jerd had returned and was regarding the last of the bread and butter she had packed for the trip. He held some of it, along with a cooked squirrel, out to her.

"Hungry enough to try this?" he asked.

"I could eat anything," she said, accepting the food. She sat on a spot of grass, took a bite of the damp bread, and chewed. After she had swallowed, she smiled at him, broke off a chunk of meat, and put it in her mouth.

He watched her soberly, and began to eat his own portion. After they had finished, he helped her turn the drying blankets, putting the bottom sides up. Then, while she made the rounds of bushes and rocks, shifting the articles on them, he settled down to cleaning his rifle and her pistol.

Later, comb in hand, she sat near him and ran it through her half-dry hair, flinging it up and out to the sun at every stroke.

He glanced at her and said, "I reckon you're put out about what happened to your plunder."

"It can rain on anybody," she said. "And nothing was ruined."

"That's good."

"Will we go far today?"

He shook his head. "By the time we dry out, and I get us some game and we cook it, night'll be on us."

"How far did we come yesterday?"

"Close to twenty miles."

"Is it a hundred miles to where we're going?"

"Better than a hundred. Why?"

"Then it'll take us five or six days to get there."

"It takes five days for a man alone and traveling hard. But it's tougher going from here on, so I don't figure we can make more than ten miles or so a day after this."

"Because of the cow?"

"Yes."

"A cow doesn't move fast."

"And it ain't best to push this one. I don't want her to calve ahead of time."

"Shall I graze her in the valley again?"

"No, it's best to keep her under cover in full day. She can make out with the grass along the creek bank."

After he had cleaned their firearms to his satisfaction, he warned her to keep her pistol handy, and disappeared into the trees. She went down to the creek, slipped out of her clothes, plunged into the water, and bathed. Afterward, she drew her dried clothing onto her wet body, braided her hair, pinned it up, and returned to camp, refreshed.

She sat gratefully in the sun, letting it bake the stiffness out of her joints and heal the rawness that had begun in her throat. Once she turned her blistered heel up to it. Occasionally she heard the sound of Jerd's rifle; at intervals she wandered about the clearing, examining the sunning articles, folding such as were dry, alert always for any sign of danger.

Jerd must have ranged far, she thought, some time after he had left. She was under an oak, and she sat erect, alarmed as she realized she hadn't heard his rifle for some time. After deep listening, she got the distant sound of it and, relieved, leaned back against the tree trunk and relaxed.

She came awake with a start, snatched her pistol, and darted a look around the clearing and along the creek, where the cow was grazing placidly. Everything looked the same, even to the lay of sun and shadow; apparently she had dozed only momentarily.

Thereafter, she remained determinedly awake, busying herself with her drying project, turning every page of every book, making sure all were bone dry before she closed them and stacked them together. She had everything folded and in tidy heaps when Jerd padded silently out of the woods, carrying his game.

The sun was slanting its last shafts into the clearing, and he strode through toward the creek, saying, "You might fetch a knife and give me a hand."

He was already squatted at the water's edge, skinning a rabbit, when she joined him. He showed her how to slit the fur, how to cut the rabbit open and gut it, how to throw the offal into the downstream flow so it would be swept away from the campsite, and how to dip the meat into the rush of water for its final cleansing.

Devora set her jaw, took a dead rabbit firmly into her hands, and worked along with him. She finished the last two squirrels while he gathered wood and built a fire, then she carried all the dressed game up, making two trips. She knelt at the fire with him, roasting the meat on sticks, and when the first was cooked, they ate while they roasted more.

"This is a lot of meat," she said.

"I figured on a big mess."

"It's enough for several days."

"Two days, anyhow . . . more if it don't spoil. When it gives out, we'll do on the dried meat in my pack. I don't want to make a racket with my rifle as we go deeper into Indian country."

She stared at him, openly admiring. "You think of everything!"

He turned the squirrels he was roasting. "The man that don't has a way of not lasting long," he said.

It was dark by the time the meat cooled. After she had packed it away, Devora brought her leather bag of money to the fire and put it in Jerd's hands.

"What is it?" he asked.

"My inheritance from my father."

"Well?"

"Amos didn't . . . I thought it could be my dowry."

He stalked over to her belongings. She heard the bag plop to the ground, and the money in it clank. He came back and stood looking at her in the firelight, his face stern.

"I didn't marry you for a dowry," he said.

"I know you didn't, Jerd. But I have it."

"I'll take no part of it."

"But what can I do with it?"

"Use it for yourself . . . give it away . . . throw it away."

He left abruptly and went to the creek. When he returned, he was leading the cow. He tethered her, and added wood to the fire. He piled rocks around it, hooding it, as he had done the night before.

"We'd best fix down our pallets and grab some rest," he said. "We'll start early without eating and make a few miles afore day comes and any stray Sioux or Osage wakes up and takes a notion to go on the prowl."

Tonight Devora fell asleep as soon as she lay down. At intervals, she was aware of the tiny fire, of Jerd putting wood on it, of the cow, and the hooting of many owls. Once she thought groggily that she should relieve Jerd at the business of sleeping with one eye open, then sank helplessly into oblivion, unable to do so much as murmur his name.

The far-off stars and the winking coals of their fire were the only sparks of light in the world when he shook her awake. Sneezing, she stumbled after her footgear as he worked swiftly at making up their packs. She returned to the fire-spot, sat on the ground, wrapped a folded handkerchief around her sore heel, and began to pull on her stockings.

When she stood up, her slippers felt stiff as wood, and as she thrust her pistol firmly into her belt and shouldered her pack, she wished violently to drop it all, to fall to the ground herself, and sleep. Yawning, she took her place at the end of their small caravan, switch in hand. It was like that first morning, except that now she knew what to expect, and could not see her surroundings, could only follow the black hulk of the cow that followed the tall shadow that was Jerd.

The valley grass was wet with dew, and the forest beyond loomed thicker and darker than that around their camp. She looked back, and could see only the dark outer rim of trees. She trudged on through the wet grass, sighing, for it was only now, when she must leave it, that she realized the clearing had become a home to her.

They kept to the outside edge of the timber, making good progress. At dawn they took cover in the woods and were forced to proceed more slowly. Devora was wide awake now, and beginning to enjoy the new morning. Her spirits rose, and she walked lithely, feeling free as air in spite of frequent sneezing.

Their fresh meat lasted two and a half days, then they ate sparingly of the dried meat from Jerd's pack for two days. Twice, after that, he caught a big catfish, and these, baked in hot coals, varied their diet and filled their stomachs for three days, all told.

In travel, they followed the pattern established the morning they left the clearing, that of keeping to the open during the predawn hours, walking on hard ground, avoiding swampy places, going into the cover of the trees at daylight, making camp before dusk. Always they moved with caution. Jerd said there were thirty thousand Indians along the Missouri—Osage, Sioux, Pawnee, Ponca, and others—and carefully he avoided their trails, stayed wide of the villages in which they lived, and watched endlessly for any sign of them.

"Even with the Osage on the warpath with the Delawares and them, we ain't by no means safe," he explained to Devora. "At home, in our own cabin, the redskins having trouble amongst theirselves makes it easier on us, but here in their territory, it's something else altogether."

At night they took turns standing watch. They rarely talked, for they were busy, alert for danger, needing to rest. Yet Devora began to feel she had known Jerd all her life. His resourcefulness, patience, and endurance instilled confidence in her, and left her at ease with him.

During the first days, she had grown increasingly tired, but gradually, as her cold disappeared, she toughened until she could do her full share of everything without suffering extreme fatigue. She developed an awed affection for the forest, marveling at its beauty, admiring the great walnut and cottonwood trees, which were sometimes as much as six feet around and forty feet up to the first branches. She learned to identify various sounds and signs, and watched with interest the vagaries of the rowdy Missouri.

By day, this was a treacherous, shifting river of flowing mud scarred with dead tree trunks and bars and islands of ugly sand, bordered by shores of crumbling dirt. But in twilit dawn, rosy evening, or moonlight, it softened into beauty, gleamed with purity and wore the sparkling stars, and the woods grew dreamy and tender with love for it, and held every twig and leaf clear against the sky.

Thus Devora no longer remembered the clearing with regret, or thought with expectation of arriving at Jerd's cabin. The moment at hand filled her. To look everywhere at once—ahead, to each side, and to the rear—watching for the slightest quiver of a bush that might conceal an enemy, to listen eternally for the breaking of a twig or a rustle or footfall not their own, to breathe the forest smells, to see Jerd and the cow moving slowly ahead of her, safe for now, these things were all there was, and they were enough.

She counted off the days by notching a tough little hickory stick she carried in her pack. The thirteenth day out of St. Louis was like the others, a little cooler, but it followed the pattern. Perhaps she was a bit hungrier than usual, for they had eaten only small portions of dried meat the past two days, but that was the only difference.

They walked through evening, nearing a campsite Jerd had selected on his way to St. Louis. He said tomorrow would be their last full day of travel, for they would reach his cabin by the next noon, so now, for the first time since her wedding morning, Devora was able to think ahead to their destination with something like excitement.

They were making their way through a stand of cottonwood when the arrow came silently from behind them, lodged in the cow's neck between her shoulders, and sent her jumping sidewise, bawling wildly. Instantly, Devora grabbed the lead rope and pulled her hurriedly toward a thicket, as Jerd had instructed her to do in the event of attack. As she went, she heard the crack of his rifle.

Her ankle turned and she almost fell, but righted herself and kept going until there was a depth of growth behind her, where she stopped between two cottonwoods, the cow still bawling. Breathing hard, she got behind one of the big trees and peered back in the direction from which she had just come.

She heard the rifle again.

Jerd was not in sight.

The cow kept bawling and plunging, making a great deal of noise. Devora dropped her pack to the ground, turned, gripped the arrow shaft that quivered with every move of the cow, and yanked. Blood welled from the wound, which was shallow, the cow quit her bawling and flung her head from side to side, her tongue out in a futile attempt to lick the spot on her neck.

Devora threw the arrow aside, and tied the lead rope to a sapling. She drew her pistol, got behind her tree, and waited. There was no one visible anywhere. The forest stood motionless, blurring into dusk. There was no sound but her own knocking heart and the licking noises of the cow.

Cautiously, she moved out from the cottonwood, stole toward a big walnut farther on, nearer to where she had left Jerd, eyes roving, ears straining.

She reached the walnut, paused behind it, then ventured on, heading now for another cottonwood, and surely when she got there, if she got there, she would be able to locate Jerd, and he would be alive and safe.

Seconds later or hours later, she left the safety of the cottonwood and slipped quietly on, nostrils flared, knees trembling. If Jerd wasn't here, he wasn't anywhere, and she had no idea how to find him, how to help him.

She was taking her third cautious step when she got the swift, smooth animal motion of bronze and blue streaking from behind brush growth, and at the same instant glimpsed Jerd, on one knee, wrenching an arrow out of his thigh, his rifle on the ground behind him.

She halted, not breathing, and the bronze and blue savage went leaping at Jerd, tomahawk lifted. Jerd staggered to his feet, blood darkening his trousers, and hurtled to meet the Indian. He jammed his right shoulder under the savage's heart and smashed his left fist into the arm that wielded the tomahawk. The impact threw them to the ground, two big men, Jerd on top.

The wild legs wound around the buckskins, the wiry brown torso bucked and twisted, muscles knotted on the arms, and the tomahawk flashed up. Jerd, neck cords standing out, lips skinned back, pushed mercilessly against the lithe body under him, gave the descending arm a crushing, backhanded blow, rammed his right forearm across the savage's neck, forcing the chin up, grabbed for the tomahawk wrist.

With a fluid movement, the Indian legs unwound, the soles hit the earth in a tremendous shove, throwing Jerd off balance, the half-naked body writhed, rolled, and was on top, raising the tomahawk.

Unaware of having moved, Devora found herself standing over them, gripping her pistol. She felt her fingers stroke trigger and pull, heard the shot and smelled it. She stared at the blossom of blood growing on the Indian's back, then closed her eyes and stood, pistol dangling, mouth open, saliva running down her chin, breath trembling.

The thrashing at her feet got louder, and her eyes flew open. Jerd was on top now. He wrenched the tomahawk away from the Indian, and then chopped down on the savage's throat. The head dropped to one side, rolled gently, and lay still in a widening pool of blood.

Devora's breath tore into her lungs and caught. The pistol dropped from her hand.

Jerd stood up deliberately, pulled a knife from the Indian's belt, put one foot on the upturned cheek, and took the hair in his left hand. He gave it a vigorous twist that yanked the skin up from the head, cut it swiftly all around with the sharp point of the knife, then turned to Devora, the scalp hanging from his fingers.

His breath rasped in and out. Blood shone on his face, smeared his weathered hair, stained his sleeves and hands and moccasins; his own blood spread on his trouser leg.

He jerked his head toward the dead Indian and said, "Osage."

Devora's lips parted. Her breath came on a rush, and with it, words. "What man are you?" she whispered. "I don't know you . . . never saw you . . ."

His rage was still on him; he stared at her through it.

"Killer . . ." she whispered out of her dry throat. "Murderer . . . torturer . . ."

The rage dropped away, leaving his face stern. He thrust one foot under the blue breechcloth of the Indian and flipped the body over. His eyes guided hers to the flowering, bloody hole in the dead savage's back.

He asked, flatly, "What does that make you?"

She stiffened. A shiver trickled over her.

"Well?" he said.

"You're right. But did you have to . . ."

Her voice trailed off, and helplessly she indicated the mutilated neck, the bloody head, and the scalp he still held. He flung it down on the Indian's back, and the coarse black hair fell across the hole she had put in it.

Never taking his eyes off hers, he said, "He'd of done worse to you."

"I suppose."

"And to our cow."

"Yes."

"And to me."

"Yes, Jerd . . . but to be so brutal . . ."

"This ain't a gentle land or a easy life," he said shortly. "It comes natural for a man to chop up a killing varmint. As for his scalp, that's to make it look like he tangled with another Indian. Now we'd best get rid of him and all sign of fight afore his hunting partner, if he's got one, happens along."

Devora nodded, unable to move.

Swiftly he loaded his rifle, made a quick survey of their surroundings, picked up his hat, and clapped it on his head. With an effort, Devora retrieved her pistol, loaded it, and thrust it into her belt. She got the dead Osage's knife and tomahawk and carried them to Jerd.

Moving fast, he took a blanket from her pack, wiped the bloody knife and tomahawk on leaves, dropped the leaves into the blanket, and slipped the weapons under the band around her pack. She reached inside, pulled out the first thing she touched, and gave it to him.

It was her white shawl.

He held it, staring at her.

"For your leg," she said, "to keep the blood from leaving a trail."

Amber flecks showed briefly in the darkness of his eyes. He said, his voice rough, "I reckon you're the spunkiest woman I ever knowed, bar none," hurriedly folded the shawl into a wide bandage, wrapped it around his thigh, knotted it. Next he spread the blanket near the Indian, lifted him, and dumped him in the middle of it.

Working desperately in the failing light, Devora found the spent arrow, and helped scoop up bloodstained soil, sticks and greenery, throwing everything onto the blanket with the body. Last, they covered the trampled area with a scattering of sticks and earth, leaving it as natural appearing as they could.

Jerd rolled the blanket around the dead Indian, hoisted the load to his back, and made his way carefully through the forest toward the river. Devora followed, carrying the pack.

When they reached the spot where the cow was tied, he said, "Wait here," and kept walking. After a few more strides, she could no longer see him.

She dropped the pack, drew her pistol, and looked cautiously about for the arrow she had tossed aside, locating it near the base of a tree. She thrust it into her pack, and stood beside the cow, stroking her head. Faint sounds of Jerd's progress continued to reach her, and then there was silence, with only forest noises coming into it.

The cow lowed, and Devora grabbed one of her horns and steadied her, listening deeply. Jerd loomed noiselessly out of the young darkness. Devora started, and began to tremble.

He said, "The river's got him . . . swift current along here."

He shoved the folded blanket he'd brought back through the band around the larger pack, shouldered it, untied the cow's lead rope, and began to move.

"We'll take to the open," he said, "and walk all night."

Devora lifted her pack, broke off a switch, and followed. "But the cow's neck," she said, "and your leg . . ."

"They'll have to wait," he said. "We've been around here too long already. Getting away is all that matters now."

❧ *Chapter Eight* ❧

THE MOON slowly climbed the sky.

The quiet, creeping cold got worse.

Devora trudged resolutely, hoping the exercise would keep her from growing so chilled she would be forced to stop long enough to unpack her pelisse. She worked her fingers constantly to get the numbness out, and occasionally cupped one hand over her face and breathed into it to warm the tip of her nose.

The moonlight was thin, but Jerd stayed close to the outer line of forest trees, keeping in shadow, though there had been no sign of Indian since the Osage attacked, hours ago. He walked more slowly than he had during the day, but as steadily, with no trace of a limp from his wound, and apparently no thought of eating some of the dried meat as they went.

Devora's stomach rumbled, and she swallowed miserably, but would not break the silence that was a part of their safety to ask for food. She moved her feet interminably through dewy undergrowth that grew colder at every step. The air she pulled through her nostrils was damp and cold, and after a while the moonlight gave trees, bushes and grass a silver look as the dew on them congealed into ice. Eventually, frost lay everywhere.

She was beginning to think she could not take another step, when Jerd stopped in a small grove. He tied the cow and dumped his pack, and Devora dropped hers, and sat down on it.

He said, his words a murmur that barely reached her in the ear-splitting silence, "We'd best put on our wraps."

She poked her hand into a side gap of her pack, felt around until her wooden fingers recognized the texture of her pelisse, and maneuvered it out. She put it on, buttoned it, and felt in her pack again for her black shawl, which she tied over her head.

When she had finished, Jerd gave her a portion of the dried meat. "We'll rest a spell," he said.

She put some of the meat into her mouth and began to chew.

The cow lay down clumsily.

"It'll rest her, too," Jerd said. "I don't like the way she moves."

"I expect she's hungry."

"That's sure."

"Can't she graze?"

"Not on frosty grass. But her mind ain't on eating."

"You mean—?"

"I reckon it's the trip, but it looks like she's going to calve right soon, a good week ahead of her time."

"Then shouldn't we make camp? Your leg needs care, too."

"That can wait," he said. "We'll travel till daybreak if we can keep the cow on her feet."

"But Jerd, we've come miles from where we . . . killed that Osage."

"We don't know but what there's more around," he replied. "And it's said to be Indian nature to attack in daylight, something about him being scared to die at night for fear he can't find his way to the happy hunting grounds."

"I've heard of them attacking by night," she said.

"Me, too. But I figure we anyhow ain't as easy seen in the dark. I've covered a good many miles by night afore this, and I ain't had no real trouble yet."

He began to eat, and Devora put her attention on her own scanty meal, chewing slowly, making it last as long as she could, wishing for more when it was gone.

It was after sunup, and the frost had melted and evaporated by the time they made camp not far from the river bank. The air gradually warmed and was pleasant. Before noon, the cow produced a heifer calf, and Devora, who had helped Jerd at his midwifery, was staggering with weariness.

She stared at the wobbly-legged newborn creature, wondered, almost in tears, how long it had been since she and Jerd had slept, tried to estimate the hours, and could not. There was a trembling in her bones, and her head was aching in long, dull throbs.

She watched Jerd walk over to his pack, take her shawl off his leg, and lay it aside. He picked up his rifle.

"If you'll keep watch," he said, "I'll go to the river and wash this place on my leg. I'll scout for Indians so you can take your turn."

She nodded, drew her pistol, and watched him move away through the trees. She turned wearily in her tracks, searching into the forest, not daring to sit down and risk falling asleep. Her eyes burned, and she had to hold them wide to keep them open.

The cow was licking her calf dry. She could hear the wet sounds and smell them, could see the big tongue come down, stroke, lift, come down again.

She jerked her eyes away and began to walk from one end of the campsite to the other, stumbling every few steps, not permitting herself to yawn.

When Jerd reappeared, she stopped.

"Your leg?" she asked.

"I cleaned it up, and put on a mud pack to draw the poison. It ain't a lot worse than her neck." He motioned toward the cow.

Later, she recalled saying she didn't believe she cared to go to the river to wash up, that she'd eat later, thank you, and could spread her own blanket down. The next thing she knew, he was shaking her awake.

She opened her eyes. His face was above hers, anxious.

"You all right?" he asked.

She pushed up groggily. The sun was shafting through the trees from the west.

"Oh, Jerd," she said, "why didn't you call me sooner?"

"I halved our sleeping time," he told her, "giving you the edge because you're new to this life. Besides, I had me a chore to do."

She stood, walked over to his pack, and sat down, smoothing her hair with her hands. She began to eat and drink the meat and water he gave her; he stretched himself full length on her blanket, pillowing his head on his arms.

"I've watered the cow," he said. "She's grazing right yonder on that patch of grass where you can keep an eye on her. Wake me when dark begins to fall."

He closed his eyes, and she could tell, from his breathing, that he fell asleep at once.

Rest and food had cured her headache, leaving her only tired. While Jerd slept, she tidied herself as well as she could. The remaining time, she sat on Jerd's pack, resting and keeping watch.

It was good to be doing this, to let her husband rest, and guard his sleep. He was defenseless now, not at all the man who had fought the Indian and hacked him in burning rage. What he had done no longer horrified her, for she recognized, sitting here and thinking calmly, that the safety she felt with him came directly out of his ruthless strength and out of his ability to turn as savage as the wilderness in which he lived.

She had to speak his name only once, quietly.

He came to his feet, rifle in hand.

"Trouble?" he asked.

"No. It's almost dark."

"Time to leave," he said.

He took her blanket to her pile of goods and readied her pack. Then he pulled forth a contrivance made of two slim poles fastened together at a sharp angle, with crosspoles between, padded with the folded, bloodstained blanket they had wrapped the dead Osage in.

While she watched, puzzled, Jerd removed the cow's lead rope, lifted the calf and returned, the cow trotting after him, lowing. He laid the calf on the blanket, tied it to the cross poles with Devora's shawls, then knotted both ends of the lead rope to the angle of the poles, forming a loop. He stepped into the loop and pulled it up around his waist. This raised the point of the angle to his back, leaving the diverging ends of the poles on the ground, the calf at a slant on the improvised litter.

Devora smiled. "So that's the chore you did while I slept," she said.

He nodded. "I hate to use your blanket and stuff. But the critter's so young it's got to be pampered."

"That's all right, Jerd."

"This was the only way I knowed we could travel. The calf's too new to walk far, and we can't wait here for it to grow up."

"But how about Dawn?" Devora asked. "How can we keep her quiet?"

The cow was nuzzling her calf, lowing.

"She'll fuss a spell," Jerd said, shouldering his pack and taking up his rifle. "But she'll quieten down when she sees her calf's safe. We won't need no lead rope for her now, that's one thing, and you won't have to carry no switch. She'll follow wherever her young goes."

He began to walk, limping some, leaning slightly forward, pulling the litter. Devora swung her pack up and took her place at the rear.

The cow trotted, lowing, beside her calf, licking at it. Finally, resigned, she quit lowing, and fell into a walk, still watching her offspring anxiously.

It was dawn of the next morning when they topped the rise that overlooked a little valley.

Jerd said, "We're here . . . that's my place."

Devora moved to the edge of the rise and looked upon her new home.

The valley was back from the river a distance, and it was oval, held by gentle wooded slopes. Within its encircling split-rail fence, it was laid out in patches, both harvested and unharvested, one with its black soil plowed open. There was a garden, a young orchard, and fenced pasture land with a creek running a sparkle of silver through it. In the four corners of a railed barnlot, stood a barn, smokehouse, corncrib and out-house, all of log.

In the center of its own grassy yard, was the double-cabin, built of hewn logs. One roof linked what was actually two separate buildings, with a breeze-swept passage, or dogtrot, connecting them. The section on the left of the dogtrot was the smaller, and had only one room; the other had two rooms, one of which was rawly new. Both original cabins were weathered, and each had a rock fireplace at the outer end.

Rough shutters covered the window openings, flower bushes waited beside the door, and vines laced the fence.

It was a cabin for living, and it was lonely.

Devora's heart trembled.

She turned to Jerd. Her weariness slipped away, she let her eyes shine up into his, and spoke with sober lips, but with gladness in her voice, "It's so complete."

"I aimed for it to be," he said.

"Fences, outbuildings, cellar, flowers . . . and three rooms! You didn't tell me there were three rooms, Jerd."

He pulled his eyes from hers and looked across the valley, his mouth suddenly grim. He said, "The neighbors come afore I left, and raised the new room."

"I'm glad to have it, but two would have been enough."

"I figure we need it."

Troubled, she glanced at him, then searched beyond the valley to find what he was staring at, could not, so looked again at the lonely cabin.

She asked, "How do we get to it?"

"Down this slope," he said, starting to walk, "through the trees, and across."

They arrived in silence.

She waited at the rail gate between barnlot and cabin yard while he turned the calf loose. The cow began to lick at it, lowing nervously. Jerd gave her a pat, then made a round of the buildings, trying the boards nailed over the doors.

When he came to Devora, carrying his pack and dragging the litter, his face had lost its hardness, and he spoke naturally. "There ain't no Indians been meddling," he said. "Now we'll open up the cabin."

He closed the gate, put the litter and his pack beside hers, took the dead Osage's tomahawk, and went around to the front of the cabin. Here he ripped off the boards nailed across the puncheon window shutters, then moved to the door, which was also boarded up. Using the blade of the tomahawk, he prized loose the end of one of the boards, carefully pulled out two long nails, and gave them, along with those from the window, to Devora.

"Look after these," he said. "I ain't got but a few, and I have to save them for such as this here."

She stood taking the nails, one by one, as he removed the boards and stacked them, followed him to the dogtrot, and waited for the nails while he unboarded the second door. She observed that the entrance to the single room, at the end of the covered passage, was also nailed shut, but Jerd did not go to it.

He said, "We'll have to use the front way in. This door's barred on the other side."

He led, limping slightly, carrying the tomahawk, and she followed him into the cabin. The room smelled of ashes and mice, and was so shadowy she could not make out anything in it clearly. She could see Jerd at the dogtrot door, hear the lift and clunk of a wooden bar, and a squealing noise as he pulled the door open. He went directly to the window and tore away the boards over it, swung the glass portion inward, unlatched the shutters and pushed them outward, and at last the room was revealed.

It was gloomy, but that could be from the drab colors of the stone fireplace, the bare puncheon floor, the loam-daubed walls, and the thin morning light, which was coating everything with gray. A generous mantel shelf held a silent wooden clock, candles and gun-clutter; on the hearth was a jumble of cookpots. There was an iron-doored bake-oven built into the fireplace, and to one side of the chimney stood a wood box filled with wood, to the other a low, thick-lidded chest. Jerd's garments hung on wall pegs above the chest.

A bunk, covered with a faded quilt, was nailed to the front wall, reaching from the window to the door. Above this, ready to the sleeper's hand, were slanted wooden pegs for his firearms.

Opposite the bunk, wall shelves stocked with tableware and food containers began near the ceiling, swelled into a work table at the center, and ran to the floor. A bare slab table took up the middle of the room, with two chairs pulled to it, and nothing on it but dust, mouse tracks and droppings. Set at random angles on either side of the dogtrot door, were two wooden armchairs and a stool.

Jerd indicated a puncheon door diagonally across from the front entrance, where he was standing. He said, "That's yours—I'll fetch your plunder," and was gone.

Uncertainly, Devora went to the door and pushed it open. The pungency of new wood hit her, making a glad contrast to the musty smell of the older room, and she entered and groped to the nearest window. She unfastened a wooden hasp, pushed tentatively to learn if Jerd had freed the shutter, and he had, for it swung open. Quickly she crossed to the opposite window, and flung back its shutter. There was no glass in the openings, not even greased paper, and a quick sweep of sun-tinged air came flooding through, and she turned eagerly to view the room.

Nailed to the unbroken north wall, were the heads of three bunks, the middle one long and narrow, the others child-size, with tall sides. On them were straw-filled sack mattresses, their fresh aroma mixing pleasantly with the raw wood odors. There was a line of wooden pegs for clothing on the kitchen partition, and that was all.

The back of Devora's neck prickled.

She stared again at the bed that was hers, then rushed into the other room. Jerd's bunk was only a trifle wider than her own. Involuntarily, her eyes closed and she recalled the wide, soft, sweet-smelling bed Amos and Reginal shared, their daughters closed off in a separate chamber.

Her breath trembled, and a desperate weariness enveloped her. What had Jerd Warner married himself—a wife or a nursemaid?

Ashamed, she opened her eyes and turned away from the bunk. It was unmaidenly, disloyal, and unfair to think of Jerd in such a manner.

When he limped in with her pack, she was briskly lifting coarse, clean sheets out of the fireplace chest.

He went into the bedroom and called back, "I see you got the shutters open."

She joined him, the sheets on her arms. He was standing awkwardly beside her pack.

"Oh, yes," she said.

"Will the cabin do? Does it suit you?"

"It's fine, Jerd."

"I didn't know just how you'd want the bunks," he said. "But I figured with two babes . . . like I put them would be easier on you. In cold weather particular, it ain't comfortable to run around a cabin barefooted. This way you won't have to get out of bed."

"That's right . . . I won't."

"It ain't a fancy room."

"I'm not a fancy woman."

"I didn't have no way to get window glass, even. Maybe in the spring I can get some."

"There's no hurry."

"But it's sound, the room's sound."

[92]

She glanced down at the puncheons. "The floor has a pretty grain," she said.

"It's oak. We split the puncheons out of eighteen inch trees and broad-axed them smooth. They're fastened down with wood pins on sleepers, so you don't never need to worry they'll rock or shake or rattle. None of the floors will."

She laid the sheets on one of the baby bunks, smiling into his earnestness. "It's a good, comfortable cabin, and I like it," she said. "Now I'm going to cook you something hot to eat."

"We had that dried meat not two hours ago."

"How about some mush?"

"I ain't about to starve. Are you?"

"No."

"And you've been walking hard for fifteen days, and you ain't used to it."

"That doesn't matter, Jerd."

"I've got no intention of making no work-ox out of you. Fix your bed and get some sleep."

Her eyes began to sting, and she held them wide and smiled her tears away. "Sweet," she whispered.

He turned, halfway through the door. "You say something?"

Still smiling, she shook her head.

"I'll fetch you some water," he said, and left.

She made up the bunks quickly, doubling the sheets for the small ones, arranging them so the upper fold would serve as a cover. She was spreading back the quilt on Jerd's bunk when he walked in and set the water bucket on the work table.

"I'll be out back a spell," he said. "I'm going to unboard the crib and give the cow some grain and fetch her another bucket of water afore I turn in."

As soon as he was gone, Devora opened her pack and found soap, cloth, and towel. She hung a clean dress on a peg, took a night robe, and went into the front room. Here she closed the outer doors, poured water into a wooden basin, stripped off her travel-stained garments, and bathed from head to foot. Clad in her night robe, she opened the dogtrot door, ventured out on the dirt floor of the passage, threw her bath water onto the grass beyond, and hurried back inside.

She set the basin on the work table, left soap and a fresh cloth and towel for Jerd's use, and went into her room. Sitting on the side of her bunk, she took down her hair, combed and braided it, letting the braids hang down the front of her shoulders. She frowned uncertainly at the door to the kitchen, which was standing open, then lay down and pulled the sheet to her chin.

The sunny breeze played across her, moving the hair at her brow, fluttering against her closed eyelids, stirring the clean smells of soap and straw and wood, and she felt herself drifting into sleep.

～ぬ～ *Chapter Nine* ～ぬ～

THE SMELL of burning hickory roused her.

She identified it and lay resting, still half asleep. Lazily she opened her eyes, and found herself looking directly at a window, which was a square of brightness. The breeze had slowed and warmed, and she turned to her back, stretching luxuriously, pleasantly aware of a mixture of tiredness and relaxation throughout her body.

A clatter of iron brought her full awake. Her feet smacked the floor, she ran to the partition, scrambled into her clothes, pinned up her braids, and walked barefoot into the other room.

Jerd, wearing fresh clothes, was at the fireplace. He swung a crane so that the iron teakettle hanging from it was clear of the intense heat of the fire.

"Good afternoon," Devora said, smiling, "or whatever it is by now."

"It's evening," he said, "getting along toward sundown."

"Mercy, I didn't mean to sleep so long!"

"I ain't been up but a while myself."

"I'll bet you're starved."

"I am a mite hungry."

"You sit down and rest your leg. I'll have supper in no time."

He walked to the dogtrot door. "My leg'll stay limbered up better if I don't favor it," he said. "And there ain't no rush about supper—I've got to milk out what the calf ain't sucked afore I can eat."

"Oh, yes . . . of course."

"You'll find meal in that keg on the floor next to the shelves," he said. "It's got a tight lid, so the mice can't get at it."

He left. She pulled out the keg and looked inside, and it was nearly full of coarse yellow meal. Dropping the lid back in place, she straightened and stood surveying the room. Everything was dusty, mousy, and in disorder. Jerd had spread up his bunk, leaving lumps and wrinkles, and she smiled at that, but did not remake it lest he notice and think her faultfinding. His discarded clothing was folded and placed on the arm-chair where she had put her own.

Feeling strange, almost like an intruder, she took stock of the work-shelves, found a second wooden basin turned upside down, carried it to the fireplace, and poured some of the boiling water from the teakettle into it. After she had tempered this with cold water, she rubbed a little chunk of hard lye soap between her hands until she built up a light suds, then laid it aside, taking care that it did not rest in a pool of its own drippings to melt wastefully.

First, she washed the things she would use for supper, scoured the tops of both tables, then dumped the water into a wooden bucket to save for scrubbing, the way she had seen Viney do in Amos's kitchen. She put her soapy utensils into the empty basin, poured scalding water over them, and lifted each one out to be wiped, saving the rinse water for supper dishes.

She had mush bubbling and tea steeping when Jerd walked in, carry-ing a second bucket of water. While he washed up, she moved a crane, swinging the iron pot away from the heat, and filled two wooden por-ringers with mush.

Jerd took his place at the table, facing the back wall, and Devora sat across from him, looking toward the window. While he laced his mush heavily with molasses from the wooden pitcher, she filled their mugs with tea.

"I think I'll leave the table right here," she said conversationally. "It catches the breeze on a warm day, and isn't too far from the fire when it's cold."

Jerd nodded agreement, dipped his wooden spoon into the edge of his mush, tested it for hotness, put it into his mouth, and swallowed. "Tastes good," he said, and spooned again.

"One night on our way here, I dreamed about eating bread and po-tatoes," Devora said. "Anything but meat. Mush, Jerd! Isn't it wonder-ful to have mush?"

He glanced at her, and she thought his eyes softened, so she smiled at him, picked up her own spoon, and began to eat hungrily.

When they had finished second helpings, she said, "There's plenty more."

"Not for me, thanks," he said. "Fry it for breakfast. I'll fetch some bacon from the smokehouse afore we turn in. That flavors it."

He stood up, walked to the mantel, rummaged, found a pipe, and filled it. Using tongs, he lifted a coal from the firebed, held it to the tobacco, and sucked on the pipe. When he came back to the table, he was puffing gently.

Devora widened her nostrils under the good tobacco smell.

"You're full of surprises," she said. "I didn't know you smoke."

He sat down, holding the pipe in his hand, regarding it. "I never do on the trail," he said, "and not too much at no time. But I like a pipe after supper, when I ain't got much left to do in the way of work."

She smiled, sipped at her tea, watched him draw on the pipe, and asked, "What's for tomorrow?"

He looked at her questioningly.

"The babies, I mean. Do we bring them home?"

He frowned, considering. "I reckon not," he said thoughtfully. "They need milk, and tonight wasn't but the fifth milking since the birth of the calf."

"When do you begin to use the milk?"

"After the ninth milking."

"That will be two nights from now."

"Then I'll leave for the Pikes' place day after tomorrow afore light," he said.

"You don't want me to go along?"

"You'll need to keep watch of the cow, and Mahala wouldn't let you lift a finger to help her. She'll likely ride back with me to see that the babes get here safe, and to make sure you're fit to handle them according to her lights."

Devora smiled at his description of their neighbor.

"Did you say she'd ride, Jerd?"

"In my wagon. I left it and my oxen over there."

"I see."

"Hauled my pigs and chickens, and drove my sheep over for Prosper to tend. Left my hard money and my dog and other rifle for safekeeping. We trade neighboring like that."

Devora looked at him, his big frame relaxed, legs crossed, hands busy with his pipe. She looked around the dusk-filled room, her eyes lingering on its glowing heart of fire, and the wonder and simplicity of the wilderness rose up in her.

"It's a good way to live," she said softly.

"It suits me," he said. "I ain't about to swap it off."

She had trouble going to sleep that night. By listening hard, she could detect Jerd's deep, regular breathing through the open door, and knew that he was asleep. Outside, bugs and distant frogs set up two separate concerts; inside, as the night quieted, the mice began to stir.

She listened to their scampering, checked over in her mind the safety of her clean utensils, which were turned upside down, and the mush, covered in its pot, and thought she must speak to Jerd about getting a cat.

Finally, she fell asleep.

She was up and dressing in the dark the minute she heard Jerd moving about. The fire was blazing when she came into the room, but he was already outside. She lit candles, and began her work.

They had finished eating when dawn broke.

Before she had her wash water hot, Jerd had carried a big iron boiling pot from safekeeping in the barn, set it in the yard to one side of the dogtrot, partially filled it with water he carried in buckets from the creek, and built a fire under it. His next trip produced a bench, which he set against the kitchen wall of the dogtrot, and when he returned again, he brought two wooden tubs, which he put on it. He carried more water in buckets until there was enough.

"There's barrels in the barn yet," he told Devora. "Once I get the oxen home, I'll haul water in them. They belong ag'in that wall across from the bench."

"I keep being amazed," Devora said. "Until you told me about all this, I assumed I'd do the washing down at the creek."

"There's back-breaking work aplenty on the land without you doing that."

"But it's as much work for you to haul water."

"One haul of two barrels lasts near a week," he said. "And saves both of us toting it up by the bucket every day."

"Well . . . yes."

"I figure clothes washed in hot suds come cleaner."

She laughed, throwing back her head, the sounds of her laughter climbing the sunny air. When she had finished, she saw he was watching her, puzzled. A sudden, tender longing to reach out and caress him as she would an earnest, small boy took her, and she clasped her hands.

"Oh, Jerd . . . Jerd," she said, her voice still quivering. "You're such a big man . . . so much a man . . . yet you know all about making a home . . . like my father knew. And he'd kept a home without a woman's help from the time I was born."

He said, soberly, "A man learns by doing."

"A woman, too. I'll be a help to you, Jerd."

"That's sure," he said, looking full into her eyes, "that's real sure."

She washed clothes vigorously, the good hot suds jumping up her arms, the breeze twisting her skirt and skittering over her bare feet. She boiled the white things, punching them under the roiling water with a stick, time and again. She draped clean, rinsed garments on bushes, hung sheets along the fence, and spread her white shawl and her blanket, the bloodstains rubbed dim, on the grass in the full sun.

She took her suds and scrubbed the front room and everything in it, including furniture, bunk, shelves, mantel, hearth and window, until it was damp and soap-smelling, and then she poured the water out, well away from grass it might harm. And still, when Jerd wound the mantel clock and set the hands at straight-up twelve, going by the sun, she had a meal of potatoes, cabbage, bacon, and cornpone ready for the table.

When they had finished eating, she mentioned getting a cat.

"I've got one already," Jerd said. "Big tom, and a good mouser. I reckon he took off somewhere to do himself some sparking while I was gone. He'll turn up—he always does."

She said, watching him, "About the other room . . . the one at the end of the dogtrot."

His face closed, and he looked past her, that fear in his eyes.

"If you'll unboard it, I'll clean it this afternoon."

"You've done aplenty for one day."

"I'm not tired."

"It's still aplenty," he said, pushed back from the table, and left.

She sat alone.

When she stepped onto the dogtrot a moment later, he was already beyond the barnlot, striding toward the corn patch, hardly limping. Her eyes came back to the boarded-up room, and she stared at it for a long time.

Sighing, she returned to the kitchen.

She spent more than two hours making the connecting rooms her own. First, she gave the bedroom floor a good scrubbing, using the water she had boiled clothes in, to remove the last vestiges of the fine wood dust left from building, and while it dried, worked in the kitchen.

She put clean sheets on Jerd's bunk, and topped them with a bright quilt from the chest, then sorted the remainder of its contents. She laid her marriage paper on the bottom of the chest, put the other articles back carefully, towels on top, her bag of money in a corner. Next, she arranged tableware and food containers attractively on the shelves, hung cookpots on the proper fireplace cranes, and set the trivets, skillets, and other implements neatly along the hearth.

She sorted Jerd's gun and smoking supplies and lined them up, ready to use, at the window end of the mantel shelf. At the other end, she stood her books in a row, and laid her writing materials and sewing equipment back of them, along with her pistol and hickory-stick calendar.

She stood off and studied the room, then dragged the table and benches a couple of feet toward the dogtrot door, and pulled the armchairs to the fireplace, putting one at each side of the hearth. The stool, when she drew it alongside the chair nearest her bedroom, became a low table, and on it she placed her Bible and a candle. She set other candles around the room, one at each end of the mantel, one on the eating table, and one on a workshelf.

She took Jerd's garments off the pegs above the chest, carried them into the bedroom, and hung them up. She shook out her own clothing and hung it beside his. Then, her hands unsteady, she made her bunk, pulling the top sheet tight, folding her blanket across the foot. Tonight, she was thinking, her cheeks ablaze, tonight I'll wear my new night robe, the one with the lace trim.

Her toilet articles and hand glass, she laid on a kitchen shelf. Last, she heated irons, pressed the things she had washed, and put them away. Her sweet-smelling, fluffy woolen shawls she folded at the foot of the baby bunks.

Jerd did not appear until supper was ready. She greeted him gaily, called his attention to the room, and watched him study it.

"It looks different," he said at last. "That quilt belongs—it wasn't never kept in here."

"I found it in the chest. It's too pretty to keep hidden."

His eyes came to her, troubled. "You moved the chairs."

"It's cozier to sit by the fire."

"They used to be in the way of cooking."

"I'll make pads for them, seats and backs both, when I find materials," she said. "And a window curtain and table cover, as well."

His eyes remained on her, and he frowned.

"Don't you like it, Jerd? Don't you like the room?"

"It's just that it'll take some getting used to," he said. "You've made it handsome, that's sure."

He walked over and inspected the vacant wall space on either side of the dogtrot door. "I've got some walnut out in the barn," he said. "When I get home, I'll fix you a indoor washshelf on this side, and a set of shelves on that one. I'll make some benches, too."

"I don't know of anything," Devora told him, a bit shakily, "I'd rather have. Thank you, Jerd."

But of course he's asleep, she thought later, in her narrow bunk, in her new, lace-trimmed night robe. You can't expect any man, especially a young widower, to plunge into the kind of marriage a woman dreams about . . . with all its love and tenderness . . . when his first wife hasn't been dead a year. He's not over her . . . I knew that. And he's trying . . . he's meeting me halfway wherever he can. He'll get around to everything in his own good time.

She smiled to herself in the cooling night, and wondered if ever before a woman had married a stranger, and waited in such unmaidenly boldness for him to begin his lovemaking. Her mouth tender from the smile, she fell asleep.

It was still utterly dark when she gave him breakfast and made up a packet of cornpone and bacon for him to take. They stood together in the darkness outside the dogtrot before he left.

"I'd feel better satisfied," he said, "if you'd swap me your pistol for my rifle."

"You're the one apt to see an Indian or a panther," she said. "I'll be in the cabin, and the pistol will do fine."

"Keep it handy," he cautioned, "and don't be backward with it."

"I won't be."

"I should get home afore sundown," he said, "but if I ain't, be sure you latch the shutters like they are now, and bar the doors."

She touched his sleeve. "You be careful, Jerd."

"Well," he said, shifting awkwardly, the movement taking him away from her, "I reckon I best get started."

She didn't see or hear him leave, but when she reached out to touch him again, he was gone. She called, softly, "Good-by," but he did not answer, and she stood looking into the nighttime of morning for any sign of him, and after a while went into the cabin, barred the door, and began to clear the table.

The one candle and the fire gave only a whisper of light to the room, and the outer darkness and the silence of darkness were greater than she had ever known. She recalled how lonely the cabin had looked that first dawn, and now she was lonely in it.

Black wilderness surrounded the little valley; if Indians were lurking at its edge, she had no way of knowing, and if they were to come creeping up to attack, she had no defense other than the pistol.

She laid it on a shelf in front of her, and washed dishes, handling them carefully, listening. The clock on the mantel swung its pendulum loudly. When the dishes were done, she tiptoed across the floor in her bare feet and made Jerd's bunk, half-holding her breath, ears straining.

She had just settled down in her fireplace chair, the pistol on the stool-table beside the Bible, when, beneath the ticking of the clock, she heard it. She sat quiet, her ears reaching desperately for a repetition of the noise.

It sounded again, a barely audible scratching at the dogtrot door. She came to her feet, pistol in hand, and stood holding her breath.

The scratch was repeated, followed by a throaty, "Me-orw!"

She wanted to move, but her feet would not budge, and she noticed how cool the puncheons were against her soles. Now she was sucking air in gulps, and it was drying her throat. She tried to close her mouth, but her jaw hung inert.

Her mind went wild. Indians often imitated a turkey to decoy a victim, but did they know the habits of the domestic cat? What was on the other side of the door . . . cat or Indian?

She had to know. She couldn't stand here until daybreak, not knowing. She willed her legs to move, and by the time she got to the door, her fingers were sweating on the pistol, and it had a tendency to quiver from the strength of her grip. Silently she lifted the door bar with her free hand, silently lowered it.

She laid her ear to the crack. Her heartbeat vibrated into the wood, and reverberated in her head. There was no sound. Then, so suddenly she started, another "Me-orw," reached her.

Cautiously, she eased the door inward an inch, and a loud purring set up, mixed with frequent "Me-orws." Pistol ready, body poised to slam the door instantly, she cracked it more, waited, felt a light push at the bottom, heard the continued purring. Breathless, she pulled the door wider, looking toward the bottom, and saw there the eerie glint of eyes.

She swung the door back, quietly laughing and crying. "Cat," she whispered, "cat, come in!"

He was a huge animal, she could see that even in the shadows, and he was deliberate about entering, taking time to purr, halt, talk, and move again. When he was inside at last, she closed the door and barred it, still hysterical, tears running down her cheeks.

She returned to her chair, sank into it, letting the pistol rest in her lap, and leaned her head back. Gradually her laughter ceased, then her sobs, and she was sitting there utterly limp.

Finally she peered into the shadows and said, "Come on out in the open, Indian."

"Me-orw," the cat said, and remained where he was.

"Let's get acquainted. Come on, Big Tom."

A full minute passed, the clock ticking, the fire snapping. Then the glinting eyes passed slowly and deviously among the table legs, around Jerd's chair, and the cat seated himself on the hearth and stared at her with his pointed yellow eyes.

He was black as night. He lifted a wide paw, flicked it daintily with his tongue, and rubbed it down his face. He was tall, rangy, thin, and scarred. His head was square, with ragged ears, and his bobtail, as he stood now and walked to another hearth-spot, was held up so high by his knobby legs that his rear end resembled that of a big rabbit.

"You're quite a Tom," Devora told him.

He sat down again, said "Me-orw," and began washing his face in earnest.

"You've scared me my last scare," she told him. "Real danger hits without warning . . . like that Osage."

He quit licking, and gazed at her.

"I've a job to do here, and I can't be swooning behind a barred door every time Jerd has to leave me by myself."

"Me-orw . . . me-orw!"

"You want to eat, do you? All right, Big Tom, come along."

She laid down her pistol and walked briskly to the shelves. She crumbled cornpone onto a small wooden trencher, broke up and scattered the cooked bacon she'd saved for her noon meal on top, poured bacon drippings over it all, and set it on the floor.

Big Tom made his way to it, smelled it in a leisurely way, glanced up at her, then began to eat with the utmost daintiness.

Devora smiled at him. "You won't get that every morning, my boy," she said. "You've work to catch up on, and so have I. So . . . let's see what it's like outside."

She flung open the front window shutters, and all the valley and the forest beyond was dewy gray. She opened both doors and stood on the dogtrot for a moment, pulling the damp, free air into her lungs, then went to her bedroom and threw back the shutters, resolving never again to let terror force her to lock out the night.

She made her bed, wandered back into the kitchen, feeling its good cleanness, and blew out the candle, liking its hot smell. The clock ticked quietly, Big Tom nibbled his food, and a sense of homecoming descended upon Devora.

She paused in the middle of the room, the thick gray light from the open doors revealing it to her, and regarded the bright quilt on the bunk, her books standing on the mantel, the orderly shelves and the eating table, experiencing, for the first time in her life, the feel of being woman in her own home, mistress of the fireplace, keeper of the family.

She stood accustoming herself to her new stature, then, with brisk decision, took her pistol, picked up the Osage's hatchet from its place beside the wood box, went out the dogtrot door and directly to the room at the end of it, where she set to work. One after another, she ripped the boards from across the shutters and the door, stacking them at one end of the dogtrot, and carefully saving the nails.

But when she had finished, she stood looking at the door a long time before she raised the latch and entered.

⤝ *Chapter Ten* ⤞

SHE WENT THROUGH the musty gloom to the window, avoiding the shadowy outlines of the furnishings, ripped the boards loose, swung the glass inward, unlatched the shutters, and pushed them open. Not yet permitting herself to look at this room which Jerd had virtually forbidden her to enter, she returned to the doorway, wheeled, and gazed around it searchingly.

The walls were whitewashed, and the floor was covered with light-colored braided rag carpeting. At the far end, a big stone fireplace centered the wall; upon its wide mantel stood a glass and gilt clock and silver candelabra. Starting well above the wood box at the right of the fireplace, puncheon doors reached almost to the ceiling; on the other side, similar doors began at the floor and matched them in height.

At this end, to Devora's left, the head of a wide double bunk was fastened to the wall, its foot extending to the small, high-set window. The bunk was covered with a pale blue and pink coverlid, and when Devora pushed tentatively, she got the softness and give of a thick featherbed underneath.

To the right of the entrance was a homemade washstand, equipped with a big, white, violet-sprigged china bowl and various matching dishes and pitchers.

Beyond the bunk, on the far side of the pink-ruffled window, stood a mahogany chest of drawers, littered with silver toilet articles. Above it hung a fine mirror. To the right of the hearth, were grouped a small, homemade chair, footstool and table, onto which needlework spilled out of a sewing box.

Finally, against the unbroken wall to her right, Devora's eyes came to an article of such luxury that she cried out involuntarily, and went running to it. It was a Spinnet, its graceful, gilt case standing on three delicate legs, music books piled on the floor beside it.

She opened the lid and looked at the pastoral scene painted on its underside. Entranced, she struck a key, held her finger on it, let the fragile note linger, then closed the lid. She had never before touched a Spinnet, never seen one, except in a picture.

Now, moving quickly, she opened the puncheon doors above the wood box, and on the shelves were stacked sheets and towels and quilts and blankets and lengths of uncut materials. Behind the long doors on the other side of the fireplace, hung dresses, pelisses, and bonnets, and on the bottom were two rows of slippers. In the drawers of the mahogany chest, were ornaments and accessories, lingerie, and a wealth of needle-work supplies. There was even a folded, white, lacy shawl, very similar to Devora's.

She pushed shut the last drawer and stood dazed, looking at the array of silver on top of the chest. A web of hairs, yellow as butter, was caught in the brush, and more were in the comb. A wedding ring lay near one end, its brightness hidden under dust.

Devora put her back to the chest, stared about the astounding room again and thought, What kind of girl was she, this Sarie? What had this locked-off place become to Jerd—an altar or a tomb?

A sense of haste took her. Mahala Pike was due to arrive this evening, and the room, sacred though it might be, and fine, was a disgrace. It cried for a thorough cleaning; it must be shining sweetly when her neighbor set foot in it.

Energetically, she plunged into the task, and when she had finished, Sarie's mark was off the room, and hers was on it. She had traded positions of the Spinnet and chest, and grouped the chair, footstool and table in the middle of the floor. She had stripped all the flat surfaces of clutter; the table held only a silver candelabrum filled with new candles, the chest only the other candelabrum, and the mantel was bare except for the clock, which was now running.

She had put a bright coverlet on the bed, and the starched window ruffles, their pink boiled to white, added a crisp note to the room. The china pitcher held water, the soap dish a new chunk of yellow soap, and on the wall pegs hung freshly ironed towels.

The clothes cabinet and the drawers of the chest were completely empty, ready for a guest's belongings. The dead girl's things were stored on the shelves above the wood box, the doors buttoned shut.

Devora gave the completed room a final glance, left it open to the breeze, and returned to her kitchen fireplace where her supper cooking was in progress. This was no time to speculate as to whether Jerd was going to be relieved or sorrowed because signs of his dead wife had been removed from the room at the end of the dogtrot. There was still work to be done before she would be ready to greet Mahala Pike and the babies.

She tended the cow and calf, left them shut in the barn, and strained the milk into wooden bowls in the cellar that was located halfway between cabin and barnlot. Inside again, she set the table, Big Tom getting underfoot, and then, throbbing with good fatigue, she bathed and dressed, putting on stockings and slippers for the first time.

It was sunset when she sat down in her fireplace chair to wait.

It had been dark for more than an hour when she drew a shawl around her shoulders and walked out into the yard, Big Tom following. The sky was black, holding the glitter of far-up stars, and there was a smell of frost. The bracing cold drove out the last of her weariness, and she stood at the fence, the fingers of her left hand prancing eagerly along the top rail.

First she heard a dog yap, then the murmur of a voice, later the squealing of pigs, and the quarreling of sleepy hens, and last of all, the creak of a wagon. Peering through the starry darkness, she made out slow moving black shadows, and went running to the barnlot and threw the big gate wide.

Jerd, driving a few sheep ahead of him, led the oxen through.

"Hello there," Devora said.

"You all right?" he asked.

"Yes . . . oh, yes."

"That's Mahala Pike on the wagon."

"Evening," said a voice that was music.

Suddenly Devora was troubled.

She had married Jerd with the understanding that she was to mother his twins; to that end, she had come through wilderness, killed a human being, and rid the cabin of a dead girl's personality. Yet, even as she waited to receive these babies, she realized that for months, which was the whole of their lives, they had known this other woman for mother. Now they were to be deprived of the loved and trusted and left to the unknown, and there was no way to give them understanding or comfort.

She swallowed against the beating in her throat and said, "Welcome, Mahala Pike. Get down and come in. Here, let me carry one of the babies."

"No. I'm handy at pairs," said the music, bright and fast.

There was movement down over the front wheel. A thin shadow reached up to the wagon seat for two small shadows, then walked toward the cabin so rapidly Devora had to half run to get there first to open the door.

Mahala Pike stopped in the full candleglow, holding the wrapped and hidden babies, one on each hip. She was the plainest woman Devora had ever seen, forty or over, with sharp features and colorless lips. She wore linsey, and when her shawl fell away, it revealed brownish hair skinned back into a tight round knob.

Her face showed tautness and suspicion. Her eyes, which were as bright and lovely as her voice, played like blue flames over Devora. "Show me where to lay them down," she said. "They're sound asleep."

Devora gestured toward the bedroom, took a candle, and led the way. Mahala lowered the babies into the same bunk, removed the blankets in which they were wrapped, and covered them, her hands lingering.

One child stirred, whimpered, quieted.

"The boy," Mahala whispered.

He had yellow curls, a thin face, and skin so white and delicate that even by candlelight Devora could see the blue tracery of veins. His lips were barely pink.

The girl had a warm brown tumble of ringlets, a plump face, and high color. Her half-open little mouth was rosy.

Mahala turned abruptly and left the room. Devora followed, pulling the door almost shut behind her. The older woman took the candle from her hand, held it so the light fell full on Devora, and again the bright, lovely eyes searched.

"You ain't what I feared you mought be," she said at last.

"And what was that?"

"Young, to commence with."

"I'll be thirty in May."

"I can see that. And you ain't silly-pretty, like some."

"No one ever called me pretty."

"You ain't ugly . . . nor really handsome."

"No."

"Oh, I speak out, you'll learn that. I got my idees, and I stick to them."

"Good for you."

"You ain't useless."

"I hope not."

"It takes elbow grease and know-how to take a cabin that's been let go like this one was, and get it to looking homey, the way it does now."

"Thank you, Mrs. Pike."

"Don't thank me. I'm only giving you your due. I ain't made up my mind about you yet."

"What else were you afraid I might be?"

"Feather-headed."

Devora smiled. "My brother thinks a little of that would improve me. He wanted me to marry a St. Louis man and live an easy life."

Mahala studied Devora for a long moment, the candlelight flickering on her plain, suspicious face. The tautness around her beautiful eyes loosened, and her mouth gentled.

"Them babies has been used to a lot of care—and loving."

"They can't grow without it."

"You know about babies—their wants and needs?"

"Yes, Mrs. Pike. I've always lived with my brother, and he has two little girls."

"Was they sickly?"

"No."

"The boy in there, he's a puny one. I've had to do for him night and day, to keep the breath of life in him. It's his heart. Has them bad spells when he gets downright blue."

"Jerd didn't tell me."

"He never come near them. Do you know how to do for that kind of a baby?"

"You must keep him warm, rub him to help circulation."

"When he has a spell, how about then?"

"I helped with such a baby in St. Louis—I know some things to do. You can tell me the rest."

"You like babies."

"No better than you do."

"Only I won't never have one. I wanted these, but Jerd wouldn't hear to it. And Prosper upheld him."

"It's natural for Jerd to want his children."

"It's duty he feels, not want. He don't know them, and they don't know him."

"They'll get acquainted now, you'll see."

"He ain't never really looked at them babies, not to this day."

"I suppose they remind him . . . of her death."

"Even so. He could of anyhow named them."

"What do you call them?"

"They answer to 'Baby.'"

"What would you name them if they were . . . yours?"

"Frank for my Pa, Lillian for my Ma."

"Frank Warner . . . Lillian Warner."

"It would've been Frank Pike and Lillian Pike. I willed it to be. I even prayed Jerd couldn't find him no woman willing, though in my heart I knowed it was wrong."

"Oh, Mrs. Pike."

"Fiddle, it ain't none of your doings!"

"Jerd says I can name the twins, Mrs. Pike. So it's going to be Frank and Lillian—with your permission."

Mahala's eyes swam with quick tears, her lids batted, she put the candle on the table, and began to roll up her sleeves.

"Pshaw," she said, "suit yourself. Names is free, and the world's full of Franks and Lillians, but call them that if you want. Now, tell me what to do to be of some use around here. I ain't one to set and hold my hands."

Impulsively, Devora asked, "Have you made up your mind about me?"

"Don't get in such a rush," Mahala said, her face earnest. "I ain't never been a hand to make a snap judgment, though I ain't slow, neither. You do look like a right one, and talk and act likewise, but them babies I have to give over to you is like a part of myself. I got to have a breathing spell afore I'm ready to give out my friendship and trust along with them. But you can drop the 'Mrs. Pike' and call me Mahala like everybody else."

Devora smiled. "Thank you," she said. "I hear Jerd coming. Do you want to start dishing up?"

Mahala was darting purposefully between fireplace and table as Devora went onto the dogtrot to meet Jerd. She relieved him of two rifles, two small packs and said, "If that big pack is the babies' things, you might put it in the bedroom," returned to the kitchen, dropped one small pack on Jerd's bunk, laid the rifles along the wall pegs above it, and put the remaining small pack, which was a handkerchief containing hard money, into the chest.

When she turned, a long-tailed white dog was sniffing at her feet. She held her hand to him, and he smelled it, ears slicked back, then began to wave his tail and whine.

"That's Jerd's dog, that's Spot," Mahala said. "Jerd raised him from a pup. He don't make up easy, as a rule."

Devora patted the dog. "Hello, Spot," she said, "hello, fellow." Then, to Jerd, as he crossed toward the outside door, "Supper's on."

"Soon as I've milked. I've put the stock up already."

"I milked."

He stopped, glanced at her in surprise.

"Father taught me how when I was a little girl."

"Well," he said, "thanks. I don't hardly know how to act, things so ready and waiting. I'll wash up, then."

But before he did so, he turned a long, deep look around the room. She saw him note the hearthfire, the chairs drawn to it, the bright plumpness of his bunk, the supper table. When his eyes came to her, she could see the amber flecks in them. He smiled, and she knew, instinctively, that she had made his cabin into a home such as he'd never had, and that he sensed this.

They sat long over their meal, commenting on the flavor the ham nub had given the cabbage, potatoes and beans, eating cornpone and molasses for dessert, drinking tea.

Mahala accepted her third nogginful.

"I don't make it frequent," she told them. "Prosper, he claims it don't stick to the ribs, and I reckon it don't, but it sure goes down easy. If you'll learn me your way of brewing it, Devorry, I'll be much obliged."

Devora agreed, and while she and Mahala cleared the table, they chatted about cooking and gardening. Jerd sat at the fireplace with his pipe, his head leaned back, his eyes half-closed, the dog stretched out at one side of the hearth, the cat at the other.

Presently the babies began to cry. Mahala stopped in midword, and stood holding the forgotten dish towel, a hunger on her face.

"Won't you go to them?" Devora asked quickly. "So the cabin won't seem so strange to them?"

Her face shining, Mahala hurried into the bedroom. When she returned, carrying a baby on each hip, Devora was kneeling at the hearth, filling two small noggins with the milk she had set there to warm.

Mahala dumped the girl on Jerd's lap. He grabbed the back of her gown in his fist, looking bewildered and uncomfortable. The baby glanced up at him with round hazel eyes, stared solemnly, and then her little mouth curled, and she gurgled and laughed, and made a bouncing motion.

Devora smiled. "You see, Jerd," she said, "it's a case of love."

"That one likes her men," Mahala said, settling herself with the boy. "When you got twins, the pa's got to do his share of the feeding and holding, and it'll be a big help, her taking to Jerd. She's always set a store by Prosper."

"When do I meet your husband?" Devora asked.

"Tomorrow. He'll be after me."

"So soon?"

Mahala paused to spoon milk for the blue-eyed baby on her lap, offering it gently, waiting for his listless acceptance of it.

"A woman's place is with her man," she said, "and every family belongs alone. We'll leave right after dinner dishes—have to, to be sure to be home in time for chores."

When the twins were settled, Jerd got to his feet, knocked the tobacco out of his pipe and said, "Mahala, you use my bunk. That'll put you near the babes in case they cry for you."

"Where'll you sleep at?"

"Out in the barn."

"There's no need for that," Devora said, unable to look at either of them in her embarrassment over such obvious display of their separate beds. "I've a bed ready for Mahala."

"I don't see where," Jerd said.

Mahala's eyes left Jerd, settled for an instant on the bedroom door, then searched Devora's face. She picked up her bundle and said, "Show me where at. It's best we try getting through the night without the twins seeing me, because tomorrow night I can't come to them, no matter what."

"This way," Devora said.

She took a candle, and shielding its flame, led briskly out the door and along the dogtrot. She heard Mahala's gasp, and then the pat of her feet on the dirt floor as she ran to catch up.

Devora went into the room she had cleaned that day, lit all the candles, and turned to Mahala, who was standing with her back against the closed door.

"There's a fire laid if you want it," she said.

Mahala's bright eyes were skipping all over the room. Her pale lips were slightly open.

"You've changed it, bettered it," she said.

"I wish you were going to use it longer."

Mahala grinned, and the breaking of her plain face into such friendliness gave her, fleetingly, the look of a twelve-year-old. "Me, too," she said. She stepped to the bunk and pressed on the featherbed appreciatively. "I wasn't never in here but the onc't, when the twins was born."

"There'll be other times."

"Jerd. Does he know about this?"

"No."

"Oh, my."

"Good night," Devora said.

"Good night," Mahala whispered.

She waited until Mahala barred the door, then walked the darkness of the dogtrot to the kitchen, feeling safe in the company of Spot, who had followed. Noiselessly, she raised the latch, and entered.

Jerd was standing at the fireplace, staring into it, feet apart, back rigid. She lifted the door bar and dropped it into place with a deliberate clatter.

Slowly, he wheeled.

His face was set. His chest rose and fell. His mouth was clamped, and there was none of that fear in his eyes, only anger.

In silence she crossed to her bedroom door, and turned. "Well," she said.

"I nailed the room shut."

"I ripped it open."

"I shut it to stay."

"I opened it to use."

She heard his breathing now, saw his neck cords stand out, and his great, white-knuckled fists jerk, but could barely hear the words that came through his clenched teeth.

"If you was a man . . ."

"I'm your wife."

"I built you a room."

"You asked me to mother your babies."

"I aim to fix up that room for you . . ."

"You said nothing about your Bluebeard's chamber . . ."

". . . with glass windows . . ."

". . . but I won't live with it, and you can't, either!"

"I can't what?"

"Live with your memories nailed into that room!"

"It ain't that."

"You can't bury a room, or forget it, by boarding it up."

"That's for me to say, in my own good time."

"Meanwhile, you have no right to expect me to keep a dead woman's tomb at my elbow."

His fresh anger took him so completely he went white and stared at her in terrible silence. She stared back at him, swept by her own rage, her body rigid.

"I'm your wife, Jerd Warner, and don't you forget it," she said. "I'm married to you for keeps, and nothing, not Indian, or sickness, or fire, or drought, or flood, or any other woman, living or dead, not even you yourself is going to change that!"

His lips moved, shook, fell apart.

She went into her room, closed the door, and leaned weakly against it.

When she could move, she undressed and got into bed. There had been no sound from the kitchen; if Jerd had gone to the barn for the night, he had departed noiselessly. That would mean the door was unbarred, and any prowling Indian could enter, but Devora would not venture in, because Jerd might still be there, and she was in no condition to meet him with dignity.

She pulled her blanket to her chin, and stared up the darkness toward the ceiling she could not see. Spot would bark if an Indian came sneaking up; that would give her time to run into the other room and get her pistol.

She listened to the breathing of Jerd's children, the son and daughter of his dead Sarie, over whom she had quarreled so bitterly with him. She lay trembling endlessly, and even after this ceased, could not sleep. Frank began to cry, continued to fret, and she took him into her bed, rubbed his cold little feet and legs, and when he was warmed, kept him in her arms close against her bosom, and he slept, his tiny breath moving on the hollow of her throat.

Holding him thus, she reflected upon how uneventful and undisturbed, with the exception of her father's death, her old life had been. She remembered the serenity of her family relationships, and wished to smile over the turmoil she was now experiencing, and could not.

Her anger at Jerd was gone, but it had left such hurt she was dismayed. She thought back to the day he first came into her life, a huge, untamed, dark-eyed man with an uncanny attraction; she let her memory slip down along all the days since, dwelling upon his friendliness and strength, the time he had held her in his arms in the rain, the promise of tenderness she had felt in him, the feeling of safety his mere presence brought, and her eagerness for his return when he had to be gone.

All these things she lined up carefully with the hurt, added them together, closed her eyes, and moaned with truth. She had begun to love this man to whom she was married but who was not yet truly husband; such love could never lessen, but was bound to grow until, unless matched by one as true, it would eventually consume her.

Chapter Eleven

SHE SLIPPED OUT of bed at the first hint of dawn. The air was icy and the floor cold to her feet as she closed the shutters and dressed. Before she left the room, she moved Lillian over in bed, carefully lifted Frank into the warm spot his sister had vacated, and covered them snugly. They stirred and whimpered, and she leaned over them for some moments, patting and soothing, before they quieted.

The kitchen fire was blazing, the teakettle hanging over it, and Jerd's bunk had been slept in, though he was gone. Quickly, while she had the room to herself, Devora combed her hair and made up the bunk before she turned her attention to the preparation of breakfast.

She was cooking mush when Mahala entered, hurried directly to the fireplace, and demanded, "How'd they do?"

"Frank cried once. But not for long. I took him into bed with me and warmed him, and he was all right."

Mahala jerked her head in an approving nod, then searched Devora's face. "Didn't sleep much yourself, did you?" she asked.

Devora hesitated, then smiled. "Not a wink," she admitted.

"Humph."

"Do I look so awful?"

"Tired around the eyes."

"I've been up all night before."

"With the sick?"

"Yes."

"There wasn't no sick here last night."

"No."

"I done some pondering in that bed of hers."

"Oh?"

"And I come to the conclusion to stick my nose in."

"Mahala."

"I'd owe it to any woman in your shoes. I knowed he'd be bucking. About the room."

"It's natural for him to be disturbed."

"It didn't disturb me none. I laid there and pictured myself her—lazy, and being waited on hand and foot. It felt fine."

"Oh, Mahala."

"True."

"Even so."

"I ain't spoke no actual wrong of the dead."

"No."

"He carried on something scandalous at the time."

"It was a shock."

"Wouldn't let nothing in there be touched, and then he nailed it up. Wouldn't look at them babies, not even onc't, acted similar to a crazy man."

"His world had fallen apart."

"Now he's brung you into her mess."

"I didn't expect things to be easy."

"They ain't going to be. Well, I've said my say, and my conscience is clear. Even if you get mad."

"Do you want to set the table, Mahala? Jerd will be through choring any minute."

Mahala looked at her steadily, then clacked her tongue and went darting about the room, making herself useful.

When Jerd entered, carrying a wooden bucket with a small amount of foaming milk in it, the open door admitted frosty air, and he closed it promptly. That set look was still on him, underlaid with a visible quiet rage. He set the bucket on the workshelf, pulled off his coat, hung it up, and took his place at the table without a word or glance for either woman.

While Mahala dished up, Devora strained the milk into a pitcher before she sat down in her usual place. Mahala used an armchair pulled up to one side of the table, her back to the fireplace.

Devora looked at Jerd, seeking his eyes, which were downcast as he poured molasses over his mush and into his tea.

She said, determinedly, "Jerd, will you please ask grace?"

His eyes came up instantly, black and hard and raging. Slowly, he set down the pitcher. His mouth clamped, then he bowed his head and mumbled, "Lord-bless-this-food-to-our-use-amen."

He didn't look up after that.

Mahala ate as she had the night before, heartily, with neat, bird-fast movements, her eyes quick between Jerd and Devora. All the while, she kept chattering brightly about the habits, requirements, and admirable qualities of the twins.

When he had finished eating, Jerd put on his coat and went outside. A wash of cold air hit Devora as he pulled the door shut, and she shuddered involuntarily.

Mahala said, "We had us a frost last night."

"Yes."

"I wouldn't fret myself, if I was you. Most men has their times when they act like a thundercloud, even Prosper."

Devora nodded absently, scarcely hearing, for she was quivering inwardly over the estrangement between herself and Jerd. On the previous occasions when she had inadvertently hit upon some painful memory, he had simply walked away. When he returned he was friendly, because, once he'd considered, he knew she had not intended to pry or intrude. This time, however, she had broken deliberately into his sorrow and destroyed its shrine, and he was not going to forgive her easily or soon.

If ever.

Any reconciliation was strictly up to her.

Yet if she had yesterday to live again, she knew she would still open the room. Sometimes, she thought, the only way to cure a sore that keeps festering is to cut into it until it bleeds, after which, slowly, it will heal, from inside out.

Abruptly, she pushed back from the table, and began to clear away the dishes. The babies were fretting, and Mahala went into the bedroom after them. From that moment, the two of them were so busy Devora didn't try to speak to Jerd, even casually, as he came and went, carrying wood, stacking it along the dogtrot, hauling water, and filling the barrels.

By midmorning the sun had melted the frost, dried every trace of it away, and warmed the earth. A mild wind was blowing the tree branches so they tossed their red and yellow and orange leaves gaily, and was knocking the shriveled brown leaves to the ground and scuttling them into fence corners.

Through this atmosphere came a sudden great barking from Spot, and a hallooing from a distance. Mahala dropped the potato she was paring, set her wooden pan on the floor, and darted out through the dogtrot. Devora followed and stood in the passage, the wind blowing her skirts against the backs of her legs.

Talking excitedly, Mahala ran across the barnlot and threw open the gate for a man on an ugly gray horse. He rode inside, and while Mahala closed the gate, dismounted, slid the bridle off the horse and hung it on the fence.

When he started toward the cabin, Devora could see that he was a square-built, solid-fleshed man with a heavy step. Mahala, still chattering, was literally hopping along beside him, looking thinner than ever in contrast, and slightly taller than he was.

She hustled him right up to Devora, and stopped.

"This's Prosper," she said.

"Hello," Devora said, smiling, and held out her hand.

He gripped it in his rough palm, gave one shake, let go. "Miz Warner, I reckon," he said, and grinned. He had a wide, warm grin in a wide, rosy-cheeked face. His eyes were green-flecked hazel, and his brown hair made ringlets all over his head.

Devora laughed. "I'm 'Devora' to friends," she said.

"Devorry, it is. That's more like it. Where's my babies at, where's my little girl?"

"Asleep now, Prosper Pike!" Mahala cried. "We only just got them down, so you leave be! She's put names to them a'ready, Prosper—Lillian and Frank!"

Prosper's grin vanished and he said, gravely, "You didn't have no obligation to do such as that."

"It was a privilege," Devora said. "Any names I might have settled on without help would have had no real meaning."

"Thanks, Devorry, thanks."

"Come in and eat."

"I et afore I started. Where's Jerd at?"

"Getting in his corn," Mahala said.

"I'll just step down to the patch then, and see to it he does it right," Prosper said. "We'll be up to put our feet under the table, come noon."

Mahala stood beside Devora and watched her man disappear into the corn rows, her mouth gentle. When she could no longer see him, she darted back into the kitchen, took up the potatoes, and began to peel rapidly.

They sat down to dinner at noon, two couples and two babies. Jerd said grace of his own accord. Lillian, on Prosper's knee, ate whatever he spooned into her, gurgled, hugged him around the neck upon request, and laughed when he tickled her under the chin. Devora, watching them, thought idly they might be father and daughter as far as coloring and disposition were concerned.

Frank leaned against Mahala's flat bosom throughout the meal, rejecting the food she offered. His big eyes were the color of opened violets as they regarded the strange room.

Devora, painfully aware that Jerd had not looked at her or addressed one word to her, was relieved and grateful when she found that he talked naturally with Prosper, and even with Mahala. He ignored the

[118]

twins, and didn't so much as glance at Lillian, even when she became her most hilarious and engaging.

The men went outside immediately after the meal, and when the dishes had been put away, Devora and Mahala settled in the fireside chairs, each with a baby. Devora held the girl, who stared up at her, smiled, closed her eyes, and promptly went to sleep. It took longer for Mahala, patting and crooning, her eyes dry, but tears in her voice, to lull the boy to sleep.

They put the twins to bed and tiptoed from the room, pulling the door shut. Mahala got into her wraps, picked up her bundle, and turned her beautiful eyes on Devora. "I got my mind made up," she said.

"Oh?"

"You're what you seem to be."

"Oh, Mahala, I hoped you'd feel that way!"

"Pshaw, it'd take a plumb fool not to see it. You got grit, you got spunk, you got everything—and I'm on your side."

"We're friends, then!"

"For keeps. And seeing as I got to turn them little angels over to some-body, I'd ruther it's you."

"Mahaley!" bellowed Prosper from the distance. "Mahaley, come on!"

"I'll come arunning if I'm needed, Devorry," Mahala said. "I'll be over frequent, anyhow." Her face broke into its rare, gamin smile, and then she darted out, a merry "Good-by!" drifting back from her.

Devora followed slowly, but stopped at the edge of the dogtrot, for Mahala was already clambering onto the horse behind Prosper. She put her arms around his waist, glanced brightly back to the cabin, and nodded vigorously. Devora waved, and Prosper lifted his hand to her as he walked the gray horse through the gate that Jerd had swung open.

He shut the gate and returned to his corn patch, but Devora watched their neighbors out of sight.

Lonely, she went into the room Mahala had occupied, and which she was trying to think of as the guest chamber, intending to set it to rights. She found that Mahala had left it so tidy there was nothing for her to do, and she closed the door, speculating as to whether Jerd was liable to nail it up again.

Working in a leisurely manner, she sorted the baby clothes Mahala had brought, and put them in the quilt chest, first removing a blanket and a quilt to make room, folding these into a pad on the wooden top. She thought of the empty drawers in the mahogany chest in the guest chamber, and wished she dared move it to her room for the little garments, but did not consider it seriously.

When the twins awoke, she spread a blanket on the floor in front of the hearth, carried them to it, and poked up the fire. The boy soon tired, fell over and lay sucking his thumb, and she took him onto her lap. The girl crept about, pushing a big wooden spoon, hammering it on the floor, jabbering.

Devora studied them both, but could find no trace of Jerd. She played with them, keeping her movements gentle and her voice low, and they seemed to accept her, for they did not cry or fret, though even the girl had her flashes of solemnity when she quit playing and stared penetratingly at Devora.

She had them fed and asleep before Jerd appeared for supper. Again he said grace of his own accord, again ate without word or look for her. When she asked him to pass the molasses, he did; when she offered him tea, he accepted by pushing his mug across the table.

She ate sparingly, trying to determine the mental state underlying his behavior. There was not the same rage in him as last night, but the granite hardness remained. He was not sulking or even truly unfriendly; rather, he was utterly and deliberately indifferent to her, and this was harder to bear than either rage or enduring anger.

She studied his weathered hair and the way it grew off his brow in bold, wide strokes; studied his broad, long eyebrows, his big nose, the strength of his jaw, and his stern mouth. She watched his hands, and how ridiculously small his knife and spoon looked in them, wondered if ever they would reach to her in tenderness, and sighed.

This interrupted the quiet of the room so sharply that she looked at him in open dismay, but his eyes were on his trencher, and his face did not change, and she sat quivering in strange relief.

She hurried through her dishwashing, and sat down across the hearth from him, determined to end his silence. He was not smoking tonight, but just sitting, with his hands on the arm of his chair, staring unseeingly at the fire, not appearing to notice when Spot licked his fingers, or when Big Tom jumped to his knee, stretched himself out, and began to purr.

She said boldly, "I have a thing to say."

His eyes left the fire and moved to the tips of his moccasins. She accepted this as token he had heard and would continue to listen, so went on speaking, softly and clearly.

"Surely we can come to an understanding about that room."

He sat silent.

"I have no intention of using it or anything in it for myself. Only for guests."

He stared at his moccasins.

"If I hurt you, I am sorry, Jerd."

His eyelids batted once; he stared fixedly at his moccasins again.

"There is more. Mahala tells me Frank has bad spells with his heart."

Now his look came at her, hard and black and swift.

"There are things to do for him," she said, "and some babies outgrow the condition."

He waited.

"To begin with, he must be kept warm."

He nodded.

"Which means he can't stay in that unheated bedroom during the day. And this floor, even here at the hearth, and on a quilt, is too cold for an ailing baby."

For the first time in twenty-four hours, he spoke to her. "Have you figured a way we can fix him up?" he asked.

Her heart lunged into a terrific pounding. Her voice stuck, and it took effort to bring it out matter-of-factly.

"Yes, I have," she said. "If you'll put two more legs on one of the little beds, we can bring it in here close to the heat. He can stay in it daytimes and never be exposed to the drafts on the floor."

"And nights?"

"I'll hold him in my arms and rub him, like I did last night."

His eyes held hers for seconds, and some of their hardness left. Her heart kept thumping in her neck.

"I'll see to that job first thing in the morning," he said, got up, took his coat off its peg, and went outside for his evening rounds.

She was in bed, the frail baby snuggled to her, when he returned. Her door was standing wide, and she heard him throw an extra log, a big one from the sound, onto the fire, and felt the sudden springing of tears she could not weep.

Even in his loneliness for the young wife he had lost, and his anger at the new one he had taken and not taken, he could be thoughtful for the comfort and welfare of the sickly boy whom he as yet neither knew nor loved. Jerd, she thought, swallowing her tears, there is always another love . . . there is love for you now . . . here . . . when you are ready for it.

Worn and disturbed, she slept only fitfully, waking repeatedly in jumpy concern over Frank. Thus she was full awake some time before Jerd lit the morning candle and began to move about the kitchen, putting on his clothes, building up the fire.

She dressed in her dark room, relieved that another day had come. Now she could be about the business of living and homemaking and mothering, of completing Jerd's reconciliation to herself, of wooing him to love her.

When she stepped into the kitchen, he was already gone.

Later, returning with the milk bucket, he looked at her casually, but without yesterday's cold indifference, as he crossed the room.

She said, "Good morning, Jerd."

He set the bucket on the workshelf before he spoke. "I strained up some milk in the cellar," he said. "There's plenty here for the babes."

By midmorning he had completed his task of carpentry and gone to the corn patch to resume his work there. Devora established the twins in the bed, and went about her duties methodically, listening to their noises, the anticipation she had felt on her first day as mistress of the cabin lacking.

When Frank fell asleep, she covered him, and lifted Lillian to a blanket in front of the hearth. The rosy-cheeked baby crept immediately to Jerd's armchair, pulled herself up, and began to walk around it.

"You'll be running all over the place in a few weeks," Devora said, smiling down at her, and the baby looked up, made a bouncing motion, and cooed.

The following days fell into a routine. If Jerd rarely spoke of his own accord, at least he never failed to reply to Devora's comments, and when he needed to ask for or give information, he did so readily enough. His bitterness over the room at the end of the dogtrot had leveled off, and he ignored it as if it did not exist.

He did not return to the warm friendliness he had shown during the trip, nor did he pay any but necessary attention to the twins. He held Lillian at meals, fed her gravely, never smiled when she laughed into his face, never gave her a gesture of affection. Frank he scarcely glanced at, leaving him entirely to Devora.

One night Lillian literally banged her way into his friendship.

As had become their habit, Devora and Jerd were sitting in the fireside chairs, each holding a baby, lulling it to sleep. Lillian, on Jerd's lap, was chewing at a long handled wooden spoon and kicking her heels. Suddenly she sat up, lifted the spoon, brought it down on Jerd's head. She threw herself back on his arm, stared into his face, gurgled, laughed, and chewed the spoon again.

Jerd's mouth twitched, broke into a slow, uneven smile that sent creases fanning out from his dark and shining eyes, and made indentations in his cheeks. He cupped one big hand under the baby's chin, gave it a shake and said, "That hurt, you little . . . girl, you!"

His low, chuckling voice curled into Devora and warmed her. Entranced, she watched this unexpected transformation of the stern and troubled man she had married.

He swung the baby's cheek up to his and held her, patting her back clumsily, and looked across at Devora, still smiling. His eyes went past her, stopped on the listless, yellow haired boy in her arms, and his smile vanished and his face went stern. Lillian jumped boisterously on his lap, demanding attention, which he had to give to her, and gradually, in so doing, his face gentled.

Devora kept looking at him, her hand stroking the ringlets of the child she held, her heart aching both for the man who had lost his yellow haired wife, and for the unloved boy whose misfortune it was to resemble her.

After that, Jerd paid considerable attention to Lillian when he was in the cabin, for she expected it. She puckered her face and screamed if he didn't take her up, and laughed enchantingly when she got her way. Inevitably, he shortened her name to Lill.

When Devora mentioned the fairness of playing with Frank too, he replied soberly that he was afraid to handle the boy because of his fragility. She knew this was true, but knew also the deeper reason. So, when he romped with Lill, she gave the boy all her attention.

Often she would find herself staring longingly at Jerd's broad shoulders, at the width of his chest, and the hardness of his arms. How would it be . . . if he were to hold me? she wondered at these times, and sought his eyes shyly, helplessly, because she must. And more than once she found them so intense upon her, before he turned abruptly away, that her heart thudded painfully. He wants to, she thought. In spite of himself . . . in spite of the fact that it hasn't been a year since Sarie— He wants to hold me.

But he never did.

November advanced swiftly. One morning when she took her water bucket to the dogtrot barrels, the icy air burned into her lungs. Startled, she looked upon a world of ice; all the grass and every bush was coated, and the trees—trunks, branches and twigs—glittered with it. After that, as the last of the brown leaves drifted to the earth, the days became more consistently cold.

They worked from dawn to dark, Devora at her homemaking and nursing Frank through his frightening spells, and Jerd outside. He stored grain and hay for the stock, and potatoes, pumpkins, squash, turnips, and cabbage for their own winter use. He chopped wood interminably and stacked it in a long, high wall along the open north length of the dogtrot, where it served the double purpose of windbreak and convenient fuel supply for the fireplaces. He planted his wheat. He was feeding two of the hogs heavily, to fatten them.

"We've got meat to do us," he told Devora, "along with what game I can bring in with my rifle. So we'll wait till we can count on cold weather holding—say after Christmas—and then butcher. After that, we won't have nothing to do afore spring plowing but cure and smoke our meat."

∞ *Chapter Twelve* ∞

MAHALA and Prosper Pike appeared unexpectedly just after daylight on Thanksgiving, greeted by an uproar from Spot. Mahala darted inside when Devora opened the door, crying, "Where's my babies . . . where's my angels at?"

When she spied them playing in their bed at the hearth, she dropped the cookpot of food she was carrying on the table, swooped at them, gathered them into her arms and began to hug, kiss, and weep, along with chattering and cooing and calling them by name. Then Prosper entered, followed by Jerd, and he, too, had his session of hugging and cuddling.

At the dinner table, Mahala chattered so fast no one else could say much. Devora saw how Jerd's dark eyes kept moving from Mahala to herself to Prosper, noting every word and gesture; once she saw him half-smile, and was happy over his pleasure that his wife and his neighbors were friends.

"The Doerflingers," Mahala announced excitedly, "and us is coming here for Christmas dinner, seeing as Frank ain't strong enough for you folks to go nowhere, and we're bringing all the grub, Devorry. You ain't to turn a hand!"

"Oh, no, I'll make pies, and—"

"Pies then, seeing they ain't easy to carry a horseback, but nothing else. Vonnie Doerflinger, she told me to tell you she's in hopes you ain't put out that they ain't been yet."

"Goodness, no," Devora said, smiling. "They live so far away."

"Fifteen miles, if it's a inch. We was to their place a week ago Sunday."

"Oh?"

"He's had blood pizen in his foot, and that throwed all the work on her, and they couldn't do no going at all."

"Of course not."

"They'll have to put up here Christmas night, if that suits," Mahala said, staring pointedly at Jerd. "If not, we'll make a pallet to our place, and give them our bed."

Jerd met her eyes, looked briefly at Devora, then at his trencher. "We've got a bed for them," he said. "They're welcome."

It was that night, after Mahala and Prosper had gone and the twins were asleep, that Devora inaugurated her bedtime custom of reading aloud from the Bible. Jerd sat in his armchair, legs outstretched, and smoked, his eyes on her face, dark and quiet and intent.

When she finished the chapter, she closed the Bible, laid it on its table, stood up, and said, "Good night, Jerd."

He came to her, put his hands on her shoulders, holding them, searched into her eyes and said, a little roughly, "Devora." Suddenly a ghost of that old fear came into his look, his hands dropped, he went abruptly outside, and she stood alone, shaking.

She was in bed, holding Frank to her warmth, when Jerd returned from his barnlot rounds. She listened to him bar the door and throw a log on the fire; she saw her doorway go black when he blew out the candle.

For a long time she lay watching the occasional flicker of light the fire made in the darkness. Before she slept, tears had slipped down her cheeks and dried in stiff little pathways.

The days fled past.

December began cold and clear, with another hard freeze. Devora kept the kitchen fire hot, the twins' bed situated where it got the best warmth. She left the front door barred, and her bedroom shut off until late afternoon, at which time she built up the fire and opened the door by degrees to take off the worst chill of the room before bedtime.

Jerd stayed indoors more now, and at his request, in the afternoons after he had helped her get the babies fed and asleep, and the supper beans or soup or stew simmered over the fire, she read aloud to him from *Poor Richard's Almanac,* and they smiled together in appreciation. And each of these moments they shared set her heart to glowing and herself to seeking for something more, something she never quite found.

His eyes were on her frequently, softly dark and intent, but whether it was friendliness they held, or wistfulness, or love, or reproach, she could not determine. He never withdrew them when she looked full into them, but rather studied her openly as he had on that St. Louis day so far separated by forest and events from the here and now. Once she smiled, deliberately and hopefully, when their eyes were holding, but he did not smile in return, and when she moved across the room, she could still feel his eyes on her like a touch.

She could not bring herself to ask him what this meant.

She could not even permit herself to think that he was holding himself in restraint against taking her into his arms.

There was nothing she could do but wait.

Now, as Christmas approached, she was unexpectedly, piercingly homesick. She wanted Amos, Reginal, the little girls, Viney, Ned; she longed for the comfortable, familiar house, the pathways and walkways of the village she had committed herself never to see again. But even as she yearned for the things of the past, she knew she didn't want them above her want for Jerd, and that she would not leave him for them or for anything else.

She made what Christmas cheer she could. By the morning of Christmas Eve, her preparations were completed, and she inspected them secretly while Jerd was hauling water.

For Prosper Pike and Doerflinger, she had two large new handkerchiefs, one red and one blue, from her own belongings. For Mahala Pike and Vonnie Doerflinger, she had taken her two best white handkerchiefs, which were large and soft, and made them into collars edged with fine-knit lace.

For Jerd, she had knit a pair of stockings from wool raveled from her black shawl, putting the remaining yarn away for future knitting.

For the twins, she contrived a toy, making one for each of them. She sewed two small white bags cut from a towel, stitched a dog on one and a cat on the other, filled them loosely with dried beans, and sewed them shut. When handled, they rattled satisfactorily, and when hammered on the floor or even on a table edge, would not break.

She looked over the gifts, hid them in the kitchen chest again, and started her tasks for tomorrow's dinner, firing up her oven, making a row of pies, loaves of wheat bread, and churning fresh butter to spread on it. She took the pinfeathers out of the turkeys Jerd had shot and dressed and put in the cellar to keep.

While she worked, she thought carefully through the period since she had married Jerd, evaluating the various stages of their relationship. She could appreciate now, after better than two months of seeing him retreat into himself over any reminder of his lost wife, the enormous step he had taken when he journeyed to St. Louis to seek another wife, when he asked her to marry him, and went through the ordeal of the ceremony itself.

The thing that had first puzzled her following their marriage, had been the fear in his eyes, its unexplained recurrences, and its gradual disappearance. Next in importance had been his angry withdrawal whenever she had inadvertently violated some privacy unknown to her; offsetting this, had been his friendliness during the trip, and his helpfulness after they arrived at the cabin, which had led her to hope that, once they were settled, and his grief for Sarie had passed, he would take her as wife in the natural manner of man.

Drastic change was hard for him to make. That this was a result of his bereavement was evidenced by the fact that she'd had to tear into a forbidden room or live indefinitely with it as a constant reminder of his sorrow. Even baby Lill had to hit him on the head to get his notice, and to this day he virtually ignored Frank.

He had progressed as far in their marriage as he was apt to, at least for a very long time. He was companionable, provided for her, ate with her, listened to her read the Bible, his dark eyes eternally watching her.

Beyond this he would not go. Unless she herself brought it to pass. And this she could not do by wooing him as she had been wooing, loving him in modesty, yearning for him in secret, waiting to submit to him in womanly sweetness.

The moment in which he took her for wife, if ever it arrived, would be unexpected, sudden, and violent. She felt a rush of warmth sweep up her neck, over her face, and into her scalp.

She was waiting in her fireside chair when he came in after supper, carrying a bucket of water. He closed the door quickly against the inrush of cold air, and set the bucket on the workshelf.

"Smells like snow out, and feels it," he said. He hung up his coat, and swooped Lill, who toddled at him in her long night robe, into his arms. He sat down across from Devora, and glanced at the yellow haired boy held close against her. "Asleep?"

She nodded.

He put Lill up along his shoulder, patted her, and nuzzled her dark curls. The hairs on Devora's neck lifted, her breath shortened, her cheeks warmed, and her lips moved. She closed her eyes, leaned weakly back in her chair and burned as she had burned lying awake at night, with a fire for his arms, his lips, for more, for all there was.

Her love for him grew another measure.

And tortured her.

She opened her eyes. He was swaying Lill, making a cradle of his arms, and presently her dark head tumbled over against his neck, her red little mouth crumpled and parted, and he tiptoed into the bedroom with her. When he returned, he lifted Frank from Devora's lap and tiptoed out with him.

It was the first time he had voluntarily touched the boy.

When he came back, she had her Bible open to the Christmas story. As he settled into his chair, she picked up the candle and held it, as she always did, so its light wavered on the printed page. The words of the story felt good to her tongue, came over her lips softly, and when she had finished reading, she looked into Jerd's eyes, and this time, when she smiled at him, he smiled back.

"Last time I heard that story, I was a youngun," he said. "Back in Car'liney my Mammy read it out to me the last Christmas she was alive. It sounds just as good tonight."

"Thank you, Jerd."

She averted her eyes in sudden confusion, put aside the Bible, and set the candle on the mantel.

"Well," he said, rising from his chair, "reckon I'll take my look outside."

Not knowing she was going to move, she found herself standing with a hand on each of his arms, whispering, "Merry Christmas, husband," her face lifted to him, lips parted, her eyes seeking his.

She felt him go rigid under her hands, saw his mouth stir, and make no sound. For a heartbeat, she thought he was going to sweep her into his arms. Then, visibly, he forced his lips to move a second time, and they said, "Merry Christmas," and he wheeled, grabbed his coat and was gone.

Mechanically, she got into bed.

She said her prayers, delayed taking Frank out of his warm nest against Lill, and lay in a suspended state, not waiting or thinking or planning or feeling.

Jerd was outside longer than usual, and when he did come in, it was seconds after he had barred the door that she caught the smell of snow. He was longer, too, about retiring, and she thought he must be sitting before the fire, and then she smelled tobacco, and knew he was smoking.

She lay on her back, eyes closed, seeing how he looked, his great, strong legs outstretched, his big head leaned against the chair, his mouth sucking on the pipestem, and wondered if, should his lips come onto hers at this instant, they would taste of tobacco or of smoke or of both. Her breath became heavy, her breasts began to tingle, and a hunger for him that was like pain went through her, through her lips and her breasts, and into her loins, and it centered there and grew and pulsed and beat back up her body on her blood, and down again, and back, and down, bigger and swelling and growing, and she was swept by love.

Only dimly aware that he was moving about the kitchen, she slipped from her bed, slid to her knees, leaned her forearms against the mattress, her brow on her fists, and prayed, not with words or thoughts or supplication, but with the pain and throbbing, with the hunger in her loins, prayed with the marrow of her bones, the heat of her blood, and with some unknown thing that might be her soul.

And when she arose, she dropped her night robe off her shoulders, felt it slide down her body and collapse at her feet. She stepped out of it and stood naked in the cold darkness of her bedroom, consumed by shame, her body flaming, her braids hanging between her aching breasts, and naked she walked into the kitchen.

He was in his night garb, standing at the mantel, reaching for the candle, ready to blow it out. She made no sound crossing the floor, but he knew of her coming, for he turned. She stopped beside her fireside chair and stood, holding her chin steady with an effort, and his dark and shining eyes traveled her up and down, and then he blew the candle out, and they stood with just the firelight.

She moved again and went to him, and stopped so close that all her whiteness followed and curved to his great, hard body. She lifted her hands to his hair and wound her fingers into it and gave a slow tug, and then she trailed her hands down his cheekbones, feeling the drag of new beard, and brought her fingers lingeringly across his mouth and felt it shake, then pulled his head toward her own uplifted and ready-parted lips. His arms came around her, hurting her, and clamped her to him, and his mouth struck hers, tasting of tobacco, and covered it and ground and bruised, and his tongue penetrated, and his body was quivering, and he dragged her to the bunk and threw her on it and himself upon her.

His hands were on her, huge and hurting and seeking; his mouth was on her, open and exploring and caressing, and hers answered it, and her hands were on him, eager and instinctive. He was covering her, there was the quick, sharp thrust of pain, and then it was over and gone, and she wanted him, all of him, body, lips, mind, and she was trying to get into him and contain him at once. There was bigness and hardness and motion and darkness and the throbbing and the pulsing and the singing of loins, of breathing, of moaning, his moans and her moans, blending into a music that ended in a blinding, brilliant crescendo.

He fell away from her and panted, and she lay apart from him and gasped. Then he gathered her tenderly and naked into his arms, and held her to his strong, relaxed body and stroked his hand over her breast that was quieted now, and stroked her brow and traced her eyelashes clumsily with his finger. The clock on the dark mantel tocked, and he stroked her breasts again, gently, and he kissed her mouth and her breasts, and there was the motion and the music and the panting again, and a long time later, after he had covered her with the quilt and cradled her in his arms, he said, huskily, "I've got to tell you how it was. I never knowed a woman could be like tonight . . . with love . . . you're my wife . . . you've got a right to know how it was."

"And I want to know," she whispered, her lips against his ear, the smell of him in her nostrils, the brush of his hair on her face. "Want to know, want to, want to."

The lassitude of plenty, the sense of a hunger fed, was all through her. Here was the texture of love—this rough tenderness, this repletion, this sureness that would be another time, and another and another, all with love, this knowing there would be the in-between companionship, deep and sweet, and the working and the sharing, even of grief. This, then, was love, was marriage, was being twined and tied in flesh and heart and soul.

"Tell me," she whispered into his ear, kissing his ear and whispering and kissing, all at once, "tell me from when you were born, into when you were a lad, to now and beyond. Don't leave out anything."

"My mammy was a New Bern girl."

"North Carolina?"

"Car'liney. And she was handsome and headstrong and quick in heart."

"Like you . . . like you."

"And when she clapped eyes on my pappy, the day after he come to town from out Beaufort way—"

"Carolina?"

"Car'liney . . . him on a journey to see what the town was like, she wouldn't have no other man, same as he wouldn't look at no other girl, town or country."

"Oh, good girl . . . good girl!"

"And I reckon the girls was for him, him being a great big man, and strong."

"Like you . . . like you!"

"I reckon I take after him some, for Mammy said it, and she was truthful, to the bone. She was a poor relation, working out her keep for a second cousin, but she was a lady all the same, like you. And she lived in a fine town house, like you—teacher to her cousin's younguns. And she walked straight out of it, and went to Beaufort with my pappy."

"Good girl . . . brave girl!"

"She was a fisherman's wife as long as she lived, working with her hands, dressing plain but proud. But it wasn't for long, me being only seven, maybe eight, when she sickened and died."

"Poor Jerd . . . poor little boy."

"Poor Pappy, you'd rather say. Never looked at another woman. He'd just sit ashore in our shanty house, drinking whiskey when he didn't have to be out on his boat, and he'd look across the dunes and kind of stare and stare."

" 'Dunes,' Jerd?"

"Sand dunes. Beaufort's way out at the end of nowhere, way down east in Car'liney. He'd look at the dunes that once he'd loved, and he'd get full of whiskey, and then he'd cuss them. He'd keep I reckon anyhow three-quarters drunk and cussing all the time he was ashore. But he anyhow tried to raise me up to her liking—he was kind to me—and when it comes to not lying, and not being scared of work, and being able to read and write, I reckon she'd be satisfied."

"Oh, she would . . . good father, good, poor sick man!"

"I reckon you would say my pappy's a good man, and I turned out wrong in his sight."

"Not you . . . never you . . . never wrong." She kissed his ear, kissed it again and again, little, soft, hardly touching kisses, loving him, dipping and dipping into her never-ending wealth of kisses.

"Yes, me and no other but me, for I didn't take to the sea, and I didn't take to fish."

"Poor Pappy . . . poor orphan boy."

"I got seasick on a boat, and I hated the dunes. She'd hated them too, my mammy. Maybe hated ain't the right word, but she sure didn't have no love for them . . . just for my pappy, and for me."

"He loved them, and she loved him, so she loved them too, with a kind of hate."

"Could be, but I hated them . . . hated their slick look and how bald they was . . . and the way they'd change their size and shape and even their whereabouts under the wind or from the water when a storm throwed the waves high. I stayed there, duty-bound to my pappy, stayed 'til I was a man growed, and more . . . 'til I was thirty . . . because Pappy wanted me to. But I made out. Done some boatbuilding, found me a patch of black dirt and planted, put money by, but it didn't end the calling in me for the far wilderness and what it holds for the man who comes after it."

"No, no . . . never . . . no."

"Pappy begged me to get me a wife and settle down close by him so he could know my mammy's grandbabes . . . and his. But somehow I couldn't bring myself to sparking none of the girls thereabouts, and I broke with Pappy at last. I waited 'til he sobered up from his last drinking, and then I put a pack on my back, shook his hand, and walked, walked away from the dunes, walked forty miles across nowhere into New Bern, gawking around. . . ."

Chapter Thirteen

HE TOLD HOW he walked with a sense of homecoming into his mammy's town, though he had never been there before. He walked in early summer morning up the street that ran northwest from where the rivers Neuse and Trent came together, found the street that crossed it, running from river to river, and saw how the two formed a crucifix under blue sky and new sun.

He walked brick paving beneath shadowing oaks, past massive brick houses, stately Georgian houses, and houses with widow's walks, and under more trees—poplars and elms and pecans. He passed clapboard cottages curtained in wisteria, and these he liked the most.

He kept going, his pack on his back, his legs moving in long, easy strides, up and down the narrow streets, across and back again. He paid no mind to the townsfolk, who glanced at him with amusement, wonder, scorn, but kept on purely gawking at the town, absorbing it into himself, listening to its sounds, smelling its smells, sensing its people, feeling its texture.

When he was ready, he went directly to his mammy's girlhood home. Situated two streets back from the river Neuse, it was a two and a half story frame clapboard structure, the kind he liked, only bigger, with wisteria lacing its sides. It had a galleried portico held up by two tiers of square, wooden columns, protected at the second story by a wooden railing. There were brick end chimneys at the left side, and a service ell and portico in the rear.

He stood across the street, taking it into himself through his eyes like his mammy had poured it into his childhood self through his ears, and so truly that today he had found it without searching. Thinking so, he recalled the long and lazy hours when he sat against her in their Beaufort place, the little shanty that leaned away from the wind, and he heard her voice telling, softly telling.

He quit his remembering, and stared at the house. While he was trying to pick which had been her bedroom window, the front door of the house was flung open.

A girl ran onto the gallery, across it to the top step, and stood there, shapely, poised as if she might run back at any movement, and looked toward him, looked through morning sun toward him.

She was small, slight as a breath, and she had pure yellow hair. She wore it pulled straight to the top of her head, bound tightly, and released in a waterfall of curls that swayed and danced at her slightest move. She was dressed in white, sheer, soft, fluffily clinging white, and as he watched she spun, her white-slippered feet feather-light, and whirled along the gallery, her soft skirt swirling and turning back upon itself. She poised again, arms outflung, threw back her yellow head and laughed, the sound taking to the air like bird notes, and then she went running back into the house and slammed the door.

Jerd let out his breath.

He turned, moved away with decision, and rounded the corner on to another street. He went faster, with a sudden sense of freedom, with the feel of being, at last and late, his own man among men, and he walked with joy and a quickening expectation.

He went to the river front and hired out to a boatbuilder. He got a shed to live in, rigged a cooking place, and spent only enough of his wages to buy food. The rest he saved, giving himself a year to finish getting his stake together.

At night, when other men went home to family, or abroad to roister, he holed up in his shed, ate his meal, smoked his pipe, and speculated upon just where he would go in the unknown west. Afterward, he slept, sometimes dreaming about the yellow haired girl on the gallery of his mammy's house. She was a girl such as he had never imagined, and in the mixed-up way of dreams, she got so confused with his mammy he couldn't tell which was which.

But mostly he slept deep and dreamless, refreshing his big and powerful body for the next day's toil, which would bring him nearer to his goal. Now that he had seen New Bern, he was restless and impatient to leave.

Thus close to a year passed.

It was on a bright Sunday in late spring that he took his long, slow walk, looking at the riot of green that was everywhere—on tree, bush, ground, in the fields. He was drinking in the qualities of this gay and enchanting land that had produced his mother, and since it was so lovely, it seemed natural for it to begin to sing.

He grinned at himself. It was human singing he heard, some distance away, up the road, around the bend and beyond. He kept walking, not changing pace, and eventually, ahead a piece and to the right, was the source of the singing.

It was a revival meeting. Even from here, he could make out the arbor, built in a pecan grove, blotches that were carriages, and moving spots that were horses staked out to graze.

As he came nearer, the singing got louder, and he could see the details. There were smoldering cookfires, and lunch baskets on the seats of carriages. The arbor itself was brand-new, the people sitting on rows of plank benches inside it.

Because his Sunday walk had begun as a kind of pilgrimage, and because his mammy had loved religion, Jerd walked to the arbor, took off his hat, stepped inside, and sat down on the back row. The singing swelled and engulfed him. His legs were uncomfortable in the narrow space, and he moved them cautiously, trying to keep his knees from prodding the backs of the people on the bench in front of him. He was painfully aware of the sidelong glances from the singing people on either side of him.

Hanging his hat and his hands between his knees, he looked at the preacher, who was standing behind a rude pulpit, frowning at the open Bible upon it. He was a tall man in rusty black, and he was excessively thin and sharp-featured, with white skin, fiery hair, and an appearance of being about to pounce.

The singing ended.

The preacher's eyes snapped up, fixed his congregation. There was an instant pall of silence. A fly droned, someone coughed, a baby whimpered; each culprit was pinned swiftly by the eyes, and each ceased his wrong-doing forthwith.

The preacher lifted both hands and began to pray in a voice that was sharp and fiery and fierce. After the prayer, he read the scripture verses, and went from them into the sermon, which was as sharp and fierce as the voice.

Jerd listened without listening. As the words were flung into the face of the congregation, he knew what they were, and as soon as they were drowned out by the ones to come, he forgot them. He wasn't interested, but neither was he bored. This was one of his few times at any service since his mammy's burying, and he felt it was a worthy thing to sit under a preacher again and let holy words beat upon his ears.

Certainly those around him were engrossed. They listened raptly, as if the preacher's voice was water quenching their parched thirst; their mouths moved in unconscious aping of his, or hung apart in absorption.

Some of them were beginning to mutter "Amen" to his words, some were beginning to moan it, some to singsong it under their breaths, and one or two to shout it out and sway upon their benches and weep from the stirring of the Spirit within themselves.

Abruptly the preacher lifted his hands again, and when the congregation's head was bowed, prayed briefly, said, "A-a-amen," then called out, "Dinnertime, folks, dinnertime! Time to eat in Holy Brotherhood! Stay, all of you stay. This afternoon we have our big sing, and after supper I promise you a sermon that'll send the Devil back to Hell and keep him there while we bring every soul to Christ." His voice was still sharp and fiery and fierce, but with friendliness now. "There's food to eat, aplenty for all. Come, friends, come brothers and sisters and strangers, let us partake of Christian food together!"

Jerd moved clumsily out from his bench, caught in a slow tide of bonneted, chattering women. Before he could escape, one of them had him by the hand, pumping it, her earnest, chubby old face beaming up, and she was saying, "I'm Sister Guthrie, young man, pleased to have you with us, what's your name?"

"Warner, ma'am, Jerd Warner."

"Where from?"

"Beaufort I reckon, ma'am."

"You've come to the right place to get acquainted, young man, right place for salvation, right place for eating. Sister Lewis, meet Mr. Warner, he's from Beaufort way. Sister Spencer, Brother Pender, Sister Pender, and little Miss Fannie Lee Pender. Sister Lemon—Sister Lemon's our revival preacher's wife—and this's Hilary Lemon, Mary Jane Lemon, and Frances Elizabeth Lemon. Mr. Buford Williams . . ."

Jerd stood in a bewilderment of names and handclasps. His head was a whirl of faces and words. He nodded, tried to smile, and failed; he muttered acknowledgments and longed to purely bust out of the crowd and get away, and he shook hands with a portly, white-haired gentleman who was, he believed, Mr. Buford Williams, and who said pompously, "My niece, Miss Sarie Williams, from Wilmington."

When he saw that Miss Sarie Williams was the yellow haired girl, and her tiny, vibrant hand came to rest on his hard palm, his arm tingled to the elbow, and the last thing he wanted to do was get away.

Her eyes were blue, soft, dusty, powdery blue. She wore a cluster of blue posies tipped onto the back of her head, and they fanned into a blue poke that revealed her yellow curls. Her neck was a beautiful white stem rising from a soft, clinging kind of silky dress of the same wonderful blue as her eyes. Her lips were pink, a dusty pink, her skin was so white, and much too delicate ever to touch.

He felt like a great, blundering, overgrown lout standing before her, her little hand in his, and he couldn't get out the first word in response to her uncle's introduction.

Her eyes flickered up and down and over him, her pink lips curled in a smile, and she said, "My, you're a great big tall man!"

She left her soft hand in his, and carefully, so as not to hurt her, he released it.

Her uncle chided her for speaking so boldly, and she made a dimple beside her pink mouth, fluttered her yellow lashes and said, "I vow, Uncle Bu, if you ain't a case! Why, I was just bein' sociable! Wasn't I, Mr. Warner?"

"W-why, sure," Jerd croaked.

She looked up at him out of the corners of her eyes and said, "You're sure enough stayin' for dinner, ain't you?"

"Why," he said, "I . . . I reckon not."

"Why not, for goodness' sake?"

"I'm a stranger, to commence with."

"Oh, I know! You didn't fetch a basket! That's just it, Uncle Bu! He don't want to stay because he didn't fetch one! Ain't that it now, Mr. Warner?"

"Sarie child, watch your tongue."

"Uncle Bu, you're scoldin'!" She pouted her mouth into a rosebud which her smile unfolded for Jerd. "We brought simply stacks of fried chicken and baked ham, Mr. Warner! So you've just got to stay! Make him, Uncle Bu, 'cause nobody expects a lone man to fetch a basket—and he is a lone man, ain't you, Mr. Warner?"

"That's sure."

"So there now! Tell him, Uncle Bu!"

She clung to her uncle's arm, gazed imploringly into his face, and he smiled at her indulgently.

"You'll have to overlook this dear child's enthusiasm, Mr. Warner," he said. "She's used to having her own way. I fear, when she goes home to Wilmington, my brother Robert is going to write back that I've spoiled her."

"Pa spoiled me first his own self, and you just tell him that, Uncle Bu! That'll fix him!"

Mr. Williams chuckled. "Yes, yes. Stay, Mr. Warner, stay, do. We welcome all, townsfolk, countryfolk, kin, friends and strangers, for this is a religious gathering. And there's food aplenty, never have a fear about that."

"Ooh," Sarie cried, giving a little bounce, "you're angels, both of you, perfect angels!" She looked up at Jerd, suddenly beseeching. "You'll fill my plate for me, won't you? And sit with us? Please, oh please?"

Jerd glanced uncertainly at her uncle, who spread his hands in a gesture of surrender, then nodded dumbly at Sarie, who immediately lowered her eyes and stood in shy, sweet silence.

Now Jerd answered the older man's tactful queries, couched in the guise of chitchat, as to his mother's identity, his own origin, background, and present occupation. Mr. Williams recalled the cousin Jerd mentioned, and said he'd bought the house from him. But when Jerd said that he worked for a boatbuilder and was leaving soon for the wilderness, the portly old gentleman's expression grew coolly polite.

While the three of them had stood together at one side of the arbor, the congregation had scattered over the grounds. Women were bustling at the cookfires, from which the aroma of coffee was lifting, the men were putting up makeshift tables, getting in the way of still more women, who were in a hurry to spread the tables with linens and the contents of many baskets.

Children were running, playing, screaming; babies were crying, crawling, toddling, nursing, sleeping. Young couples were pairing off, and those who had not yet done so, were standing in separate groups, eying each other secretly, the young men uncomfortable in Sunday atmosphere, the girls giggling and whispering.

Sarie, glancing toward the young men, drew in her breath. "Why, I vow, Uncle Bu," she said delightedly, "if it ain't Clifford Talbert and Duffy Willis, standin' there big as life!"

"Eh?"

"Over yonder with George Ottis and Valentine Bridges and—"

"So it is. Good day, young men, good day," Buford Williams called, nodded to the group, then returned his attention to Jerd.

The young fellows, five of them, moved forward in a body. Sarie's voice went out like a silken, glistening ribbon, drawing them to her faster.

"Why, I told you two, you Cliff and you Duff," she said, "that I didn't never 'spect to see you at any revival meetin'!"

"But we're here," grinned the first one to arrive. He had sandy hair, freckles, and slightly crossed eyes.

"We wanted to say hello sooner," said a dark haired one, "but you was busy."

"And we didn't want to push in," offered a third.

"We've agreed to ask you to favor us by choosing which one of us you'll eat your dinner with," said another.

"Oh, I'm so sorry," Sarie said regretfully. "But I already promised to eat my dinner with Mr. Jerd Warner, here!"

"But Miss Sarie," said the sandy-haired Cliff. "You good as promised you'd eat with me if I'd come to the revival meetin'!"

"She did not!" said the dark haired Duff angrily. "She promised me!"

"Why, I declare!" said Sarie contritely. "I was only foolin', 'cause I never dreamt you two'd actually— Jerd these gentlemen is too many for me to name without mixin' you all up, but they've all been ever so gallant to me since I been visitin' Uncle Bu! Gentlemen, meet Mr. Jerd Warner."

The five nodded and murmured. Jerd acknowledged them, feeling foolish, struck by their youthfulness, sure Sarie couldn't really prefer to eat with him.

Her uncle began to frown politely, and they took themselves off. The group of girls was no longer giggling, but shooting indignant looks at Sarie, who was completely unaware of them. Cliff and Duff were arguing violently.

Jerd regarded the girls briefly as the other three young men meandered toward them, and thought they were nice enough to look at, but couldn't find it in himself to censor the five for trying first to win the company of the enchanting and unbelievably pretty Sarie.

She laid one hand on her uncle's arm, the other on Jerd's and asked, brightly, "Why don't we pick us out a nice place to ourselves, and then you two go and fill our plates? Ooh, ain't this fun?"

When Jerd returned, carefully managing both her plate and cup and his own, she was sitting on a grassy spot under a big pecan tree, her skirts spread charmingly. She had removed her bonnet, and sunlight coming through the tree was dappling her hair, once striking a fiery glint in it when she moved her head. This was as surprising to see as a streak of flame in a dish of yellow butter.

She set her plate on the grass, shook out her napkin, and laid it across her lap. "Why don't you sit down, Mr. Warner?" she asked. "Who you lookin' for?"

"Your uncle."

She laughed. "That Widow Thompson got him, and they're eatin' with the preacher and them. Won't do her any good, pursuin' Uncle Bu. He ain't about to get married."

"I reckon not," Jerd said, and sat down.

"Uncle Bu's a born bachelor. He says my pa won Ma out from in under his nose, and now she's dead and he can't win her back, why he'd as lief have me for his sweetheart. Me and my sister Sudie."

"You've got a sister."

"I got a twin."

Jerd stopped eating. "I never met a twin afore," he said, and grinned.

"She's exactly like me—we're the same girl made twice. Same hair, same eyes, same voice, same dresses, we even think the same and act the same and get sick the same way, same time."

"Well."

"We mostly take turns visitin' Uncle Bu, 'cause Pa gets lonesome by himself in Wilmington."

"I reckon so."

"But when we're both at home in Wilmington, on the plantation," Sarie said gaily, "we have such fun! The boys come flockin' and we just mix them all up. They can't tell which one they're with or which one they told what to or which one promised what . . . me or Sudie!"

"You're too young to be playing games," Jerd said soberly. "You ain't but a little girl. You've got time aplenty for such as that."

"It ain't always games," Sarie said, her laughing face suddenly quiet. "And I ain't a child. I was nineteen a long time ago."

"How long ago?"

"More'n a month."

He grinned again.

"You ain't a grandfather yourself," she said.

"I'm thirty-one. Too old for you to bother with."

Her face had remained quiet, and now her blue eyes darkened. "You ain't old," she said softly. "You're just grown up. You're a man . . . not showin' off like Tommy Manners was, or like Cliff and Duff, even. Look at them now . . . just look!"

The two young men, who so recently had been vying for her company, were walking past at some distance, solicitously escorting two of the girls who had stood apart giggling, waiting, glaring in turn. Both men cast a sidewise glance toward Sarie, who lifted her hand and waved, smiling wistfully. The two girls, their attention caught, shot angry glances at her, jerked their heads and walked faster, talking animatedly to their escorts.

"I simply don't understand the girls in this town," Sarie said, dropping her hand. "That Mable Louise Howard, she does me that way all the time. And the other one, the fat-like one with Duff, she's Docia Bell. She's the same way . . . and I only want 'em to like me."

"I reckon they don't take to being second choice," Jerd said, smiling.

Suddenly she laughed, dancing her eyes at him. "Now, then, you tell me all about that Beaufort place where you come from!" she said. "I'm dyin' to hear!"

"It ain't nothing but some houses in the sand," Jerd said. "I'd like it better for you to tell me about Wilmington."

He listened to her account of Wilmington, hearing her voice and not her words, he was so taken by how they were wrapped in the layers of sunlight and blue sky and spring breeze and wild flower scent that made up her voice. It was the lingeringest, softest, prettiest sound he'd ever heard, as lovely as her face and hair and eyes.

Because of her, he remained for supper and evening preaching, promised to return the following night, and did. He went the next night also and the next, until it became habitual for him, after his day's work at boatbuilding was finished, to bathe, put on his best clothes, and go to the revival meeting.

Sometimes he sat with Sarie, but most of the time he did not, because generally either Cliff or Duff, both of whom had abandoned their erstwhile Sunday dinner partners, had got there first. Whichever one sat with her, shone with triumph; the other, sitting where he got a side view of her face, glowered and pined. Twice, when the two of them had been defeated by still another rival, Jerd saw them almost come to blows.

Jerd made no effort to compete with them or any of Sarie's admirers. They were all years younger than himself, all infinitely better suited to claim her hand. Yet he continued to attend the revival. And it was not religion that pulled him there.

As the time drew near for him to leave New Bern, he was reluctant to go.

The days passed, the revival took on impetus, and the tension between Cliff and Duff mounted. Sarie's uncle was always frowning anxiously now, was looking worried, was staying close to his sparkling niece.

The various girls eyed her, but Sarie herself, Jerd observed, was unaware of their undercurrents of jealousy. She had no idea, either, of the violent passion she innocently stirred in the immature youths who pursued her, particularly Cliff and Duff.

Thus recognizing her lovely purity, Jerd's heart melted toward her. And she spoke to him always with a special tenderness.

And he continued to sit, night after night, Sunday after Sunday, at the revival. And the gospel singing filled the arbor, and the preacher's fervor mounted, and the sinners came into the fold, shouting, weeping, dancing, and were saved.

⟪ *Chapter Fourteen* ⟫

IT WAS the first Sunday in June.

Jerd had set today as his last Sunday in New Bern, and, as he walked to the meeting grounds for morning service, determined it must also be his last attendance at the revival.

He had to quit seeing Sarie, or he'd never start west. Already, influenced by her dismay when he spoke of leaving, he had delayed until he was going to be hard put to reach his destination, get his land and raise his cabin before winter set in. So today he'd say a definite farewell to Sarie, and that would be an end to it, for anything else was impossible.

She was standing outside the arbor, surrounded by young men, when he got there. Buford Williams was at the outer fringe of the group, speaking courteously to people arriving for the meeting, glancing worriedly at his niece now and again.

She sat between Cliff and Duff at morning preaching, and she ate her dinner with them, her uncle having been captured by the Widow Thompson. Jerd, sitting apart, saw that Cliff and Duff were on bad terms. They were strained and anxious, competing fiercely for Sarie's every smile and slightest attention, ready to spring at each other's throats. Idly he wondered if they had been drinking, and a swift admiration went through him at the demure and laughing manner in which Sarie, young as she was, kept them in hand.

After the meal, she jumped to her feet, and the boys sprang to theirs. She put a hand on the arm of each, looked from one to the other, smiled, spoke quickly, left them, and came running to Jerd.

"Hello!" she said, coming to a breathless stop in front of him, lifting her dusty blue eyes.

She was wearing pink today, the same dusty pink as her lips, and her bonnet was pink, and her curls were yellow flames against it. The unbelievable, dear enchantment of her got him by the throat, and he could only grin down at her, as bemused and certainly more inarticulate than any of the youths he considered so shallow.

"Would you sit with me at the sing?" she asked, making a dimple beside her smile. "See, they're goin' in a'ready."

Clumsily he offered his arm and escorted her to the arbor. Cliff and Duff had disappeared, much to his relief. The sing commenced, and he sat beside her, sang beside her, his bass covering the bright charm of her voice until he could not hear it.

Afterward, he ate supper with her and Buford Williams. They sat under the same pecan tree where they'd eaten that first Sunday dinner. Jerd marked every charming look and word she gave him, for this was the last time, and he wanted to remember it all.

Presently she began to glance so repeatedly out over the grounds, that her uncle spoke of it.

"You looking for someone?" he asked.

"Sort of."

"Who?"

"Oh, just Cliff and Duff."

"What for?"

"They vowed they was comin' back."

"Good riddance if they don't."

"Why, Uncle Bu! That'd make somethin' terrible out of me, your very own niece!"

"Why?"

"I told 'em they couldn't come back 'til they quit arguin' and quarrelin'."

Buford Williams frowned, Sarie resumed her dainty eating, and Jerd his admiring, comfortably aware of the pleasant warmth of the lowering sun and the contented buzz of talk that filled the grounds.

Into this peace, two sharp, nearly simultaneous shots cracked. The grounds went deathly quiet; people froze in position—sitting, chewing, standing—and listened.

The encircling trees stood quiet.

Now a hysterical laugh arose from their depths, a crashing sound began, drew rapidly nearer, and a figure plunged into the clearing, dark hair awry, clothes disheveled, mouth twisting and crying out hoarsely.

Jerd stood up slowly, Buford Williams coming to his feet on one side, Sarie on the other. She put one hand to her throat and whispered, "It's Duff. Oh, Uncle Bu . . . where's Cliff? *What have they done?*"

Duff staggered to the middle of the crowded clearing, stood unsteadily and peered vaguely about. He fought away from the crowd and stumbled toward Sarie.

[144]

"I did it! I did it!" he screamed as he came. "We agreed . . . the one that shot first . . . so name the day, because I've won you, Sarie . . . won you!"

Crying and laughing swept him, and he stood swaying before her, the smell of whiskey strong, and men grabbed his arms and dragged him, struggling and cursing, away. Suddenly he quieted and fell into their arms, and they carried him, and a woman's voice shrilled, "Drunk! Dead, disgustin' drunk!"

Other men came out of the grove, bearing a prone, sandy-haired figure. There was blood across the white shirt front of the figure.

A girl screamed.

She tore loose from the clutch of a matronly woman and went flying to the bloody figure, pressed her hands against her mouth, stared, whirled, and raced to Sarie.

Even while she was still running, Jerd recognized her as the girl named Docia.

She stopped in front of Sarie, her plump breasts heaving. Her round face was contorted, and she wept, "You murderess . . . you temptress . . . you . . ."

Sarie backed off, and Docia followed. "Don't you dare try and get away, you nasty flirt! We know you . . . we've heard! You wouldn't stay where you belong. No, you had to come here, take all the boys, make my Duff kill his best friend, all for fun! I hope God strikes you down . . . down . . ."

The matronly woman had trotted up and seized Docia by the arm, and now she pulled her away. Some of the crowd was gathering around the bloody Cliff, some near the unconscious Duff, the rest gaping at Sarie.

Her pink mouth quivered. Her eyelids fluttered; she crumpled. Jerd caught her and lowered her to the grass where so recently she had sat eating and chattering and being gay.

Uncle Buford knelt and fanned her with his hat.

She opened her eyes.

With Jerd helping, she sat up. Her eyes flew to the excitement at the far side of the grounds, and one hand fluttered to lie over her left breast. She lowered her eyes, breathing unevenly.

Buford Williams, still fanning, asked, "Feeling stronger?"

"I vow," she said, lifting her eyes first to him, then moving them beseechingly to Jerd, "whatever took that Docia-girl?"

"She was out of her mind," Buford Williams said.

"She didn't mean it," Jerd said.

[145]

"Duff had been drinkin'," Sarie said sadly. "I smelled it on him . . . on Cliff, too. So I told 'em to go off and quit that drinkin' if they ever wanted me to speak to 'em again. Oh, Jerd . . . do you s'pose he really did . . . kill him?"

She paled.

"I'll find out," Jerd said.

When he returned, he was feeling such relief as he had never before experienced. "He's bad hurt," he told Sarie, "but alive. There's a doctor with him . . . they're taking him home."

"Then everything's all right?"

"He's only got a chance," Jerd said, "barely a chance."

She looked up at him, holding her breath. At last she whispered, "What about Duff?"

"They've took him home."

"He'll not be bothered if Cliff lives," Buford Williams said.

"And if he don't?"

"He'll be a murderer."

"And me . . . what about me, Uncle Bu?"

His hand rested on her curls. "Don't bother your pretty little head about it, sweetheart."

"Will I be a murderer, too?"

"Of course not."

"But people'll gossip, won't they? It'll be like it was about Tommy Manners?"

"Worse, my sweet."

She lifted her hands to Jerd. "Help me . . . hold me up," she said softly.

Her hands were so small in his, and there was no weight to her as he half-lifted her to her feet. She was trembling, but her wide-eyed face was tearless.

"I'll fetch the carriage," her uncle said.

"No, Uncle Bu."

"You must rest, child."

"Run away, you mean. I can't . . . I won't. I'm stayin' for the meeting . . . 'cause I've got to . . . don't you see . . . got to!"

No amount of pleading or even demanding shook her, so they sat halfway up the arbor, she and her uncle, and Jerd took his place on the back bench where he'd sat that first Sunday.

The congregation, whetted by weeks of revival, was at high pitch from the suppertime excitement. The people sat their benches, alert. Their singing was loud. Their eyes avoided Sarie Williams, or stared openly, or slid secretly at her.

The preacher's voice, when he began to speak, was hoarse and husky, loud and shouting, whispering and clear. Its text was, "Thou shalt not kill." It accused and threatened, soothed and begged; it predicted and denied and berated. It went into a singing rhythm and he pleaded with his salvation, and promised with it, and bargained and battled with it, and after a while he began to sway with it, to shout and dance. The various ones on the benches sat and stared, or moaned and sang, or even wept and danced, and the choir went to singing a hymn as the preacher leapt down from his pulpit and stood waiting, hands outstretched, and exhorted the sinners to come forward and be saved. And in the flickering lantern light they flowed to salvation—men, women and children. They knelt at the front benches, dropped their heads, and lifted their one voice in supplication.

Sarie, in her dusty pink dress, her curls paled to gold by the lanterns, arose from her bench, her sweet figure melting into the shadows. She tipped her head back, revealing the pure white of her throat, and began to sway to the music of the song with a grace that set the hairs on the back of Jerd's neck to prickling.

Now she moved into the aisle and up it, only a slow step at a time, pausing to sway to the music, face uplifted. When at last she reached the front, she put out her hands, and, with the preacher holding them, went to her knees before a bench and dropped her head upon her arms.

The preacher knelt with her and prayed, stood over her and prayed, raised his hands and prayed, sang and wept his prayer. Others, both men and women, young and old, prayed over her, with her, beside her.

Occasionally she lifted her face, wet and beautiful with her tears, and they asked if the Spirit had entered into her yet, and she shook her golden head and wept afresh, and hid her face again and they prayed again, over her and over the others.

The night cooled, the horses moved restlessly in the darkness, whinnied and waited. The lanterns burned low, and their chimneys blackened and the singing and praying went on, and Jerd remained.

When at last Sarie came to her feet down there at the front, just below the pulpit, he half-rose from his bench, then sank back. Her eyes were closed, her curls had fallen to her shoulders, and she was swaying to the singing, swaying slowly—one sway to two beats of music, her arms backthrust like an angel's folded wings.

Suddenly she whirled, much as she had done in her dance along the gallery that first morning, only just the one whirl this time, so that she faced the benches of the arbor. Her eyes opened, large and far away, seeing things unseen by others, and her voice came out over the singing and praying, and these muted as she spoke, her words pulsing and aching.

"The Spirit's in me . . . I'm saved from my sins . . . my scarlet sins . . ."

". . . praise the Lord . . ." cried the preacher.

". . . the Spirit's tellin' me to confess . . ."

". . . hallelujah, hallelujah . . ." chanted the choir.

". . . and get off the road to Hell . . ."

". . . a-men . . ." prayed the praying ones.

". . . my sin was Vanity . . ."

". . . praise the Lord . . ."

". . . and not tryin' to make myself plain . . ."

". . . hallelujah, hallelujah . . ."

". . . so's the young men'd gather to the other girls . . . not just me . . ."

". . . a-men . . ."

". . . but I liked it . . . I was havin' fun . . ."

". . . praise the Lord . . ."

". . . sinful, selfish fun . . ."

". . . hallelujah, hallelujah . . ."

". . . like today . . ."

". . . a-men . . ."

". . . jokin' and carryin' on . . ."

". . . praise the Lord . . ."

". . . with drinkin' men . . ."

". . . hallelujah, hallelujah . . ."

". . . wantin' me to marry 'em . . ."

". . . a-men . . ."

". . . and now one's a-bleedin' . . ."

". . . praise the Lord . . ."

". . . and the other's a-tremblin' . . ."

". . . hallelujah, hallelujah . . ."

". . . and I'm repentin' . . ."

". . . a-men . . ."

". . . of Tommy Manners . . ."

". . . praise the Lord . . ."

". . . back in Wilmington . . ."

". . . hallelujah, hallelujah . . ."

". . . that hung himself . . ."

". . . a-men . . ."
". . . because I was foolin' . . ."
". . . praise the Lord . . ."
". . . and havin' fun . . ."
". . . hallelujah, hallelujah . . ."
". . . now the Lord is showin' me the way . . ."
". . . a-men . . ."
". . . like a Heavenly light . . ."
". . . praise the Lord . . ."
". . . He's leadin' me . . ."
". . . hallelujah, hallelujah . . ."
". . . into righteousness . . ."
". . . a-men . . ."
". . . He's tellin' me . . ."
". . . praise the Lord . . ."
". . . to get married . . ."
". . . hallelujah, hallelujah . . ."
". . . to cling to one man . . ."
". . . a-men . . ."
". . . one that's big and strong . . ."
". . . praise the Lord . . ."
". . . that will be father and brother . . ."
". . . hallelujah, hallelujah . . ."
". . . friend and husband . . ."
". . . a-men . . ."
". . . that will never fail me . . ."
". . . praise the Lord . . ."
". . . that will love me . . ."
". . . hallelujah, hallelujah . . ."
". . . that I can obey . . ."
". . . a-men . . ."
". . . and never make trouble again . . ."
". . . praise the Lord . . ."
". . . He's givin' me the name . . ."
". . . hallelujah, hallelujah . . ."
". . . the Lord's givin' me the man . . ."
". . . a-men . . ."
". . . it's Jerd . . . Jerd Warner . . ."
". . . praise the Lord . . . hallelujah, hallelujah . . . a-men . . ."
said preacher, choir and those who prayed.
The others, sitting their benches, were silent except for their moaning

singing, and they seemed to hold their breaths as Sarie Williams stood swaying to their music, her face transfixed, an angel with golden hair, holding out her hands to Jerd Warner.

Unaware that he had moved, he found himself stumbling up the aisle, folding her tiny hands into his, losing them in his, and mumbling into her flower-soft curls flung suddenly and abandonedly against his chest, "Little darling . . . little darling . . . Jerd's here . . . he'll never fail you."

She swooned.

When she revived, she was in a state of collapse. Jerd lifted her into the carriage, and, arrived home, stood aside when servants appeared and helped her up the steps.

Her troubled uncle turned to him in the darkness and said, "Thank you for your help. Thank God, her pa'll be here tomorrow! I sent for him to come for her. You'll have to deal with him."

"That's fine, sir," Jerd said soberly. "Good night."

He went to his shed and waited for daylight, for midmorning, made himself as presentable as he could, and returned to Buford Williams' home to face the father of the yellow haired girl he had promised to marry.

Robert Williams was younger, taller, slimmer than Buford; otherwise, they might almost have been twins. His manner was even graver than that of his brother as he faced Jerd in the fine parlor of the house in which, unknown to them, his mammy had spent her girlhood.

"Sir," Robert Williams said, after a handshake so fleeting it was a mere touch of palms, "words fail me."

"I reckon so," Jerd said.

"My daughter is young, motherless . . . perhaps even a trifle spoiled. You can readily understand she was . . . er . . . merely carried away last night."

"She was converted."

"Permit me to extend you my sincere gratitude for helping my brother get her away from that place and safely home."

"I couldn't do no less."

"And now, if you'll pardon me, I must see to getting off to Wilmington with my daughter." He arose and stood waiting courteously.

Jerd stood up, too. "Hold on, there," he said. "It ain't quite that easy."

"I don't understand."

"What happened to Sarie last night was real."

"You're referring to her hysteria, no doubt . . . to her . . . er . . .

[150]

fancy that a husband had been Divinely chosen for her. Really, Mr. Warner."

"I ain't a religious man, sir. But she come to me with the Spirit on her, and I gave my promise. In the church. That promise a man don't break easy."

"Nonsense. She can't possibly know her own mind."

"You mean I ain't a fit husband for her."

"No father thinks any man is quite good enough for his daughter, Mr. Warner."

"I'll try hard to be worthy of her."

"You're considerably older, for one thing."

"Twelve years."

"Precisely. And at that age, you still have your way to make, for another."

"I'm going west."

"Yes, and that. My brother tells me you're planning to head off into some godforsaken wilderness nobody ever heard of."

"I'm going to St. Louis. It ain't as bad as you make it sound."

"I don't say it's bad . . . for you. For my daughter, it's impossible."

"That was my notion until last night."

"What changed it then?"

"Her hands in mine, her trust in me. I'll look after her, sir."

"You'll do nothing of the sort."

"There ain't but one thing can stop me, and that's Sarie herself."

"Which I won't . . . ever!"

The cry came from the doorway, followed by a whirl of soft yellow garments as Sarie ran across the room and turned before the marble fireplace to confront the men. Her face was white, her eyes enormous, her hair a blaze of yellow.

"How long you been listening?" her father demanded.

"I couldn't help hearin', 'cause I was comin' here from the kitchen, where I heard the slaves talkin'. So I know that Cliff died this mornin' . . . which makes Duff a murderer, and me the girl that caused it!"

"No!" Jerd said involuntarily, but the grim faces of the men confirmed the truth of Sarie's statement.

"Sarie, go to your room," her father ordered, "and dress for travel. We leave within an hour."

"You can go . . . Sudie can . . . she's dressin' . . . but not me . . . never me!"

Her father moved toward her, and she ran to Jerd. From his arms she cried, "I can't, can't, can't!" She was weeping now, tears rising in her eyes, spilling over, creeping down her pale cheeks. "You can't go against God, Pa!" The tears quickened, and she was sobbing wildly. "He told me to marry Jerd and go with him!"

"Sarie, honey," her father said, pleading, "that's like going to another world—or dying."

"Don't s-*say* that word!"

"It's so far away, Sarie."

"That's what I want—'way off!"

"Sarie . . ."

"What good did it do for me to come here from Wilmington—after Tommy Manners? It all f-followed."

Jerd saw the brothers glance at each other.

"And now, with poor Cliff . . . they'll crucify me, you know they will!"

"People forget, Sarie, in time they do."

"God told me to marry Jerd."

"You'd regret it in a month."

"I won't!"

"How about us, honey? How about leaving your pa, and your Uncle Bu, and Sudie?"

"I c-can't help it!"

"It's a long, hard trip."

"It's fun to travel!"

"The wilderness is dangerous—Indians and wild animals."

"Danger's excitin'!"

"You'll be afraid."

"I won't! I'll have Jerd!"

"You won't have slaves in the wilderness. You'll have to work hard."

"Jerd'll take care of me! God told me to go, and I'm goin'! I'm goin' to marry Jerd this very day, and leave this h-horrid place!"

And at sundown, because she would have it so, because she stormed, wept, and called upon Heaven, because she vowed she'd run away with Jerd otherwise, and he said yes, he'd run with her, she stood all in white with him, her twin, Sudie, there like another self, before that same fireplace where his mammy must have stood more than once, and the red-haired revival preacher made them man and wife. Afterward, while Sarie was upstairs changing into travel garments, Robert Williams pulled Jerd grimly aside.

"Now that you are my daughter's husband," he said, "there are a few things I mean to say."

"I reckon it's your right," Jerd said.

"Precisely. God knows why you would take a sheltered girl out of civilization, but you are doing it, and there are facts you need to know."

"Go ahead."

"To begin with, Sarie has been reared as a lady. She's always had slaves. She's never done a day's work in her life."

"I figured that."

"Furthermore, she's not too strong. A heart tendency. Slight, but it's there."

"I'll hold it in mind."

"She is in no way suited to do the work of a farm woman—in the fields, herding cattle, spinning, weaving."

"I don't expect such of her."

"You'll get no money from me or my brother."

"If you wasn't Sarie's father, I'd hit you, sir."

"I respect you for that. But it isn't entirely the way it sounds. We live well, very well indeed, but both my brother and myself are far in debt."

"Money don't worry me."

"Sarie has been through an ordeal the past two days."

"That's sure."

"You won't fail to have her well out of the country before the funeral?"

"We'll be gone tonight."

"There's been no woman to guide her. Bluntly, she is completely innocent. She has no idea what to . . . er . . . anticipate in marriage."

"I figured that."

"Then you'll—"

"I won't touch her tonight."

"Thank God."

"Or tomorrow night. Or at all, until she's ready."

"Thank you, Warner."

"It ain't needful. It wasn't no lie I spoke when I promised to love her."

Briefly they touched palms.

Sarie came running downstairs, and they all went outside to the ox-drawn covered wagon Jerd had bought hurriedly at noon. It was loaded, for the most part, with Sarie's hastily assembled belongings and wedding gifts—bedding, linens, clothes, knickknacks, a fine chest of drawers, and a Spinnet.

She flung herself into the arms of her father, uncle, sister, weeping and laughing, then held out her arms to Jerd, and he swung her to the seat of the wagon, and vaulted up beside her.

[153]

He drove north out of town through young summer darkness. Sarie, sitting close beside him, linked her hands through his arm, and chattered excitedly. What towns and cities would they see? How long remain in each? How many weeks before they reached St. Louis? Months, then? What fun—a weddin' trip that would next to never end! Never before had a girl started on such an excitin' journey with such a wonderful man. She was lucky, Sarie Warner was! Sarie Warner . . . Sarie Warner . . . that was her new name, and she sang it over and over to him until, at last, her head drooped against his shoulder and she slept.

He slipped his arm around her and held her.

What had he done, he wondered humbly. Yet how can a man turn away from his love when she flies to his arms, sent by God? As for the rigorous life ahead, when he would be breaking raw land to the plow, he'd have to work harder than most, that was all, in order to make things comfortable, to shield her from drudgery and disappointment, to give her all he could of pleasant living. He sighed, laid his cheek against the top of her head, and smiled.

After perhaps an hour, he stopped at a farmhouse. Leaving Sarie drowsily awake on the wagon seat, he went to the door, hammered up the farmer, and arranged for room and breakfast. He himself carried upstairs the bag Sarie indicated, before he went down to stable his oxen.

When he returned to the room, Sarie, bedecked in a nightdress of golden silk such as he had never dreamed of, was in the wide bed, looking up at him shyly through her yellow lashes. He blew out the candle, undressed, and lay on the far side. She came scooting into his arms, soft and sweet-smelling, kissed him on the mouth and wept, and he soothed her, and finally she slept.

As for him, he lay in torment, not daring even to touch the curve of her cheek with his finger. Hours later, when he felt himself going into troubled slumber, a great protectiveness welled in him, and he knew he would give his very life to insure his golden bride her happiness.

It was black morning when they drove northward again. If Sarie longed in secret for father, uncle, sister, she gave no sign. She was elated, talkative, interested. She couldn't wait to see what lay ahead, hear the sounds, smell the smells, cross the mountains, and float down the rivers.

That afternoon she napped on the featherbed in the wagon. She made her dimple at him in the shoddy inn where they ate supper, and flirted with him shyly after they were in their room. She came into his arms, held up her lips, and when he trembled she blushed and pulled away.

In bed, she crept into his embrace and felt his lips with her fingers and whispered, "Jerd . . . tell me?"

"Tell what?" he whispered back, holding himself still, quite still.

"Pa . . . did he have one of those man-talks with you?"

"He had a few things to say, yes."

"About me?"

"Yes."

"What?"

"Things I already knowed."

"Tell me . . . please tell me."

"Mostly it was that you're innocent."

She laughed, a small, purring sound in her throat. "I ain't," she said. He jerked to a half-sitting posture. "You don't know what you're talking about."

"I do, too. Jewell told us."

"Who's Jewell?"

"The slave girl that grew up with Sudie and me."

"She don't know, either."

"She does, too! She's even got a baby!"

"Sarie, you hush that talk!"

She snuggled into his arms, close against him, and he held her, his pulses bursting.

"But you're my very own husband . . . and I want to know . . . show me, Jerd . . . big, sweet man . . . show me."

She was little and dear, and innocent and eager, and cool and hot, and the night was not long enough or big enough to contain his joy and hers. Or the next night, or the next.

He was certain now of one thing. He had done right to make Sarie his wife. She could not get enough of him, or he of her.

There was nothing he would not do for her.

Ꭿ Chapter Fifteen Ꭿ

Unexpectedly, she changed.

They were toiling toward the Mississippi, and one night, camped in their wagon, he was fondling her and she was teasing by submitting and resisting at once, when suddenly she pushed out of his arms, saying, "No, no."

"Sarie."

"Please . . . not now."

"Sarie?"

"I'm too tired, Jerd darlin', too awful tired. Hold me nice, now . . . maybe I can go to sleep. I'm so awful tired."

He held her, and she composed herself and fell asleep in his arms. He awoke in the night, and she was still there, and he touched her hair, barely touching it, and her cheek, shoulder, breast; before she was fully awake he was past stopping, and afterward, while she sobbed desperately, he held her helplessly and called himself brute.

He was uneasy from then on.

He treated her with gentleness, striving to reassure her; he worried lest she was falling ill. Always, early in the morning, she was bright and gay, but before night she grew listless and exhausted. Yet sometimes, in the night, she'd come into his arms of her own accord, tease him, then change her mind, like as not, weeping unexplained tears. Or else she'd submit so suddenly that he was bewildered and hurried and anxious and never quite satisfied.

He told himself she'd be different in her own cabin. She wasn't strong; her father had warned him. The journey was becoming an ordeal for her. He would somehow control his want for her, not touch her at all. He'd see to it that she rested once they got to their own land.

She would become herself again.

They first met Prosper and Mahala Pike in St. Louis, and, after making final purchases of supplies in the shops, set out westward in their company. Jerd and Prosper hit it off at once. They thought alike about land

and how to treat it. Jerd liked Mahala too, though he behaved with a remote friendliness toward her because of Sarie, who had taken an immediate and feverish dislike to the older woman. Mahala, so far as he could tell, was kindly in her manner to Sarie, but his bride assured him, tremulously, that this was not the case.

"I know her kind," she sobbed, abed in their wagon. "I see her lookin' at my hair. Can I help it if it's curly? Can I, Jerd?"

"No, of course you can't."

"She's like that Docia-girl back in New Bern."

"Mahala's a good woman," Jerd said, helpless.

"She might's well be . . . she's got to be somethin'. But she hates me."

"She don't, honey. Prosper was telling me—"

"Prosper's sweet. I told him so. 'I vow,' I said to him, 'but if you ain't a rosy-cheeked sweet thing!' "

"What'd Prosper say to that?" he asked.

"Nothin'. He knew I was just teasin'. But he is sweet—always doin' some kind thing for me, to help you, 'cause he knows you got so much slavin' to do for your lazy wife."

"My wonderful wife," he whispered, and drew her to him.

This time she took him with sweet eagerness.

They didn't meet the Doerflingers and the other distant families until after the cabin was up. Then it was that Sarie must give a party, so Jerd walked over to invite Prosper and Mahala, and Prosper undertook to pass the word to the Doerflingers and ask them to relay it to the Weeds, who were to carry it to the next family, and it to another, and so on indefinitely.

It was in the deep of winter, with snow on the ground. On the day of the party, Jerd built a roaring fire in each room, moved the Spinnet to the kitchen, and turned out some fair cooking under Sarie's supervision. Late that afternoon, all the countryside appeared to meet Jerd Warner and his bride, who was said to speak with the warm breeze of the south right on her tongue, and Sarie, her yellow curls upswept, her sweet form draped in blue silk, greeted them at the door, smiled at them, and made them welcome.

She insisted that the children and babies be put to sleep on her own fine bed and on pallets in her bedchamber at the end of the dogtrot. She chatted with her guests, moving with the light grace of a sunbeam among them, and she sat at her Spinnet, and played and sang for them.

She sparkled like a jewel against the drab clothes, lean bodies and worn faces of the women, who watched her bleakly, listened to her stonily, and stood silent and apart while their men gaped, whooped, applauded, and gathered around the Spinnet. The men yelled requests for songs, and stood grinning as Sarie played on, singing the words of each piece right into the eyes of the one who had asked for it, her own blue eyes sweet and open with the frankness of an angel, and filled with innocence.

Jerd stood beside Mahala, smiling. Here at last was the gay and lovely girl he had first seen in New Bern. She was in her element now, showering beauty, happiness, talent on people. It takes folks, he thought tenderly, to bring her alive, like it takes sunshine to coax plants out of the ground.

She ate her supper surrounded by men—Prosper at her right, Doerflinger at her left, and out from them, in a semicircle, Weed, Piepmeier, and an elderly man whose lower lip hung and drooled. Jerd felt his breath go uneven with the knowledge that she was his. He glanced at Mahala, bursting with his pride, wanting to share it, and she gave him a direct look, turned on her heel and went to sit by Vonnie Doerflinger, who was looking at her husband fiercely.

Disturbed by Mahala's action, Jerd studied all the solemn women, their uneasy men, and the five around Sarie. It was the expression on the face of the loose-lipped oldster that woke him to the unhealthy situation, and a small frown grew between his eyes.

Sarie was too young to know what she was doing to these men; she was too innocent. She was a creature of impulse, like a kitten or a bird first taking to the wing.

Can't you see that? he wanted to shout at them, at the hankering men, at the women who could not understand Sarie's difference from themselves. She'll change, she'll grow up, and this warmth will be for her babes. And her turning to men like she does, can't you see that, too? She was raised by men . . . her pa . . . her uncle . . . it's natural for her to take to men . . . but that'll quit too, when she has her babes . . . and you women, when that time comes . . . you'll be friends to her.

For now, at last, watching the women's watching eyes and set mouths, Jerd came to the only logical conclusion—the women, all of them, were jealous of Sarie's sparkling wit and beauty. They were thinking spiteful thoughts about her who was only natural and innocent, and they did not even like her who wanted, more than anything else, to be loved.

His heart swelled.

He would love her enough to make up for all others.

When the last of the guests had left, she coaxed him to shut the door on the kitchen disorder and dragged him gaily along the dogtrot to their bedroom.

He sank gratefully into the featherbed, and she scampered in over him and lay next to the wall, chattering. "Don't go to sleep, not yet," she said. "I want to talk about my party . . . ever' little thing . . . and plan what I'm goin' to wear to the first one we go to."

"Look, honey," he said, "about parties. I'd best point out a couple of things—"

"Ooh, Jerd, didn't my Spinnet sound nice, and didn't they love the music, though? And out west here they dance so . . . so . . . they're different from back home. These are men . . . big and strong . . . and fierce, sort of—"

"That's what I mean, honey. Next party, you'd best—"

"Like you . . . hold me, Jerd . . . no . . . tighter. Love me, Jerd . . . love me."

The weeks, months, years passed like a summer breath. Land breaking, planting, fence building, harvesting, Indian scares, all melted away from Jerd when he returned to the cabin, to Sarie. She'd look up from her Spinnet or her needlework or from her bed, where her heart kept her at times, and always she'd smile and want to be kissed. The work he did for her in the cabin—washing, ironing, scrubbing, heavy cooking and baking—was nothing to his muscular arms, and when she kissed him gratefully, reproaching herself for not being strong, he knew he would do anything to guard her beauty and her health.

Her father died at the end of the first year, and Sudie went to live with Uncle Bu in New Bern. When, at the end of the third year, he too died, Sudie went to live with a family friend in Wilmington, and the letters from her dwindled to almost nothing. Sarie wept stormily about each death, but soon bravely pushed sorrow away and became herself again.

Sometimes she regretted aloud the lack of society, and she was lonely, but not deeply so, for she whiled away the days with her music, her needle, her room, her hair and clothes. And there were callers. Young Piepmeier, Weed, or Doerflinger, and most often, in the beginning of the fourth year, it was Prosper Pike, which was natural, seeing that he lived the nearest.

Occasionally, after a visitor had gone, Sarie would put herself against Jerd in bed and hold him with an ardor that was unending and intense; other times she would turn from him if he so much as tried to kiss her, and he knew that whichever man had been visiting had tired her beyond her strength.

Once her weariness forced her to deny him for an entire month.

It was mid-June when she told him there was to be a child.

They were lying awake in the night, and she told him, weeping and trembling in his arms, told him whispering and choking, her tears running into his mouth. He held her, himself choked, but with awe and tenderness, and he stroked her hair, her wet face, and put a gentle kiss upon her shaking mouth.

"It ain't nothing to fret about," he said, "but rather a thing to give thanks for and be happy over."

She caught her breath on a sob. "I'm s-scared to go through with it."

"I'd do it for you if I could, honey."

"There's my heart . . ."

"I'll take care of you."

". . . like my Ma's."

"And Mahala and Vonnie'll help when the time comes."

"Ma died havin' Sudie and me . . ."

"We'll all help, little wife, little sweetheart."

". . . 'cause her heart couldn't stand it."

"She had two babes."

"So'll I . . . so'll I . . . twins run in the fam'ly!"

"You'll be all right, sweetheart, Jerd promises."

"I'll be ugly!"

"You couldn't be ugly."

"And big!"

"Or big, my little girl."

"You'll hate me!"

"I'll love you."

"I'll die, I know I will!"

"Not that . . . never that . . . I swear it."

And he had no fear for her safety, only for her fear.

At first she grew thin, later she put on weight, and her beauty ripened. She scarcely left her room as winter advanced, but spent her time with music, needle, and callers, smiling gallantly for Piepmeier, Weed, Doerflinger, and the frequently appearing Prosper who just sat, with less and less to say, even about the land.

If she was making baby garments, Jerd did not know or ask. Any mention of the expected child threw her into hours of sobbing, brooding, and predictions that she was going to die, and invariably she had to take to her bed, white-lipped and weak, for rest.

Otherwise, she settled into such a sweet, youthful maturity that Jerd felt she was at last growing up, and the moment her child was put into her arms, the transition would be complete.

Her labor struck her a month before she'd thought it would, at the same moment a snowstorm sent its first flakes tumbling downward, and it heightened, tore and raged through her small body as the storm thickened, cut and whipped around the cabin. Prosper, who had stopped in on his way home from trap-setting, went rushing to fetch Mahala, and Jerd frantically stripped the clothes off Sarie as she moaned and doubled, got a night robe onto her distorted body, and lifted her into bed.

She wouldn't stay there under the slicing pain, couldn't stay, and she'd come screaming out and go plunging about the room, Jerd trailing, helpless to help. He was able only to guard her from staggering into the blazing fireplace, to lift her back into bed when the pain was briefly gone. He held her hands and smoothed her hair, frightened at her terrified eyes, the blue look to her lips, the quivering of her pulse, the strangeness of her breathing.

Mahala arrived at last, pushed him out, and barred the door. He stood there, and it all went on and on, the screaming voice inside the room, and the shrieking wind outside. He walked the snow-swept dogtrot through long evening hours, through the endless night of desperation, aware of arrivals and departures, of comings and goings between kitchen and torture chamber, though he never so much as lifted his eyes.

Prosper rushed past with a whiskey jug; Mahala kept running by with linens, mugs, spoons; Vonnie Doerflinger jogged back and forth, her great buttocks rocking, breasts swaying. Doerflinger hunkered off to one side in the darkness, mumbling to someone, himself, or even God for all Jerd knew or cared.

There were so many people around—himself, the husband; Mahala, the midwife; Vonnie, the helper; Doerflinger, Piepmeier, and Prosper, able men, all wanting to help Sarie. And there was nothing they could do but rush, run, jog, mumble, hunker, wait.

The snow fell thick and silent without the wind, and the day crept past noon and toward night.

Hands reached out to Jerd, offering food, and he pushed them aside; footsteps joined his pacings, and he hurried away; voices pleaded with him to sleep, to sit, and he did not reply, but walked the dogtrot, on and back.

When darkness of the second night came falling through the falling snow, the screams were hoarse and constant, fastened onto each other so they hung like sharp, strung beads, piercing the night and him and the smothering snow. He lunged at her door, and when someone—a man —Prosper—tried to stop him, he shoved him back, hurled open her door, and plunged through the screaming to her bed.

Mahala was pulling forth a child by the heels, and when it was yanked and torn out of the screaming Sarie, she fell as silent as the fallen snow. While Mahala was slapping, slapping the child as it hung, head down, from her grip, he stared into Sarie's eyes, which flickered once and stared up at him, not seeing him, for they were as vacant as glass. He dropped to his knees, buried his face in her breasts, and his sobs ripped him, loud and wet and ugly and blasphemous. Hands took him, dragged him away, through cold, noiseless dark, pushed him onto a bunk, poured choking, stinging whiskey down him, and when he groped for the jug, let him have it.

Night and quiet. Rustlings and whisperings. Food under his nose, steaming its stink—hit it away, suck the burning whiskey. Dawn and quiet. Off somewhere, hammering; close, the thin wail, the damned wail of the newborn.

Lie on the bunk, lift the jug, and when they try to get it away, curse them off, and they leave you be and go back to their rustling and whispering and plotting and scheming their secret doings. But you know more than they figure you know; you catch on when they're fixing to shut Sarie away in a box, and you think at the back of your fuzzy and weeping mind, think clear and definite, that she ain't to be stuck in no snowy ground in this wilderness where you ought not to of ever brought her, God or no God.

They think you're asleep, and they sneak outside, the lot of them, even the women. You sit up and put on your moccasins that somebody pulled off, and struggle into your coat and button it, standing with your feet spread wide, holding you steady as a rock. There's a whirl to the room, and a worse whirl in your head, so you take a pull at the jug, and then you hook your finger into its handle, poke your knife into your belt, pick up your rifle, and you go outside.

Snow everywhere. Vast blankets of it on the ground, hung from bushes, ridging fences, thick on trees, roof, woodpile. Mounds of it on the rolling fields, white, pure, mounded graves with pale sun on them, swell after swell, grave after grave, but none for Sarie, never her.

He pushed open her door, and she was alone on her bed. Her yellow hair was on her shoulders in curls, and her yellow lashes were touching her cheeks, and her white lips were strange. They had dressed her in white, and folded her hands, her tiny, little-girl hands, between her breasts. They'd taken her wedding ring, and he cursed them for robbers, but could not, somehow, figure a way to find the ring and get it on her finger without disturbing her rest.

He set down his jug, laid aside his rifle. He pulled the quilt she lay on tenderly up and around her, wrapped her warm, and lifted her, lifted his dead, sweet wife up from her deathbed, the girl he had killed with his love, and he hooked up his jug and rifle, and went outside again.

Nobody stopped him. Nobody was here. Nothing was here but snow and tracks they'd made in it on their way. He stepped off the dogtrot and went in long, uneasy stumbles, and he tromped the snow they'd tromped, and it led him up the ridge and to the black hole they'd dug in the white snow.

They were grouped around a raw wooden box, which the women were lining with white cloth, the men watching, all of them crying.

Jerd staggered to a halt, holding Sarie, and yelled at them, cursing about the ring, and he swore to kill them, one after the other, if they tried to use the wooden box and the grave. Prosper walked at him, tears sparkling in the sun on his red cheeks, his red lips moving on such words as "decent burial" and "drunk." Mahala's voice said, like singing, "father" and "motherless babies" and "duty." Doerflinger and Vonnie and Piepmeier threw in their voices with words on them—words, words, words.

He ran, stumbling, away from the black hole in the white snow, and he kept going, plunging, all of them after him. He stayed ahead of them by running and cursing and breathing and not breathing, and he got to the river first. He dropped Sarie gently to the cushioned bank beside his snow-covered dugout, and she made her own nest in the pure snow that was not pure enough for her, and he dropped his jug and his rifle, and turned to those other ones, his fists clenched with rage.

He heard himself bellowing, his voice thick and not understandable, tongue queer and swollen, but he made them hear, made the trees hear, and the snow and the river, even God above.

"You ain't to touch her," he yelled. "You ain't sister, mammy, pa . . . ary a one of you! Strangers to her . . . visitors. You've got no rights . . . she's my Sarie, all mine!"

The faces of the men grieved, and they moved at him in a group, cautiously, rifles up, and Prosper was saying, "We got to do it this way, Jerd . . . got to."

He grabbed his own rifle, and held it on them. "Stop! Stop where you are," he said, low and hoarse. "You won't shoot, not to kill, but I will—hear that? I will."

"Man," said Prosper, still advancing, the others with him, the women motionless, "you don't know what you're doing."

"I've killed already," Jerd said, pushing his words out from behind his teeth, "killed her. So another one . . . or three . . . it's all the same. You'd best stop . . . you'd safer back up."

The three paused.

"He means it," Piepmeier said, and took a backward step.

"Every word," Doerflinger agreed, and backed away.

Only Prosper stood his ground, eyes desperate, rifle steady. "You can't do this to Sarie," he said. "In God's name, what is it you're trying to do? Tell me that—anyhow tell!"

"I'm taking her back."

"*Back?* Where?"

"Where she belongs . . . out of this godforsaken hole where I didn't have no business bringing her."

"You can't take her clear to Car'liney, man! She'd—"

"And you ain't astopping me . . . God Hisself ain't!"

"The river's on a rise, you fool! It's a devil and a bruiser! You wouldn't get—"

"Back up, Prosper . . . all of you. Keep moving . . . women, too."

"Jerd, Jerd, Jerd," Mahala moaned.

"No talk . . . just back and back."

They kept going, their faces arguing and pleading, the women sobbing, but he would not heed, could not. Keeping his rifle always on them, he used one foot and one hand, gave a mighty kick and heave, and the dugout was on its bottom, showering snow. He threw the paddles into it, and the jug; he pulled his knife and hacked through the rope where it was knotted around a tree.

Still facing Prosper and the others, he shoved the dugout into the water, dragged Sarie clumsily to it, and half-threw her into the bow. He gave the stern a push, jumped in, dropped his rifle, grabbed a paddle, and began poling away from the bank fast.

The men came rushing, yelling, and running along the bank, but he paid them no mind. He crouched in the stern, paddling strongly across the edge of the current, heading for midstream, and as he toiled and sweated and maneuvered, he was telling Sarie how it was.

"I'm taking you to St. Louis, honey," he said, "so's you can be with folks . . . and there's folks there . . . walking the streets . . . going in and out of shops and houses . . . buying and visiting . . . singing songs . . . dancing . . . laughing . . . sleeping in rows in the burying grounds . . . so's even when you get sleepy, my darling-honey, you won't be alone . . . won't never be alone. . . ."

He wrestled the dugout into the current, headed downstream, and told her not to be scared. He explained how the Missouri wasn't no plain river running its bed, but a pure horned devil that cut crooked through the land, and for sheer cussedness its channel went crooked through it so sometimes the current would flow upstream. He told her how he was plotting against the river so's it wouldn't have no chance to outscheme him.

He excused himself to suck the jug, because he needed it so. He begged her to forgive him when the current snatched the dugout and set it to whirling, and after he got it under control again, promised to leave the jug be until he got her to St. Louis. He showed her the river's wickedness.

He explained how it wasn't fit for no kind of river craft: too deep for poles, too swift for oars, too crooked for sails. He described how it was alway rising unexpected like, lifting logs and driftwood off a thousand bars, yanking up lusty trees, hurling all downstream on its plunging flood; he pictured how the Missouri acted when its waters fell, taking the trees and logs, lodging them on bars, piling sand around and between and through them, and matting the whole mess together with quick-springing willow roots, forming rafts and islands almost overnight.

But that wasn't enough for this river. It also laid traps for boats. It wedged logs in its muddy bottom so they stuck upward, leaning downstream, sometimes breaking water, but just as often hidden, and these were what boatmen called snags, because they could pierce a boat or rip off a gunwale. But the Missouri had a better trick than that: it anchored the ends of some of the logs in its mud by their roots or branches, thus giving them freedom of movement which they took advantage of, surging up on the current, falling under with a great vibration, jumping out of the water again, and these the boatmen called sawyers, and they were real disaster. Then, tucked away in deep, secret pockets, the Missouri kept its quicksands, hungry and sucking and relentless. Oh, it was a real bruiser, this river.

Now he saw the quilt had fallen away from Sarie's head, and the sun was warming her yellow hair and patting her face, so he cautioned her against ever getting herself, her lovely self, dirtied by the filthy water. If ever the Missouri touched her, his bride, wife, darling, he'd tear it apart with his hands, and tromp it into its own slime, and it would be no more.

And while he told her these things, or thought them to her, or dreamed them, whatever it was, he paddled, steered, poled, and rounded islands and rafts, avoided snags, sensed the sawyers and dodged them and they didn't get him, not him, they didn't dast.

Until that final one, that almost-little one that kept its head under water until he was right on it, then reared up, black and sharp and shining, and tore at his bow, then tipped the dugout over. He saw the thick brown river pour over Sarie's quilt, creep through her hair and down her face, and then he himself was overboard and sinking.

When he come to the top he was sober, which the first he knowed he'd been otherwise. Sarie wasn't swimming nowhere, couldn't, because she was dead. He dove, eyes open, staring through the water that wasn't mud, the mud that wasn't water, but he couldn't see nothing. He swam and swam, looking, groping, grabbing, his hands on slick things, soft things, but not Sarie, never Sarie.

He surfaced, choking and clawing, gulped cold air that burned, and dove again, searched again, crawled the river bottom, and this he did and did, over and again. He was tired and beyond tired; he dove, swam, crawled, felt. Of a sudden he realized his crime, and accused himself of it straightway: he'd killed his Sarie not once but twice—once with his seed, once with his river—and he opened his mouth to cry his accusation aloud, to shout and demand the punishment that was his due, and then he swallowed the river and knew no more.

When he come to, he was on his kitchen bunk. His hush-voiced neighbors were in the room. He jumped up to go back to the river, but Prosper told him it was no use, they'd searched for hours after pulling him out.

Sarie was gone.

Chapter Sixteen

"MY DOINGS, none but mine," he whispered now.

Devora, lying with him in his kitchen bunk, cradled his head in her naked arms, put her kisses along his brow and waited.

"I killed her twice, and I turned ag'in her babes . . . packed them off on Mahala."

"She wanted them, Jerd."

"I got drunk ag'in, stayed drunk."

"You were shocked, stunned."

"Nailed up her room . . ."

"Talk, Jerd, talk it out."

". . . and drunk myself sober ag'in . . . sober and sick and thinking . . ."

"Yes . . . yes."

". . . until I found my duty, to bring her babes home, and get them a mammy."

"Me."

"So I raised the room, and I fixed my pack, come to St. Louis, and seen you."

"And sought me out."

"And knowed you was above what I could offer . . . like her, like Sarie."

"You married me . . . you spoke the vows."

"And in front of the parson, and after, it was like maybe it was wrong, all of it. Wrong to her . . . wrong to you . . . I was plagued by want for you, but I was scared . . . for fear I'd do to you what I done to her . . ."

"But you grew to love me . . ."

". . . if I touched you . . ."

". . . the way I love you."

". . . or took comfort in you."

"But you did, at last you did . . . and it's here now, the comfort, and the loving . . . waiting . . . all yours."

Her kissing lips went along his brow again, and she pulled his face into her breasts, pressed it to them, felt his lips take up the kissing, felt his hands again, and him, all of him, gently this time, and sweetly.

They dressed together, eyes catching, escaping, meeting shyly, smiling in embarrassment over their own confusion. They looked out their window together upon a snow-white Christmas world, and it was snowing yet, the flakes big and fluffy and coming down silent and thick.

They ate together, looked after the babies, made ready for their Christmas dinner with Vonnie and Doerflinger, Prosper and Mahala. They filled the fireplace oven with its special wood, and when it had burned to sizzling coals, scraped them out, put in the turkeys, and closed the door.

They laid the table, with a gift at each place, Spot, the dog, and Big Tom, the cat, getting underfoot. When Spot began to bark, and the knock came at the front door, they went to it together, eyes quiet now, content now, shining now, and Jerd threw it open to admit their expected guests.

Standing on the pure snow, dressed in utter black, was a tiny, shapely girl, an angel of a girl. Yellow curls showed under the poke of her black bonnet, blue eyes looked up at them, wide and innocent, pink mouth wistful in her face. Snowflakes were coming to rest gently on her black-clad shoulders, on her yellow hair, touching her face like white, pure tears. When she spoke, the ease of a faraway south was on her tongue, and she said, like a summer breath, "Jerd . . . don't you know me, Jerd? It's Sudie. I've changed my mind. I've come to marry you."

Chapter Seventeen

"SUDIE," Jerd whispered.

The silence of the falling snow beat in Devora's ears. She stared at the one back from the dead, the slender girl in widow's black, who wore the floating snow like a bridal veil. She saw, without looking, the figures of a man and horse in the background.

The cold of air and snow, the knowledge of the girl's intent, and Jerd's consternation, rolled into Devora. She moved forward a pace, touched Jerd's arm, and waited.

He said, hoarsely, "Sudie. This is Devora—my wife."

The blue eyes flew to Devora, back to Jerd, sparkled with tears, and now it was Sudie who was whispering. "How could you?" she asked. "I wrote as soon as—" She indicated her black with a helpless small gesture. "What am I to do?"

"Come in out of the snow," Devora said.

As she turned back into the room, she glimpsed Sudie's pleading hesitancy, and the way Jerd reached out, dazed, took her hands, and pulled her into the cabin. When she faced them again, they were standing apart, and a very young and bony man was stepping through the door, closing it behind him.

Sudie said, her wet eyes for Jerd alone, "It took all my money to g-get here."

"How did you come?" he asked. His face showed nothing; only his eyes, with their shock and bewilderment.

"By boat and wagon. It was such an awful trip, Jerd honey, you j-just don't know. And all by myself."

"I reckon you are wore out."

"She sure is," said the bony young man. "She's rid double on my horse from St. Louis, goin' out'n the way to bunk at settlers' cabins. And we had two real Injun scares. She's had it tough."

Jerd nodded.

Devora ignored her jumping heart. She steadied her voice, looked at the tall, sandy-haired stranger who couldn't be out of his midtwenties, and said, "I haven't met this young man, Jerd."

He looked at her absently. "This's Piepmeier, Junius Piepmeier—the one I told you about. Piepmeier, my wife."

Devora offered her hand, and Piepmeier shook it. "Pleased," he said. "I heer'd Jerd'd took a wife."

"I didn't," said Sudie.

Piepmeier turned to her solicitously. "I'd of swore I told you."

"Oh, you maybe s-said somethin', but I thought of my s-sister. I didn't dream he'd—so soon."

"You orter knowed I wouldn't fetch you to no lone widower," Piepmeier said, shocked.

"I don't know what I thought!"

"Ain't she Sarie all over, though?" Piepmeier asked, grinning from Sudie to Jerd and Devora. "I was in St. Louis to barter my pelts, so when I heer'd they was a young lady'd just got off'n the keel and wanted to be took to the Warner place, I hunted her out. And when I clapped eyes on her, I like to swallered my tongue. I told her I'd knew her sister, and spoke her name right out—Sarie'd told me what it was." His grin vanished, sadness washed through his eyes, then he was grinning again. "Warn't it like that, Sudie?"

"Oh, hush!" she cried. "Can't you see this ain't a time for foolin'?" She cast a beseeching look at Jerd. "What am I goin' to do? Where can I g-go?"

"It don't have to be decided immediate," Jerd said. His eyes came to Devora's, asking. "We've got room and grub aplenty. Devora'll make you at home. Piepmeier and me'll go look after his horse."

He took his coat from its peg and left, Piepmeier and Spot following. Sudie turned coolly to Devora and regarded her.

"Well?" she said, at last.

"Come to the fire. Get warm."

Sudie stepped gingerly around Big Tom, drawing her skirts aside.

Devora stood facing her across the hearth, feeling big, awkward and plain before such fragile beauty. She looked at the yellow curls, the innocent eyes, the pure features and pink lips, and knew she would have recognized Sudie anywhere from Jerd's telling of Sarie. She wondered, detachedly, if, had she met Sudie under other circumstances, unaware that she was the counterpart of the girl Jerd had worshiped, she would have liked her. She sighed. She was being unfair to both the dead girl and the living one to feel they were born to make trouble.

"Is somethin' wrong with me?" Sudie asked, her tone anxious, her eyes appealing now.

"I was thinking how pretty you are."

"Were you? That's sweet of you, ma'am."

"And how far you've traveled, and what a shame it was for nothing."

"I know you just perfectly hate poor little me for comin' in on you this way, ma'am."

"Of course I don't."

"Why don't you?"

"You didn't know how things are."

"Did you know Jerd long, ma'am?"

"We've been married for over two months."

"That ain't so long."

"Perhaps not, but it's as final as two years."

"I reckon s-so."

"Would you like to rest before dinner?"

"I ain't hungry."

"You can stay in your room if you prefer."

Sudie's damp eyes wandered to the table. "Is it a p-party?"

"Not really. Just neighbors coming for Christmas."

"I'm so mixed up."

"Yes."

"I'm so tired, and my head aches."

"You need rest. But if you'd like to see the twins first—they're asleep in the little bed there."

"Later. I vow I must look a sight! I ain't goin' to let 'em see me—Jerd or that silly boy either one—'til I get decent. Can't we hurry?"

Devora led the way along the dogtrot, opened the door at the end of it, and stood aside. She had prepared the room for the Doerflingers, so the bed was made up with clean sheets, fresh towels were out, the water pitcher was filled, and a fire was snapping in the fireplace. Someone, either Jerd or Piepmeier, had left Sudie's bags at the foot of the bed.

Sudie paused in the middle of the room, and turned slowly, looking it over. She glanced at Devora. "Thank you for showin' me to Sarie's room, ma'am," she said. "I'll get along here just fine."

Devora went back to the kitchen, her mouth gentle with sympathy for Jerd, her eyes puzzled over the silken girl who had, almost literally, returned from the dead. She recognized Sudie's dilemma, but her quick pity was overshadowed by an instinctive distrust.

Jerd's love had now become hers; her sister-in-law's presence was a threat to it.

[171]

She determined to get Sudie out of her cabin as quickly as possible.

She worked briskly, laying two extra plates at the table. After a moment's consideration, she made a packet of tobacco for Piepmeier, another of her own best writing paper for Sudie, and put these at their places.

The guests arrived while Jerd and Piepmeier were still in the barnlot. The men remained there, tending their horses, but the women came plodding for the cabin, baskets on their arms, heads tipped away from the snowfall, their voices preceding them on the cold air.

Devora was holding open the door when they reached it, Mahala's chatter brightening the room as she stepped inside.

"This's Devorry, Vonnie," she said. "Vonnie Doerflinger, Devorry. You a'ready know each other from my talk—you'll get along. Where's my babies? Ah, there they are, sound asleep, precious angels!"

Devora helped Vonnie off with her coat, hung it and the brown bonnet up, turned back. "Come over to the fire," she invited, "and get warm."

"I ain't that friz," said Vonnie. "Stand quiet. Want to see you."

"That's her . . . that's Vonnie," said Mahala. "If I speak out, she's even worst."

Smiling, Devora regarded the neighbor, whose kindly hazel eyes were examining her. Vonnie Doerflinger was fifty or over, and she was a sizable woman with big bones, plenty of comfortable fat, and a broad, tired face. Her hair was half gray, combed into a looped knot, and she had a barely discernible mustache on her upper lip. Her dress was brown linsey, and it put a yellow tone to her skin that was not only unbecoming, but aging.

She gave Devora a lop-sided grin, said, "You'll do," dropped the grin, and openly looked around the kitchen. "It's better," she said. "Sound. Clean. No frills."

"What'd I tell you!" cried Mahala, whose hands had been dipping into the baskets, bringing out pots and pans of food. "Things is fine in this cabin these days!" She trotted to the fireplace, set a small cookpot on a trivet, pushed it over some hot coals, came trotting back.

Devora and Vonnie helped her with the baskets, chatting, speculating as to which moment the turkeys would be done just right. For a time Devora was almost able to forget Sudie, and it wasn't until Mahala began to tell Vonnie in detail what a fine guest room she and Doerflinger were going to enjoy that night, that the shock of the girl's arrival came flooding back over her.

She was groping for words to explain Sudie, when the babies awoke and began to cry. Mahala and Vonnie rushed to them, and there was so much exclaiming, cooing, laughing and baby talk, that she gave up for the moment.

The door opened and the men came in, pausing on the dogtrot to stomp the snow off their feet. Devora glanced at Jerd, but he showed nothing, not shock or pleasure or sadness. Piepmeier appeared as he had earlier, pleased and young and a little foolish. Prosper winked at her, whooped, hugged her, and shouted out an introduction to Doerflinger.

This one was a match to Vonnie in that he was sizable, big-boned and half gray. He wasn't as tall as his wife, but he was big and bull-shouldered, and his face was rimmed with a burst of grizzled beard. His lips spread in a smile that was at once open and sensual.

"Pleased, Devorry, pleased and tickled," he said. "Smells purty in here. When do we git our chanct to find out eff'n it tastes purty, too?"

"Soon," Devora said, and smiled.

Prosper and Doerflinger were much too hearty and loud to have been informed of Sudie's arrival.

She turned deliberately to Jerd. His dark eyes met hers, and his head moved almost imperceptibly in the negative. It was she who looked away first.

Thus, it was not until they were all standing around the table, each person behind his bench, stool or chair, that she had an opportunity to tell about Sudie. Prosper noticed the vacant place and asked who was to sit there. Devora pulled in her breath, but before she could utter a syllable, the dogtrot door swung inward and Jerd wheeled so quickly that the others noticed him and looked, too.

Sudie stood there, dressed in white, bearing white-wrapped packages. Her hair was piled in curls on top of her head, her eyes were pleading, and her lips quivering with the beginning of a smile that had a tentative dimple at its corner.

Someone gasped, but whether it was man or woman, Devora did not know, for her attention was on Jerd. He was staring at the girl in the doorway as if he could not believe, draw breath, move or speak. Devora, pressed by his need and by the consternation of the others, went to Sudie, took her arm, and walked with her to the table.

"This is Sudie Bennett . . . Mrs. Bennett," she said, her voice steady. "Jerd's sister-in-law, come to visit. Sudie, this is Mahala Pike . . . Vonnie Doerflinger . . . her husband . . . and this is Prosper Pike."

The women jerked their heads; the men gaped and mumbled. Sudie, hardly noticing the wives, let her packages tumble and held out both hands, one to Doerflinger, the other to Prosper.

"Sarie wrote me such precious things about you darlin' two!" she cried sadly. "You'll just never know how much I love you both for bein' so sweet to her!" Her smile trembled back onto her lips, and her eyes clung to the men.

Jerd was staring at her as he'd been doing from the moment she entered in her pure white, and now Devora saw a tinge of embarrassment enter his eyes.

While Piepmeier clumsily got Sudie's packages off the floor and laid them on the table, Doerflinger and Prosper grinned sheepishly and murmured their "'Twarn't nothing," almost inaudibly.

Suddenly she became aware of the twins, Frank on Mahala's arm, Lill on Vonnie's.

"Sarie's babies," she whispered, tears rising. "So beautiful! The fair one's her image! The dark one's so cunnin'! Jerd! Jerd honey, can I touch them, hold them, my own twin Sarie's babies, my sweet almost-mine babies, can I?"

Devora caught the perplexity in Jerd as he glanced quickly to her, back to Sudie and said, "Well, sure."

The girl ran to Frank and put out her arms. He turned his face to Mahala's neck and began to wail. Sudie backed away, and went to her chair, almost weeping.

"I'm sorry, Jerd," she said. "I scared him, rushin' at him so eager. I'll wait. I've waited so long, this long, and I've come so far . . . I can wait a little more. Forgive me, ever'body, for disturbin' things with my notion." She looked beseechingly from man to man.

Devora broke in, asking Jerd to say grace, and they all bowed their heads speedily.

When they were seated, they began to open their packages in subdued embarrassment, a mood entirely different from the gaiety Devora had anticipated when she prepared the gifts. She herself received hemmed towels from Mahala and Vonnie, and thanked them warmly.

Piepmeier said many thanks for his tobacco; Prosper and Doerflinger grinned widely over their presents, and Mahala and Vonnie exclaimed delightedly over theirs. The twins handled their bean bags, gazed at them wonderingly, began to chew them.

Jerd, when he unwrapped the stockings Devora had knit for him, lifted his eyes soberly to hers, said, "I needed these," reached under his chair, brought out a knobby parcel, and passed it to her, his eyes asking her to like it. It was a small wooden bowl, newly made and smoothed and polished. She smiled into his waiting eyes and told him she'd use it as a centerpiece for her table, and he looked content.

Sudie, unwrapping her packet of writing paper, turned her eyes softly on Jerd. "Jerd honey," she cried, "how perfectly sweet! How darlin'! Look, ever'body, such fine paper! Open my present, Jerd. It ain't but a tucked shirt, but it's real big, 'cause I didn't forget what a enormous, fine man you are!" She turned contritely to Devora, offering her two small, beribboned boxes. "I'm so sorry I didn't have somethin' for you, ma'am, but not knowin'— Maybe you'd enjoy openin' what I brought Sarie's babies."

Devora took the boxes. Each contained a gold baby ring. She passed them to Mahala. "They're charming, Sudie," she said.

While Mahala glanced at the rings and gave them, without comment to Vonnie, who handed them to Jerd, Sudie said, "I wanted Sarie's babies to have somethin' that'd last and show my love. Did I do right, Jerd?" she added anxiously as he received the boxes into his palm and looked, not at them, but at her, speculatively.

"Why, I reckon so," he said tightly.

Devora ended the uncomfortable silence that followed by asking Jerd and Prosper to carve the turkeys. That left only Doerflinger and Piepmeier staring at Sudie, the two women guests talking together, not looking at her at all, except covertly.

After the plates were filled, Mahala put a direct question to Sudie. "When'd you get here?" she asked.

"Couple hours ago," Piepmeier said. "I rid her out from St. Louis."

"That so?"

"He was just so good to poor little stranger me," Sudie said, giving Piepmeier a smile.

"Where's Mr. Bennett at?" Mahala asked.

Sudie's eyes dimmed; she lowered them. "He—I'm a widow," she said.

"Mahaley," Prosper chided.

"My apologies."

"She couldn't know," Sudie said, lifting her eyes to Prosper. "Don't fuss at her, 'cause it's my own silly fault." She touched her white dress with her finger tips, looked apologetically at Jerd, and went on. "I didn't want to spoil your party, so I took off my mournin'. I didn't know how it might seem." She whispered the final words, stricken.

"It's quite all right," Devora said. "Eat what you can, Sudie. Food will make you feel better."

Mahala came out with a small burst of talk to Vonnie, Piepmeier joined in and so did the others, all but Jerd and Sudie. Devora gave up hope for a comfortable, friendly gathering, and tried to keep the talk flowing and thus cover the various wonders, griefs, tensions, and disturbances she sensed. She even went so far as to ask Piepmeier if he'd seen her brother, Amos Griggs, this trip, and if he had any word of him, and Piepmeier shook his head and said no, he warn't acquainted with the feller atall.

Sudie's spirits rose as the meal progressed. By the time Devora and Vonnie were washing up, she had spread her soft skirts, sat down on Jerd's bunk, making room for Piepmeier and Doerflinger on either side, and was entrancing them with her account of her travels from North Carolina to St. Louis.

Mahala and Prosper, each lulling a baby to sleep, sat in the fireplace chairs. Jerd sat a bench at the table, smoking, his eyes going from Devora to Sudie, back to Devora.

Devora, aware of his watching, wondered what thoughts he was having, and what differences he was measuring. When the others are gone, she told herself, when we are alone with this problem, Jerd will work it out. And I will help him.

In thirty minutes or so, Doerflinger and Piepmeier went brisky through the dogtrot door. Sudie wandered over to the baby bed and leaned above it, gazing lovingly at the sleeping twins.

Jerd watched her. Prosper watched her. Mahala turned on her heel and asked clearly for a dish towel so she could earn her keep.

Devora was setting the last wooden mug on its shelf when Doerflinger and Piepmeier came back, carrying Sarie's Spinnet. Sudie went to them in a little rush, showed them where to place the instrument, took her skirts in her finger tips and seated herself at the keyboard on the chair Piepmeier brought. The light from the window fell over her left shoulder, and fireglow stroked her right side.

She looked full at Jerd. "What'd you like to hear, Jerd honey? I know all Sarie's pieces, and more. Tell me what to play, what to sing."

Jerd said, "It don't matter. I ain't musical."

Sudie lifted her eyes inquiringly to the semicircle the other three men had formed around the Spinnet. They grinned and said they wasn't musical neither, and she laughed.

She touched the keys, tipped her yellow head, let her yellow lashes rest on her cheeks, and listened to the plucked strings. "It ain't as bad out of tune as it could be," she said, opened her eyes, played a melody that was both happy and quick, and began to sing.

Song followed song, and Devora became absorbed in listening to the sunny fragility of the singing voice and the quivering sweetness of the plucked strings. Seeing, hearing, she found herself thinking that Sudie, come out of the snow, seated now at the gilt Spinnet, truly looked and

[176]

sounded like an angel. She wondered, with a sickness, how Jerd could content himself with her, plain, everyday Devora, now that his lost miracle had touched him again.

Mahala jumped up and began to hustle about, breaking the spell. "Go get the horse, Prosper," she ordered. "We got to get along. It'll be dark time we're home, and you got to chore, don't forget."

Vonnie stood up. "Us too," she said. "Mr. Doerflinger, get the horse."

"But you were to spend the night, Vonnie," Devora protested.

The older woman jerked her head toward Sudie, who had stopped playing. "You got company enough."

Jerd said, from the table, "Us men can bunk out in the barn. Turn the cabin over to the womenfolk."

Vonnie stabbed him with a look. "Thanks. Mr. Doerflinger, the horse."

Doerflinger left Sudie apologetically, got his coat, and came toward Vonnie, his mouth uncertain in its nest of beard.

"We'll stay at Mahaley's tonight," she told him.

"Eff'n that suits," he agreed helplessly.

"Suits fine," Mahala said.

The men assured Sudie it'd been a pleasure, and went out, leaving Jerd and Piepmeier to comply with her soft-spoken request that the Spinnet be carried back to her room. She held the door open for them, murmuring how sweet they were to go to such bother, and she'd run ahead and open the bedroom door for them.

"She's like the first one," Mahala said, the instant the door closed.

"She's a bitch," Vonnie said.

"Don't talk like that!" Devora cried.

"Why not?" asked Vonnie. "We don't mean no bad to you, Devorry. But watch that 'un. She's after men . . . any men."

"But she's only a child!"

"She's twenty-four . . . that's woman-age," said Mahala.

"Why'd she come here anyhow, tell me that!" Vonnie demanded.

"Why, to . . . visit her sister's children."

"She don't give a snap of her finger for them babies," Vonnie said. "And she's got her a reason for leaving Car'liney and slaves and all for what we got here on the land. Even for a visit."

"Vonnie's right, Devorry."

"She's a bad 'un," Vonnie went on. "I'm warning you, Devorry. Me and Mahaley's been through it. Ain't we, Mahaley?"

Mahala nodded.

"Been through what?" Devora asked.

[177]

"Seeing our men turned into plumb fools," Mahala said.

"Her playing with them like they was a mouse," Vonnie added.

"This 'un's at Jerd now, whereas he belonged to the other 'un a'ready," Mahala said. "You seen how he went into that room of Sarie's just now, soft as butter."

"Where nothing'd drag him afore," Vonnie said.

"That he nailed up," Mahala said.

"We ain't intending to be mean or un-Christian," Vonnie said earnestly, "but us women got to hang together, Devorry. You seen them fools lop on that Spinnet, agaping at her, and not a one of 'em gives a rap for music . . ."

"Prosper can't even carry a tune," Mahala said.

". . . unless it's got yaller hair. Don't you never take your eyes off'n that girl, Devorry."

Impulsively Devora embraced them, an arm around each. "Don't you worry about me," she said, her voice catching.

They laughed embarrassedly, then scurried for the barnlot, floundering through ankle-deep snow that looked faintly blue in the dusk. The flakes were no longer coming down and Devora wondered, in some surprise, when they had stopped.

She had candles lit and the twins asleep by the time Jerd and Piepmeier finished choring. They said they wanted nothing to eat, so she sat in her fireside chair, Piepmeier across from her, Jerd on a bench he pulled up. She let one hand rest on the edge of the baby bed, her fingers lying thoughtfully along the sturdy wood, and listened to the men talk of peltries, prices, and the St. Louis market.

An eddy of cold touched her ankles as the dogtrot door opened and closed. Sudie was moving across the room to the fireplace, gracefully and unobtrusively. She was still wearing her white dress, but had put a lacy white shawl around her shoulders, and was holding this together with both tiny hands.

Piepmeier sprang up, offered his chair, and she sank into it while he pulled up another bench alongside Jerd's. They all sat with just the snapping of the fire and the sound of the clock.

Sudie said, softly, "I hope I ain't in your way, ma'am."

"Not at all," Devora said.

"I don't mean to be, ma'am. I did think I'd retire, but it was so lonesome. And I hurried so to be with . . . here . . . for Christmas. And my first night. You do understand, ma'am?"

"Perfectly."

"We warn't talking nothing but peltries," Piepmeier volunteered.

[178]

"You go right on, do," Sudie begged. "I'll just sit quiet and listen, and maybe-so I'll learn somethin'."

"Tain't worth going on with," Piepmeier said.

"Oh, you'd just say that. Jerd honey?"

Devora saw him move on his bench.

"I ain't botherin' . . . honest?"

"No."

"Well, then!" She sighed in little-girl satisfaction and leaned back in her chair. "Ain't this cozy?"

"Hain't nothing better," Piepmeier said.

Sudie's breath snagged.

"I say something wrong?" Piepmeier asked.

"Oh, my no. You're just so sweet to think of my feelin's, Juney! No . . . I just recalled what awful things've happened to me. You just wouldn't believe 'em! And I was so happy last Christmas. And with my husband after that. We had the biggest party once . . . but you wouldn't be interested hearin' about poor little me."

"We would," Piepmeier exclaimed. "Wouldn't we, folks?"

"Of course," Devora said. "Talk all you want, Sudie."

" 'Want' ain't the word, ma'am. 'Need' is more it. I need Jerd to know how ever'thing happened, all the horrible stuff, so's he'll understand. To start with, there I was, all alone—Pa and Uncle Bu and Sarie all dead—when I— When Zebbie—"

"Captain Bennett?" Devora asked.

"Yes, ma'am. Captain Zebediah Bennett. I called him Zebbie for a pet name, and he fussed, but he loved it. He was the ha-handsomest thing."

"I'm sure he was."

"He was the darlin'est man . . . so jealous of me, but that showed he really loved me."

"Go on, Sudie."

"He was so h-healthy."

"Army men are."

"Uh-huh, but then he was d-dead!"

"In line of duty?" Devora asked.

"N-no."

"Do you want to tell how it was?"

"We had this party, and eatin' and drinkin' and dancin', and it lasted —oh, 'way awful late. And after ever'body'd gone home, Zebbie was jealous . . . he was just awful . . . even after I fixed him a nice glass of wine with my own hands, he was nasty . . . so I l-locked myself in my

[179]

room . . . and in the mornin' . . . the s-slave girl woke me up a-screamin'
. . . and he was—"

"Gawd," Piepmeier whispered.

"So I c-called the doctor, and he f-fooled around, and called in those
other men—"

"What other men?" Jerd asked. "What for?"

"I d-don't know . . . what'd I know about law. I never wanted anything in this world but to be sweet and have folks love me."

"Don't cry," Piepmeier said, his voice sharp.

"And they s-said Zebbie'd been p-poisoned . . . on p-purpose."

"You mean, murdered?" Jerd asked.

Sudie nodded, dropped her face into her hands, and wept.

"They find out who done it?" Jerd asked.

The yellow head shook; the sobbing deepened.

"Who'd they think?"

"Oh, Jerd honey, I don't know," she wailed. "I didn't wait . . . I just
came straight to you! I couldn't stand to stay there with ever'body bein'
so ugly and nosey!"

She dropped her head on her arm. Sobs trembled her slight body.
Piepmeier was shaking his head, and Jerd sat in utter silence. Devora
stared at the nimbus the firelight was putting around the yellow hair.

She asked, "Did you tell anyone where you were coming?"

"No, and I never will, and I'll never go back!"

Now the silent room had the snapping fire in it, the sound of the
clock, and the weeping of the girl who had fled into the wilderness to
marry a man already married. This Devora pondered, searching for the
reason why, even in grief, especially in grief, Sudie would have come to
marry Jerd, and found only suspicion that she was hiding something.

As in a dream, she heard Jerd say, "You don't have to go back. You
can stay here as long as you want."

With the suddenness of a thunderbolt, Devora knew it was going to
be as hard for her to get this girl out of her cabin as it would have been to
evict Sarie herself.

❦ *Chapter Eighteen* ❦

PIEPMEIER escorted Sudie along the dogtrot to the door of her bedroom that night, looking in the kitchen again only to insist upon sleeping in the barn. Otherwise he wouldn't feel free to visit a few days, as they'd invited him to do. Jerd went with him, protesting, and while he was gone Devora settled the twins, hurriedly disrobed, took the pins out of her hair, and got into bed.

She lay waiting and listening. She dared not actually believe Jerd would come to her so soon after the shock of Sudie's arrival, but she hoped he would, and so in so doing, establish immediately and beyond challenge, her own priority in him.

But when he had returned and the sounds of his undressing had stopped, and the smell of tallow from the extinguished candle drifted into her room, and he did come to her in the darkness, it was not the same. Not the same, either, the next night, or the next, but almost hurried, and in silence. And after he went to his own bunk, sickening doubt took her, and she wondered, When he holds me, does he find me big and awkward . . . after Sarie? And when we . . . is he thinking of me . . . or of Sudie?

Thus, although she welcomed him, and gave him all her love, and had for herself the wonder of him, she never recaptured the glory of that first time, that Christmas-Eve time, before Sudie came.

And instead of being sure of him, she was more unsure than ever.

She was relieved to have Piepmeier around daytimes, for he kept Sudie amused and occupied. She even thought, with a stirring of excitement, that Sudie might conceivably marry him, for he was young, ambitious, and plainly in love with her.

She was encouraged in this hope one afternoon when she was at her breadmaking. Piepmeier and Sudie were in the fireside chairs, and he was speaking earnestly, his big, bony hands gesturing an inadequate description.

". . . I'll clean that cabin ontil it is raw," he was saying. "I'll sweep

it out and scrub and rub a rag all over. Get me a cat in . . . good mouser
. . . and she'll rid me of ever' last mouse . . . and I'll ride over to Weeds
and horse-trade me some whitewash, and I'll really coat them walls . . ."

"What else will you do, Juney?" Sudie asked, teasing.

"I'll smooth down that floor and give it what polish I know how, and
when I'm over to Weeds, I'll make a deal with his missus to braid me a
carpet."

"What color?"

"Light—blue mostly, with yaller streaks—ask her to put in all the blue
and yaller she can dig up."

"Umm."

"Don't you favor blue and yaller, Sudie? I sure got the idee that you
favored blue and—"

"Yes, I like them, silly! What next? Tell me more."

Amused at the boy's smitten state and Sudie's flirting, Devora finished
her bread. She added more potatoes and onions to the soup to make sure
there would be enough to fill this skinny young fellow who ate so hugely.

He remained for three days, worshiping Sudie's swinging yellow
lashes, her pink and teasing lips, her flirting eyes. Sudie, bright and
smiling, stood on the dogtrot with him the morning he left for his distant
farm. She told him good-by and thank you for bringing me from St.
Louis, prettily and touchingly.

His young mouth was split in such a helpless grin Devora wondered
if he'd be able to speak with it or tear himself away at all. He managed,
somehow, to swing onto his horse, and from there stammered and asked
Sudie if she'd be willing for him to show up again.

"After I've got my cabin slicked up, carpet'n all," he concluded.

"We-ll, I s'pose," Sudie agreed, her mouth puckering thoughtfully.

"I'll have me aplenty to say that time," he said. "Take care of her,
ma'am . . . she's so little."

Devora nodded, smiling.

She watched the smile leave Sudie's mouth as he rode away, saw it
twist downward ever so slightly. She noticed that Jerd was watching too,
with surprise on his face. Unexpectedly he said, "Don't look down on
Piepmeier . . . he ain't no fool," and then he turned and went into the
kitchen.

Sudie danced merrily after him, teasing about how his hair nearly
touched his shoulders. "Old shaggy bear!" she cried. "I bet you never
did have your hair cut, ever!"

"Oh, I chop it off occasional."

"I vow, if that ain't just like a man! If there wasn't a girl around to see after him, I don't know what'd happen! Wouldn't even fix his hair!"

"Devora's offered."

"Why didn't you let her, silly?"

"I don't rightly know. Don't like to be no trouble."

"Why, it ain't trouble, Jerd honey! Is it, ma'am? Of course not! Here, poor darlin', sit down! Sudie'll do it for you!"

She went on tiptoe in front of him, reached her hands to his shoulders, her face up to him, and pushed him backward toward a bench. Clumsily, his eyes seeking Devora in wild appeal, he sank down on it.

"Now, you just sit there!" Sudie ordered. "I'll run get my scissors . . . Sarie's scissors."

"There's no need," Devora said, crossing to the mantel. "Mine are here in my work basket, they're good and sharp, and you're perfectly welcome to use them." She handed the scissors to Sudie and smiled into Jerd's unhappy eyes to cover her annoyance. "Sudie'll make you into a regular town man," she said lightly. "I expect I won't even know you after this."

"Devora—" he said.

But Sudie already had the scissors flashing through his hair. "Sit quiet and don't talk," she said. "I want to show you how handsome you are!"

Devora washed dishes while Sudie cut, trimmed, and chattered; she dried them and put them on their shelf while Sudie discovered the cutest cowlick, parted Jerd's hair a new way, and combed it just right. She mended the fire while Sudie got the hand glass and held it in front of him.

"There now," she said, "look!"

He stared into the mirror, speechless, miserable.

"Ain't you goin' to say somethin', Jerd honey?" Sudie chided. "You didn't speak one word while I was cuttin'."

"Why . . . thanks," he said.

"Don't it look better?"

"Sure. Thanks."

"What do you think, ma'am?"

"It's a great improvement," Devora said honestly. "I like it, Jerd."

He tried to meet her eyes, didn't quite manage it, got up, mumbled something about outside work piling up, and turned to make his escape.

"Wait!" Sudie cried. "I'll go along . . . I'll help . . . ever' day I'll help!"

"No," he said bluntly.

He left fast.

Sudie sobbed once, returned the hand glass to its shelf, knelt and gathered up the heaps and swirls of hair from the floor, and Devora went into the bedroom and began to pound and fluff her mattress vigorously.

That night, as she lay abed listening to Jerd move about the kitchen, waiting for him to come to her, she was startled by a terrified scream from outside, and a frantic beating at the dogtrot door. She sat up as the bar clattered, and heard Sudie whimpering, "An Indian . . . it was an Indian, I know it, I know it!"

While Jerd rumbled and Sudie murmured, Devora swung her feet to the cold floor. As she stepped into the kitchen, Jerd, rifle in hand, was pulling open the dogtrot door again.

Spot came through, tail going, and Jerd grinned in relief.

"There's your Indian," he told Sudie. "There ain't nothing wrong or he'd be raising a fuss. I'll take you back to your room, then have me a look around the barnlot."

Sudie glanced wordlessly at Devora, clutched her lacy shawl, and pattered out into the darkness at his heels. Devora went to the hearth and sat down in her chair.

Jerd reappeared in a short time, barred the door, hung his rifle on its pegs, took off his coat, and began to undress. "I reckon Sudie's scared to sleep out there by herself any more," he said.

"Did she say so?"

"Well . . . no . . . I reckon not."

"What did she say?"

"I don't rightly recall."

"Are you judging by what just happened?"

"No . . . it's only that she'd feel safer in here with us."

"Do you think she'd actually be any safer?"

"N-no," he said, after deliberation. "I built that room solid. It'd be tough to break into, particular with the shutters fastened from inside, the way she keeps them nights."

"Well, then."

"Still, it ain't hardly right."

"Why don't you put Spot in with her?"

"She don't like him."

"He'll stay on the dogtrot, won't he?"

"There or mighty close. He's a fine watchdog, none better."

"I can't see there's any need to worry then."

"But it don't look human for us to have each other for company," Jerd said, "knowing how scared she is. She purely ain't used to this wild country."

Devora sprang up. "It's getting late," she said, trying to conceal her impatience. She walked quickly into her room, fell upon her bed and lay there, trembling. Just when she'd won her battle with the dead Sarie, the live Sudie had begun her schemes, and Jerd was blind to them. Anger beat through her, and she wished to cry, but the tears would not start.

Later, when he came to her in darkness, she heard herself say, low and with conviction, "No. No, Jerd." But it was not until she felt his hand on her breast go rigid and drop away, not really until she heard the pad of his feet leaving, that she knew what she had done.

She had allowed resentment to make her love a weapon, with which she had hurt both him and herself. She moaned in despair, sorry already, and longed for Jerd, for husband, for nearness and tenderness. And knew that her life must halt while Sudie remained, and knowing both this and the wonders of union, wept at last.

Jerd behaved with his usual quiet friendliness the following morning. When Sudie appeared for breakfast, she was wearing blue. She ate little, spoke infrequently, and then mostly to the babies, her voice gentle. They stared at her solemnly, refused to go to her when she held out her arms, but did not cry.

Over the second mugs of tea, she declared she had an apology to make for disturbin' them the night before. Nobody must get upset, and she could perfectly well sleep 'way out there in that room alone if they wanted her to. It was perfectly silly for her to be scared of the dark or Indians either one, 'specially seein' as how nothin' had hurt her yet, and it was only Spot last night, but it would be so sweet of Jerd and Devora if they'd let her sleep over here with them so's she'd feel really safe.

She came to a breathless pause. Devora watched Jerd's troubled eyes go slowly from herself to the girl and back. Finally he said, "I reckon that's for Devora to say," and she, turning to Sudie, glimpsed a fleeting slyness that melted into pleading.

"Well . . . ma'am?"

"Take my room, Sudie," she said wearily. "I'll use Jerd's bunk, and he can go to the guest room."

"I'll make out with a pallet," Jerd said.

Sudie cried that they were darlin's, and promised to use Devora's room only for sleepin', and not mess it up daytimes.

Devora got up from the table and started clearing away, her movements slower than usual. Sudie would be chattering at Jerd even more gaily, she thought wearily, if she could guess that it made no difference where she slept, because Jerd would not come to his wife in any event.

That night, when they were undressed, the twins in their kitchen bed, Devora on the bunk, Jerd ready to blow out the candle, the bedroom door swung open. Sudie, her curls falling past her cheeks to her shoulders, looked in and was sure they wouldn't mind if she left the door open so's she'd get some heat, 'cause it was so cold in here, and g'night.

Thus again Devora lay lonely, Jerd's nearness on his pallet a throb in her. She hungered and burned for him and knew that, even as Sudie had planned it, he could not come to her even if he would. And ached with the knowledge that, being Jerd, he would not come to her if he could.

The days crept past.

No neighbors came to call.

The monotony of the wilderness did not bore Sudie. She kept to her room, and often the sweet, quivering voice of the Spinnet sounded for hours at a time. She got out her sister's dresses, hung them with her own, and wore them.

Casually, on washday, she dropped her linens and garments atop the soiled clothing piled on the floor beside Devora's tub. When they were ironed and folded, she gathered them up, thanked Devora warmly for her sweet kindness, and went happily away.

She appeared promptly for meals, persisted in her overtures to the babies, and gradually they began to know and like her. Every evening she joined Devora and Jerd at the hearth and sat talking softly, brightly, sadly, whatever her mood. It was Devora's task to make the proper responses, for Jerd did not take part in these conversations.

He studied Sudie from day to day in a puzzled manner, and Devora watched him, hoping to sense his thoughts. Was he annoyed because Sudie slept with the kitchen door open every night, keeping him from Devora's bed . . . or was he relieved? Mostly, however, she sought to read from him whether he was trying to solve the problem Sudie had created.

He was unfailingly considerate of Devora, shielding her from heavy work, and he talked to her so naturally that sometimes she was certain he felt as tenderly toward her as he had on Christmas Eve. Yet, because he spoke to Sudie only when he must, she was unsure and more troubled than if he had conversed freely with the girl. But even in her disturbance, she remembered Amos, his ineptness in matters pertaining to women, recognized the same masculine trait in Jerd, and smiled to herself.

One night Sudie unexpectedly insisted upon wiping dishes. "I'm goin' to make you glad I'm here, ma'am, instead of sorry," she declared.

"You're free to do anything you like," Devora said, irked at herself for suspecting the girl's motives.

"You're the sweetest lady, ma'am," Sudie said. "If you'll only show me how to do things, I'll try ever so hard to be of some use."

The chatter ran along this line as they worked until Devora was glad to escape long enough to throw out her dishwater. She stood for a moment in the cold, clean air, hating to go back inside.

When she did, Sudie was established in a fireside chair, holding Frank. "He does love his Sudie, ma'am," she said, dimpling. "I hope you don't mind. Jerd was cuddlin' Lill, and this beautiful man-baby looked so lonesome Sudie just had to take him up. And Jerd said it was all right . . . didn't you, Jerd?"

He nodded, frowning slightly, and shifted Lill's head to his shoulder. The baby in Sudie's arms was so much like a breath of her fragile self, yellow curls the same, and wide blue eyes, that Devora's breath caught. Her gaze flew to Jerd, but he was looking into the fire, his big hand lifting and falling gently, patting the child he held.

She turned away, puttered unnecessarily, the tableau disturbing her so much she took another swift look. She saw the two at the hearth, saw the drowsing babies, heard the clock go, and the fire mutter. She sensed the joy that might have been if Sarie had lived. Or if she, Devora, had not left her brother's house to come into the wilderness.

She pulled a bench toward the fireplace. Jerd came to her, Lill on one arm, picked up the bench, placed it at the hearth and sat on it, leaving his chair for her. She settled into it, her hands waiting together in her lap.

In a moment Jerd put Lill in the bed; Sudie laid the sleeping Frank beside her and covered them both. Then she sat back down and turned her face up to Jerd, who was standing beside the baby bed.

"Jerd honey," she said softly, "I've waited and waited."

He looked at her, puzzled.

"I understand, I really do. You wanted to spare me, 'cause you know I've had so much grievin'." She touched her eyes with her handkerchief. "Pa, and Uncle Bu, and Sarie, and . . . Zebbie. And it has been more'n I ever thought I could bear."

Her breath quivered, and tears stood in her eyes.

Despite her conviction that the girl was play-acting to at least a degree, Devora felt a twinge of pity. "We do understand, Sudie," she said kindly.

"Th-thank you, ma'am. I know Jerd does, 'cause one of my l-losses was his, and—" her glance touched the sleeping twins "—will be theirs."

"Yes, Sudie," Devora said.

"Well, ma'am . . . Jerd honey . . . like I said, I know you been sparin' me, and why. But I got to see it sometime, so I thought . . . well . . . tomorrow?"

"See what?" Jerd asked.

Before the words were off his lips, Devora glimpsed the realization in his eyes, and the dread.

"Sarie's grave," Sudie whispered.

Her face was white, her eyes burning blue.

Devora looked to Jerd.

His body stiffened, legs, chest, arms, neck. He turned, reached his coat in two strides, the door in another two, and was gone.

Sudie, half-risen, sank again into her chair. Her eyes wavered to Devora and clung, honest and beseeching. Shaken, Devora knew what, in fairness to the girl and compassion for Jerd, she had to do.

She rested her hands on the broad arms of his chair, leaned her head back, and searched for wisdom. Her voice fluttered in her throat. She tried again, and the words came out not much above a whisper.

"There is no grave, Sudie."

The blue eyes questioned wildly.

Drawing a deep breath, Devora haltingly told the story.

Sudie moaned.

She sat staring at Devora, tears running down her cheeks. With her hands lying in her lap, she cried like a small girl, unashamed and without control, mouth twisting, face not lovely.

"Sarie's in that water, that awful, nasty water!"

"You mustn't think of it like that. Don't let yourself. Because she isn't in the water, not really."

"But she is, and it h-happened to her, my very other self!"

"Don't blame Jerd, please don't."

"Sarie, Sarie, poor darlin' . . . poor Jerd darlin', too! Oh, he needs to be loved, needs it bad . . . nobody knows!"

Devora closed her eyes against the girl's sorrow. There was no meeting ground here, no comfort to give. Only the blow, the helping Jerd. Swiftly she prayed that he would not return to the grief he had talked out in her arms. For if he did, he might never again come to her, his wife, in love.

~~ *Chapter Nineteen* ~~

WHEN SUDIE learned of Frank's condition next morning, she cried airily, "Oh, I know about blue-looking babies! Chet Ballinger, back in Wilmington, he was one. It ain't anything to worry over too much, I reckon. Chet vows anybody can outgrow that if he's a mind to."

Devora, studying Frank, felt a surge of alarm. He looked thinner, frailer, his skin more transparent, and surely bluer than yesterday. Glancing up, she found Jerd's eyes on her, dark and anxious, and tried to smile for him, but could not.

Within three more days, Sudie had established herself as a member of the family. Though she was eager to work, Devora suspected her motives. She took over much of the care of the twins, did part of the ironing, and was even learning to cook a few simple things.

Like a child, she ran to Jerd for approval of every new accomplishment. Devora, preoccupied by Frank's weakening condition, worried over this and found herself looking forward to Piepmeier's expected visit. If Sudie married him, so many problems would be solved. He would be the happiest man alive, and Sudie herself would not only be provided for, but spoiled and worshiped. As for Devora and Jerd, they could get back what they had only touched.

Piepmeier arrived at dawn one morning, his face red and cracked from the wind, cold riding in on his wraps, its smell filling the room. Sudie pulled him to the fire and ordered him pertly to thaw out so's a person could breathe.

After breakfast, he challenged her to go for a walk. "Air's clear, and it's clean," he said.

"We wouldn't go where there's Indians, would we?"

"Nary Injun," he promised solemnly. "Just upslope a piece. You can see way yonder, toward my place. I told you that Christmas, when I brung you, only it was snowing too heavy to really see."

"I had snow all on my eyelashes!" Sudie laughed.

"I recall," Piepmeier said. He swallowed noisily, then got her pelisse from a chair. "Want I should help you on with this?"

She let him hold it for her. She tied on her bonnet, which was as blue as her eyes. She drew on fur mittens, and danced out of the door ahead of him.

Devora stepped to the window and watched them go, smiling at how Piepmeier was trying to fit his lope to Sudie's dainty steps, and at how tall and rawboned he was, trying to hover over her as they moved along. Still smiling, she turned back to her dishes.

Jerd helped clear the table. He carried the kettle of boiling water to the workshelf for her, threw a fresh log on the fire, made sure Frank was covered. Then he pulled on his coat, took his rifle, and started for the door.

"Reckon we can use a bait of meat if Piepmeier aims to move in for a spell," he said with a grin. "I'll try to get back for noon, but if I don't you folks go ahead and eat."

He left, and Devora plunged into her work, singing.

She was mixing corn bread when she heard the rattle of hooves. She laid down her spoon and hurried onto the dogtrot, from where she saw Piepmeier galloping his horse rapidly away toward the woods that stretched in the direction of his farm.

Alarmed, she ran to Sudie's door, only to find it barred. She knocked, and there was no answer. The second time she knocked, Sudie called to please go away and leave her be.

Because there was nothing else she could do, Devora returned to her cooking. Surely they hadn't quarreled. Sudie would be quick enough to anger, she was sure, but she couldn't imagine Piepmeier, so foolishly in love, ever crossing Sudie, arguing with her, or getting angry.

She sighed, poured her batter into a skillet, covered it, and set it to bake.

Jerd did not get back for dinner. Sudie remained in her room. Devora spent the afternoon mending and playing with the twins.

Seeing Jerd in the barnlot at chore time, she swung the fireplace cranes so the pots were over direct heat, and set the table. When he came in, she started dishing up.

"I got a big turkey," he said. "Cleaned him and put him down cellar. Where's Piepmeier?"

She told him, and he looked at her in amazement.

He said nothing, but went to the washshelf, scrubbed his hands, ran a comb through his hair, then sat down at the table. Devora brought the teapot and was pouring when Sudie came in.

She slipped into place with a murmur, and ate sparingly while Jerd and Devora kept a conversation going about what he had seen on his hunting trip.

Afterward, she wiped dishes in continued silence.

She sat with them at the fire, never speaking.

Devora and Jerd decided to butcher in a couple of days.

"We're late with it now," Jerd said, "so we'd best get it over with. This cold weather's apt to hold."

Sudie made a little chuckle.

They quit talking.

"I s'pose you want to know what's wrong."

They waited.

"Juney and I had the biggest fight," she went on, and stopped.

Devora, as was customary in these sessions, responded with, "Is that so?"

"Can you ever guess what about?"

"I'm afraid not," Devora said wearily.

"Jerd honey?"

"I reckon not."

"It was about gettin' married."

Devora's heart began knocking hugely.

"Well, my sakes," Sudie said, piqued. "Don't you even want to hear more?"

"Only if you want to tell, Sudie."

"Juney's been fixin' his cabin up, you know that."

"Yes."

"He's got it finished. And he actually expected me to marry him and go live in the silly thing! Imagine!"

Devora looked at Jerd. He was gazing at Sudie, his face expressionless, his lips moving on the stem of his pipe.

"I just told him he was crazy if he thought I'd ever live in a cabin!"

"You're in a cabin now," Devora said.

"That's different! And he was so mean, and claimed I led him on, told him how to fix his old cabin, and he vowed I'd as good as said I'd marry him the minute it was done!"

Devora stared into the fire.

"So I just told him he was a big old storyteller," Sudie went on, "and that he was perfectly scandalous to ask a widow to marry him anyhow, so soon after—" Her voice faltered, turned petulant. "And then he yelled at me, and said he'd never come near me again, and got his horse and rode off, and that's all."

"I see," Devora said. "It sounds quite . . . definite."

"Oh, it is, ma'am! Why, I was only nice to him 'cause he was your friend! Yours and Jerd's. I couldn't ever marry a skinny thing like him. He's just a stick! Did I do right, Jerd honey, did I?"

"I reckon," Jerd said slowly, moving his dark eyes to Devora, "it's right for a girl to say no to marrying a man she don't want."

Sudie chuckled again, her chin ducked.

She jumped to her feet. "I'm so tired, I'm goin' to bed. Juney wore me out, he was so fierce. G'night, ma'am."

"Good night, Sudie."

"G'night, Jerd honey." Swiftly she dropped a kiss on his brow, turned, ran to the bedroom door, paused. "I told him," she said, "I'd be crazy to leave my fam'ly!"

She disappeared into the unlighted bedroom.

"She don't really mean nothing by her ways," Jerd said, very low. He got up and reached for his coat. "I'll take my look outside."

As soon as he closed the door, Devora made down his pallet. She undressed, shifted Lill to the middle of the baby bed, covered her, took Frank up, and got into the bunk, holding him in her arms.

Jerd returned shortly, barred the door, put out the candle, and bedded down. He said good night, Devora replied, and after that there was only the whispering fire, the talking clock, and her wondering about his thoughts.

Was he glad Sudie wasn't going to marry Piepmeier? Did he want her to remain here . . . like another Sarie? Devora sighed, sadly content that her nights with Jerd had not given her a child. I'd never want to hold his loyalty that way, she thought, couldn't bear to.

She cupped Frank's icy feet in her hand and rubbed his toes, one by one, rubbed the balls of his feet, and up around the ankles until, very slowly, he began to be less cold.

Jerd was calling her.

He had spoken her name more than once.

She struggled to a sitting position. He was at the hearth, fully dressed, putting wood on the fire. The flames were leaping and snapping and orange color against the darkness of the room.

"Yes, Jerd," she said, swung her feet to the floor, and stood. The hem of her night robe touched the cold boards.

The clock began to strike. It ended on the fourth bong. Jerd lit candles, and now she could make out the clock's face, and it really was only four.

"Is something wrong?" she asked.

"No," he said, "there's so much cold in the air, I figured it'd be a good day for our butchering. And the change from our regular work will be good for us. If that suits you."

"Of course," she agreed.

He went to the barn, and she hurried to close the bedroom door, her heart beating fast. He'd decided to butcher immediately because of Sudie's intimate behavior last night; he'd virtually said he wanted a change from the cloying atmosphere the girl created. Surely his turning to her for this meant he wanted to keep their marriage solid.

She dressed swiftly, excitedly, happy over the task that would busy them as man and wife, grateful that it was one into which the dainty and inexperienced Sudie could not intrude. She started breakfast, singing under her breath.

Sudie did not appear for the meal.

Devora washed dishes, tidied the room, dressed the twins, made advance dinner preparations. While she was so occupied, Jerd heated water in the washpot, which he had placed under a big tree, put a barrel there, laid knives out on a rock, set cookpots at hand, and dragged his farm sled to a spot just outside the pigpen.

Devora could hear the pigs squealing as Sudie came through the bedroom door. Sudie heard them too, ran to the dogtrot door, yanked it open, looked out, clapped it shut and leaned against it, wan and bewildered.

"What's Jerd doin' in the pigpen with an ax?" she asked.

"We're going to butcher."

The girl shuddered, and closed her eyes for an instant.

Devora said, "I've kept your breakfast warm."

"I couldn't eat, ma'am. It's my head."

"Sit at the table, and I'll bring you some tea."

She went to the fire, poured a mug of tea, and put it before Sudie. While the girl sipped, Devora settled Frank in the baby bed and covered him. Then she bundled Lill up, put on an old jacket herself, and wrapped a scarf around her head.

"Where you goin', ma'am?" Sudie asked fretfully.

"To help Jerd."

"You're goin' to touch dead pigs?"

"It's too big a job for one person."

"Ugh!"

"Lie down and rest, Sudie."

"I know you perfectly hate me, ma'am. 'Cause I can't be a help to you. It's that Juney's fault for upsettin' me so."

"Everything will work out. Lill can play in the yard, where we can watch her. Frank's almost asleep now, and I'll run in now and then to see to things. You can even go to sleep yourself."

"I'd stay in here, ma'am, except if he was to cry, it'd hurt my head."

"Oh."

"I b'lieve I'll just go to my own room. And not be a trouble. I won't even eat any dinner."

"You may get better by that time."

"Oh, I won't . . . I never do! These old headaches just last and last!"

Carrying Lill and a blanket, Devora went outside. The sharp air pressed against her cheeks as she walked toward the spot where Jerd had just arrived, the second hog on his farm sled. The washpot was steaming from the hot little fire under it. On this fire were old irons, glowing red, and chunks of rock, also sizzling hot.

Devora spread the blanket on the ground at a safe distance, set Lill on it, and put her bean bag into her mittened hands. Jerd glanced over inquiringly, and she explained about Sudie's headache and her own arrangements.

"When Lill begins to fret," she concluded, "I'll take her in for a nap. This cold air will make her sleepy fast."

Jerd dumped the hog beside the other one, moved the sled directly underneath a big limb of the tree, and rolled the barrel up. Together, they dipped the boiling water out of the washpot until the barrel was half full.

Both of them lifting, they put the first hog into the scalding water, back end down, pulled it out, lowered it again, head down, then laid it on the sled. Devora began scraping hair off it with a knife, and Jerd hurriedly dropped the iron and rocks from the fire into the barrel to keep the water hot for the second hog.

Knife in hand, he joined her, and they settled into the hurried, yet tedious process of scraping. Long before they finished, Devora's moccasins were soaked from spilled water, and her feet were numb. The wind had sprung up out of the north, and it stiffened her hands, beat her face, and cracked her lips. On her trips indoors, the cabin seemed breathlessly hot and made her head fuzzy. It was almost a relief to get back into the cold air, though the first blast of wind left her longing for the heat again.

By noon the cleaning and gutting was done, and they left the shining white carcasses hanging from the tree, Spot on guard, to get thoroughly cold.

Working together the next days, they finished the immediate butchering chores. They readied hams and side meat for curing, made sausage and scrapple, ate the tails roasted, and the feet boiled. They rendered lard, and even made up a good supply of yellow soap.

They were as companionable as they had been on their trip from St. Louis. But at night there was Sudie in the next room, the door open, keeping them apart.

Sudie rejoined the family group looking prettier than ever. She helped with breakfast, and when Jerd came in from his chores, apologized prettily for letting that silly Juney make her sick right when he needed her so much.

When Jerd left to run his trapline, she kept moving restlessly about. She picked up one of Devora's books from the mantel, flipped through it, dropped it onto the table, took another, tossed it aside. She went to the window and stood looking out; she got a drink of water, wandered to the washshelf and inspected herself in Devora's hand glass.

She did some dance steps up and down the room, humming, holding out her skirts, whirling. Abruptly, she flung herself into a chair, and sighed.

"I'm so lonesome," she said petulantly. "What'll I do, ma'am?"

"Needlework?"

She made a face.

"Music?"

"What for? There's nobody to hear it."

"Let's hope somebody will come to visit, then."

"Who? Juney won't."

"Prosper might, or Mr. Doerflinger."

"Not them. Their wives won't let 'em."

"Oh, now!"

"Sarie wrote how jealous they are."

"We might have a party. That way, you'd meet new people."

Sudie went quiet. Fear washed across her face, and she said, in a rush, "No, thank you."

"Jerd says they dance at the parties."

"They'd just tear me to pieces."

"Who would?"

"The women, that's who! Old, jealous, ugly hags!"

"Oh, no."

"They would, too. But I wouldn't let 'em bother me. Only I don't want a party. I'm satisfied right here, like this. Forever'n ever. It's just that I'm lonesome with Jerd gone. When'll he be back, ma'am?"

"He didn't say," Devora answered flatly. "But in time for supper, I'd guess."

Sudie got up, threw her pelisse around her shoulders, and went to the door. "I'll fool around in my own room 'til suppertime then," she said.

She left softly, and Devora sat on, her hands holding to each other. Sudie had declared herself plainly at last. She wanted Jerd.

But why Jerd, Devora wondered, why not some other man, one of her own kind, in Carolina? She frowned, considering. Then, irritated at herself, knowing that Sudie's reasons for coming were of less importance than a plan for getting her away, she threw such speculation out of her mind. All day, as she worked, she pondered, and came up with three possible solutions.

At supper, she studied Sudie's ways with Jerd. She watched the girl dimple, smile, sober, and listen enchantingly to every word he uttered. She observed the sweet, eager commotion Sudie made about helping with the dishes. Afterward, at the fireside, Sudie played mother to the twins, all beauty, gentleness, and love.

She sat by the entire evening and watched, clear-eyed and with full understanding, while Sudie demonstrated by tone, glance, and deed, as she had been doing since the day she began to help with the work, that here was the wife Jerd needed, wanted, once had and would have again. Here was his Sarie-Sudie, his Sudie-Sarie, his first, last, and only.

She felt her jaw harden. Tomorrow morning, as soon as Jerd went outside after breakfast, she would have a decisive talk with Sudie.

Only it didn't happen that way.

He had just gone to the barnlot, when a great barking and hallooing set up. Devora, hurrying onto the dogtrot, saw Mahala and Prosper Pike ride through the gate on their big horse, and called a welcome to them.

In seconds, Mahala's wiry arms were around Devora, and she was telling what a fine, early ride they'd had, and admonishing Prosper to be careful of them bundles now, and don't smash them, and set them down careful when he got inside. Prosper, his rosy cheeks in full bloom from the cold, a towel-wrapped bundle on each arm, grinned and nodded at Devora, unable to get a word past Mahala's talk. Jerd, who had come up from the barnlot with them, was grinning at her excitement, and, catching Devora's eye, winked.

". . . so I says to Prosper," Mahala was running on, " 'Jerd'll never think of it, manlike, and Devorry don't know, so tomorrow I'll bake up two little cakes for the party, and next day we'll ride over bright and early and have a proper celebration!' "

Devora was aware of Jerd's grin fading, and that the kitchen door had opened and Sudie was looking out at them, stricken, and that while she was doing this, cold air was flowing into the room that must be kept warm for Frank.

"What party?" Sudie asked, her blue eyes on Mahala. "What is there to celebrate?"

"The babies' party, that's what," Mahala said, instantly ruffled. "Them pore angels, it's their birthday. They're one year old today."

"Why, Mahala," Devora exclaimed, "how thoughtful! How splendid of you to do this!"

"Birthday," Sudie whispered, her mouth shaking. "Don't any of you know what today is, and not a birthday? Don't you know what you're really celebratin'?" She faced to Devora. "Don't you, ma'am? Jerd . . . it's my sister's dyin' . . . make her see!"

Devora's look went past the others, Mahala's disgust, Prosper's consternation, to Jerd. He was staring at Sudie.

His lips were pale.

His fists were clenched.

Devora went to him, put out her hand, touched his knuckles. Slowly he moved his eyes to hers, deep into hers. His fingers loosened and he said, "Devora wouldn't hurt nobody, Sudie. I wouldn't, neither. Not deliberate. But this time I reckon the babes come first."

Sudie caught her breath, ran desperately into her room, and closed the door swiftly.

ᴄ✦ᴏ *Chapter Twenty* ᴄ✦ᴏ

After the men had gone to the barn, Devora closed the door and turned to watch Mahala, who was leaning over the baby bed, hugging both twins at once, murmuring and laughing and half-crying.

At last she stood back, and let her eyes race over them hungrily. "Lill's more of a bouncer than ever," she said. "But Frank—"

"Nothing seems to help him."

"He been having spells?"

"Only twice, some time ago. And another day he got very cold. Otherwise, he just seems to grow weaker instead of stronger. Sometimes he won't even close his fingers around his bean bag when I put it in his hand."

"Pore darling angel," Mahala said, a tear sparkling on her cheek. "And that one!" She jerked her head in the direction of Sudie's room. "She don't want him to have his birthday!"

Quietly Devora took Lill up and put her into Mahala's ready arms, motioned her to a chair, and sat down herself and watched her friend, who held the rosy little girl as if she were a treasure.

"Mahala," she said, "we'll make it a good day! Tell me everything you and Prosper have been doing since Christmas, and bring me up to date on Vonnie and Doerflinger. Tell me about the other folks, the ones I haven't met yet—how many in each family, how they look, what they like to eat and wear and do. Let's make it a happy day. Oh, Mahala— talk!"

Mahala talked.

She talked as they sat at the fire, talked while they cooked and laid the table, talked when Devora returned with Sudie's rejected tray, her lovely voice making beauty and friendliness. She talked a flow of merry nonsense when the men came in for dinner, and she made a great busi-ness of letting Prosper hold Lill, the birthday girl, on his knee as they ate, and of choosing herself to hold Frank, the birthday boy, on her own lap.

And she kept up the talking and the merriment until they were all joining in, though they knew Sudie was weeping alone and that Frank, who needed food, turned his face away from everything offered, including his birthday cake. Lill, by contrast, was comically hungry. Jerd burst into laughter with the rest of them over the amazed pleasure on her face when she tasted her first bite of cake. Devora, watching Jerd under cover of her own lively conversation with Mahala, saw his spirits rise from that point, and became honestly gay herself.

While she and Mahala washed dishes, Jerd talked crops with Prosper, who held Frank on one knee and played with Lill as she walked around him, holding on. She kept grabbing and hitting at her brother, crowing and bobbing and rowdy, until he fell against Prosper and began to cry, almost inaudibly.

Mahala swooped on them, and took the child into her arms. "Shame on you, Prosper Pike!" she cried. "The idea! Letting his sister wear him out! She ain't to blame, the sweetie, but you sure know better!"

The baby lay back in her arms, his face marked by tears, and looked up at her. His blue little mouth quivered, a smile showed faintly, and he slept.

Devora's eyes smarted, and she turned away.

Prosper was now playing boisterously with Lill, and she was squealing, laughing, and hiccuping. Suddenly he hugged her so that one rosy cheek lay against his red cheek, and her brown ringlets were directly below his, and it could be seen they were alike.

The time came when Mahala said, not unexpectedly, "It's coming on late. We got a ride ahead of us, and chores to do after we get there."

Prosper yawned and said he reckoned she was right.

Mahala, sitting at the edge of her chair, her back like a ramrod, said, "Devorry . . . Jerd . . . I got a thing to ast, so I mought's well spit it out."

"Why, sure," Jerd said easily, and Devora smiled.

"It's them babies, the sweet angels. Frank ain't as well as he was. We all see it and know it, and we mought's well admit it."

"Mahaley," Prosper said uneasily, "there ain't no call for you to be so all-fired outspoke."

"Ain't no call for me to keep shut, nuther. We all see Frank's puny and Lill's rowdy as all get out and wears on her little brother. He could use some peace and quiet. Way I look at it, he'd get them things, Devorry, and you could give him all your time instead of splitting it with Lill if me and Prosper took her home with us for a spell. To say nothing of the pure pleasure it'd give the two of us."

Devora glanced inquiringly at Jerd.

He said, "It's for you to say."

She moved her look to Prosper, who was watching her expectantly, then back to Mahala's lovely, pleading eyes.

"Why, of course," she said. "Even if— Under any circumstances, we'd love for Lill to visit you! I'll get her things together."

In less than a half-hour, she was standing in the barnlot with Jerd, waving to the departing guests.

"Well," she said, suddenly at a loss without them, "I'll see to Frank. If he's awake, maybe I can get some of that potato soup down him."

"I've got some extras to do out here," Jerd said, "so it'll give you plenty of time."

She went running to the cabin, hung her shawl away, and warmed her hands and clothing thoroughly before she went to the bed. Frank was lying on his back, awake, making no effort to sit up.

Talking to him gently, she warmed a portion of the soup, took him on her lap and slowly, drop by drop, persuaded him to take a spoonful. His blue eyes stayed on her face and once, when she called him Mother's sweet boy, he smiled.

As if the smile had exhausted him, a sigh quivered through his slight frame and he closed his eyes, and she let him lie back, his feathery yellow curls against her breast, his thin little hand at the hollow of her throat, before she tried with the soup again. He refused listlessly, so she pushed the bowl aside and held him close, and while she did this, she sang. Almost at once he was asleep.

Sudie came in presently, gazed at the sleeping boy, glanced around the room. "Where's Lill, ma'am?" she asked. "I want to hold her, feel her in my arms, my sister's little girl."

Quietly Devora told where Lill had gone, and why.

The blue eyes flamed. "You sent her away, not even tellin' me? My own twin's own baby girl?"

"When I brought your dinner tray, Sudie, you told me not to bother you again. About anything."

"Did you sneak her out to hurt me, ma'am?"

"Jerd knew. She went with her father's consent."

"Jerd ain't—" Sudie broke off, weeping. "He ain't close to her, same as I am! Bein' a twin, it's like I bore her with my sister!"

"I suppose it is."

The door opened and Jerd came in with a pail of milk. Sudie gazed at him reproachfully, then made a helpful fuss about setting the table. He unconcernedly washed up for the meal.

The baby didn't wake until after the dishes were done. Devora offered him milk, but he turned from it, so she made him comfortable in her arms. Uneasy, she watched him fall asleep again.

When the cabin was settled for the night, she tried once more to spoon warm milk into him, but he would not have it, and cried feebly. She carried him to the bunk and lay down with him, rubbing his back gently, murmuring, and he slept.

She put her lips to his forehead, and it was not feverish. She strained to hear his breathing, searched out his tiny pulse, felt it wane, disappear, throb distantly. He twitched and moved, and she let go his arm and began to rub his back again.

She listened to the whispering fire and the stroking clock and Jerd's regular breathing. She listened to the rising wind rattle the shingles, felt her own breath strike the pillow and come back to touch her face.

She was too warm from the heated room, the covers, the small body against her own. Again and again she sought his pulse, felt to see if he was cold, as she had done so many times on so many nights, and still he slept. Once Jerd mended the fire; shortly afterward, the clock struck. Even as she checked on the baby's breathing, pulse, warmth, she felt drowsiness roll over her, thick and irresistible.

She awoke heavily, and sat up. Jerd was throwing wood on the fire, poking at the red hump of the night's log, the sparks dying wherever they hit. Instinctively, she turned to the baby.

"How does he seem this morning?" Jerd asked.

She slid her hands under the covers; the tiny feet were cold. Alarmed, her fingers went up the motionless little body, and suddenly she was lifting it, whispering, "Jerd . . . oh, Jerd . . . he . . . he's dead!"

Together, they made sure.

There was no look of pain on the baby face, or of struggle, or illness. Devora said, at last, "He must have . . . simply stopped breathing. It does happen that way."

"When do you figure—?"

"He was . . . here . . . when you put wood on the fire. Right after that, it struck two, and I—that's when I went to sleep. I didn't wake until now, and I sat up and looked, and he was . . . like this."

She began to tremble.

She searched his eyes, fearing that wild grief he'd had for Sarie. There were no tears, and no sorrow, only pity and regret for the ended life which had not truly begun.

"Poor little fellow," he said.

Her trembling grew.

There was a sound at the bedroom doorway, and Sudie was there, dressed, curls in place. "How is he?" she asked gaily. "How's Sudie's man-baby? I got up 'way early to take care of my darlin'." She came toward the bunk, lips curved, arms out, but midway she stopped and gazed from Jerd to Devora, the delight and anticipation dropping from her, and asked, "What is it? What's wrong with my baby?"

Jerd told her bluntly. "He died in his sleep."

She clenched her fists between her breasts. She sucked in her breath, ran to the bunk, stared at the little figure, and tears began to stream down her cheeks. Her hands went out to the baby, withdrew, clenched again. She backed off, lifted her weeping eyes to Devora, and they were hard and weeping at the same time.

"Where were you when it happened?" she asked.

Now Devora's trembling got into her throat and jaw, and she could not speak. She stood up, folded her arms, clutched them in futile effort to steady herself.

She saw Jerd's eyes on her, troubled, heard his voice. "Devora was sleeping. We all was."

"Sleepin'?" Sudie repeated. "When Sarie's own baby was—" She wept terribly, her face uncovered, with just the rain of tears down it. She stopped crying, and spoke quietly to Devora. "It happened on your hands. Did you do it on purpose, ma'am . . . did you sleep real sound, so's maybe he'd . . . and he wouldn't be a bother any more?"

A shudder swept Devora. She swayed, tried helplessly to keep from falling, and then Jerd's arms were around her, holding her, and she was lying against his chest, his broad, safe chest, and her trembling was over.

His hand was on the back of her head, and his breath moved her hair as he spoke, his voice not kind. "Stop that wild talk, Sudie," he said, "beside yourself or not. Devora can't be beat as a mother. She feels this thing as much as anybody . . . , maybe more."

While Sudie wailed and sobbed and wept aloud, crying that she simply could not understand why Jerd should talk so mean, Devora stood herself out of his arms, thanked him with a look, and asked, her voice not even, "What do we do next?"

"Why," he said thoughtfully, "I'd best go for Prosper. He'll spread the word and come right over."

Sudie ceased crying. "W-what'll I do?"

"You and Devora'll be busy."

She ran to him, grasped his shirt, threw back her head to look up at him, throat arched, curls swaying. "It ain't that I don't want to help, Jerd honey!" she cried. "It's that I c-can't! I don't know how!"

"Devora'll show you," he said.

He clamped her wrists, pushed her into a chair, stepped away, and began to pull on his coat. Devora, who saw and heard as if she were in a dream, stared at him. She felt her heart grow in her chest, rise up her throat, and hurt.

He took his rifle, said "I'll be quick as I can," and was gone.

Sudie, weeping again, jumped from her chair and ran across the kitchen. "I'm goin' to stay in Sarie's room," she cried, "no matter what!"

The door shut behind her.

The sound of the clock filled the silence. Devora was glad to have it with her, talking, a living thing in the presence of death.

She tidied the bedroom. She bathed the dead baby, dusted the tiny body with powder, slipped a white dress on it, and brushed the yellow curls. Sorrowfully, she carried him into the bedroom.

When she stepped onto the dogtrot to fill her water bucket, a horse was galloping up to the barnlot, and Spot was barking wildly. Mahala, riding behind Jerd, lifted one hand in a solemn gesture. The first tears stirred in Devora, did not reach her eyes, and lay in her like a pain.

Jerd led the horse into the barn, and Mahala came hurrying, carrying Lill on her hip. She had been crying, and though the tears were gone now, they had left their mark around her eyes and on her reddened nose.

She thrust Lill at Devora, and encompassed the two of them in a fierce hug. "There!" she said, drawing back. "Jerd's starting the box, Prosper's went to get Mitchell to ride out with the word, then he'll be here. If the pore angel had to go, it's best in the sleep, Devorry, you know it. I said the same to Jerd, and he give me one of his looks."

"It's his only son, Mahala. Come inside and have some breakfast."

Mahala followed into the kitchen, talking soberly, her voice muted. "We'd et when Jerd come running up," she said. "I made him take a bite while I was getting ready." She stopped abruptly, then asked, "Where is he . . . where's my baby boy?"

Devora gestured toward the bedroom, and the older woman went in and closed the door.

When she came out, there were damp streaks on her face. She stopped at the baby bed, picked up the bean bag Lill had thrown to the floor, and gave it to her.

"He looks beautiful," she said, "just beautiful. When do you and Jerd figure to . . . lay him away?"

"I don't know," Devora said. "We haven't talked about it. But today,

I imagine. I don't know if there's a preacher we could get, even if we waited."

"Nearest I know of'd be in St. Louis."

"Yes."

"Doerflinger spoke over Miz Weed's ma-in-law couple of years back. She died of snakebite. And Vonnie tells me he done it a time or two afore that. I don't know if Doerflinger's words would suit you folks, though."

"I don't see why not," Devora said. "I'll be most grateful, for my part, if he'll do it, and I believe Jerd will be, too."

"Hadn't we ought to get to some cooking?" Mahala asked. "We'll have no telling how many to feed afore the day is out . . . folks have a way of flocking to a marrying or— Where you keep your potatoes, Devorry?"

The first ones, Vonnie and Doerflinger among them, came before dinner, and at midafternoon people were still arriving. Each woman brought her offering of food, shook Devora's hand, tiptoed into the bedroom, returned, stayed in the warm kitchen to help, talk, sigh, wait. Each man greeted the men outside, walked to the small, open grave, returned, squatted in the windy sunlight to whittle, talk, spit, wait. Each child stared at the other children, was quiet, joined the play to run, scream, be scolded, wonder, play again.

Names, faces, voices, words blurred for Devora. She responded to everyone, kindly and absently. She said yes, what a shame, so young. She said no, Sudie has been in her room all day, please excuse her, yes, she's taking it hard, yes, it's natural that she should, yes, indeed. And please, gentlemen, just carry the box into the bedroom, will you, Vonnie and I are going to line it and do the rest, no please, I'd rather help, if you don't mind, and thank you just the same, if you'll excuse us, ladies, we won't be long . . . yes, Vonnie, I wish you would shut the door, yes, he looks quite natural if . . . death ever looks natural.

She stood beside Jerd on the windy hill in the late afternoon with the others. She looked down upon the nailed-shut box in the little grave at her feet as the singing faded, and Doerflinger started his burying words.

She listened to the sniffling women, the hawking men, the fidgeting children. She listened to the pretty sobs coming from Sudie. She did not have to look to know that the girl, wearing stark black, had moved close to Jerd and was weeping into his sleeve.

Doerflinger said, "Ah-men," and the singing took up softly as he laid the shovel in Jerd's hand. Devora allowed herself one glance into Jerd's bleak face, then lowered her eyes, saw the first dirt hit the box, jump, roll, and stop, and her heart winced.

The shovel bit again into the crumbly dirt piled beside the grave. Out of the corner of her eye, Devora saw Sudie's arms go around Jerd's waist and hold him, and when he tried to free himself and keep on with the shovel, she cried out shrilly, "No . . . no . . . you're not goin' to take him away from me . . . I won't let you."

Prosper stepped up and took her by the arms, and she clung tighter to Jerd. He pulled her hands away from his waist, pushed her toward Prosper, said, "Quiet yourself, Sudie," and the second shovel of dirt went into the grave.

She wrenched loose from Prosper, screaming, and threw herself across the grave, shielding it, fell down inside it and hunkered on the box, her shoulders quivering. A few of the singers gasped, the others kept singing, and the gasping ones sang again. Jerd thrust the shovel at Prosper, and went to one knee. He reached into the grave and pulled Sudie out, and she had swooned. He got to his feet with her in his arms, her head hanging back, her bonnet tipped off the spill of curls.

Devora thought numbly, hearing dirt thump onto dirt as Prosper wielded the shovel, watching Jerd stride away in his terrible, stern purposefulness, No wonder she swooned, she hasn't eaten since last night. But Jerd won't know that . . . he'll see just her grief, and perhaps he will comfort her, and in so doing— She closed her eyes, and when she opened them, the forms of the singing ones had become clear and steady, and she thought, It's nearly over, tomorrow it will be in the past, with only Sudie wrong in the future, but not for long . . . it's coming to an end, for I am going to end it.

Within thirty minutes after the little mound was weighted with its rocks, marked by its cross and left on its hilltop, all the people had gone home, including Prosper and Mahala, who offered eagerly to help with Lill at any time.

With Sudie in her room at the end of the dogtrot and Jerd busy at his chores, Devora fed Lill and undressed her for the night. She lit the candles and sat in her fireside chair, holding the drowsy baby in her arms, and while she did this, she sang. She sang lullabies her father had sung to her in the so long ago she had remembered them not so much by ear as by feel.

She was still holding, singing, remembering, when a surge of cold told her the door had opened and closed. She glanced up, and Sudie was standing against the door, asking, "Have they all gone?"

She nodded, singing, and Sudie came lightly across the room, dropped into Jerd's chair, leaned back her yellow head, sighed and closed her eyes, looking wan and forlorn and spent. Every line of her body, from her pulsing throat to the abandon of her slim fingers on the arms of the chair, told of her lonely suffering.

Devora, not inclined to succumb to beauty or pity, asked, "Are you hungry?"

The blue eyes opened. "Me? Why?"

"You haven't eaten since last night."

"How could I, ma'am? How could I possibly eat?"

Lill stirred, and Devora patted her, humming. Her eyelids fluttered, closed, and she was asleep.

"Did you, ma'am?"

"Did I what?"

"Eat." She made the word sound unclean.

"We did because we must, Sudie."

"Jerd, too?"

"Jerd, too."

"How could he?"

"Sudie."

"Are you satisfied now, ma'am?"

"Sudie, Sudie."

"Are you glad my sister's poor little boy died? Are you?"

"It won't help to say what you can't mean."

Tears spilled out of the blue eyes, dried away. Sudie gazed at the sleeping Lill, and the tears flowed again. "Do you hate her, too, ma'am? Even if she ain't to blame?"

Devora looked at her silently.

The tears waned. "Where's Jerd?"

"Doing his chores."

"I w-want him!"

Devora put Lill in bed, covered her.

Sudie dabbed at her tears with her handkerchief, tucked it away, folded her hands in her lap, and stared into the fire.

Devora sat down again, facing her.

"Now," she said, "we can have the talk I wanted us to have first thing yesterday morning."

"I don't feel like makin' conversation, ma'am."

"Neither do I."

"Well, then."

"We must discuss your future sometime, Sudie."

The blue eyes searched Devora's face. "Mine?"

"You've been with us quite awhile."

"Yes, I know you perfectly hate poor little me for even livin', ma'am."

"Not at all. Still, you have had some time in which to rest, think, plan."

"What plans could I possibly make?"

"We all make them. Even in the midst of our deepest sorrows, we make them."

"Not me, ma'am, not me!"

"Back in Wilmington, when you were first a widow, you did, Sudie. You planned to marry Jerd, and you came here for that purpose."

Now tears were going down Sudie's face. "Wasn't that natural? He asked me, and I didn't know what else to do, or where to go, so I came! How was I to know I'd find him m-married when I got here?"

"You couldn't have known."

"Well?"

"So it becomes our responsibility, mine and Jerd's, to help you get established."

"Oh, I know I'm a bother, ma'am! And I've tried so hard to be a h-help, truly I have! Do you think it's k-kind for you to harp on gettin' rid of me?"

"Crying won't solve things, Sudie."

"Oh, why're you so m-mean? I want Jerd!"

"He has no plan for you. I have."

The tears stopped. The last ones trailed down Sudie's cheeks as she stared at Devora, fear rising in her eyes. Her lips quivered, and she asked, "D-don't you think I want to be safe and taken care of? That I'd do somethin', if I had the least idea what?"

"I have three suggestions."

"You, ma'am? How could you, possibly, for me?"

"You can marry Piepmeier."

"Never! I'd die first!"

"You can go home to North Carolina."

The fear deepened. "I've got no money."

"I have. Money of my own, to do with as I like."

"What do you mean?"

"If you want to go home, I'll give it to you. Or is there some reason you can't go back?"

Sudie gave her head the suggestion of a toss. Her voice was breathless as she cried, "I never heard of such a perfectly silly idea! I'll never go back there, you can't make me, nobody can!" But the fear was still in her eyes, along with her defiance.

"I don't mean to force you into anything, Sudie. I'm trying to help. If you don't like my other suggestions, you can go to St. Louis."

"Whatever for?"

"To live."

"And what would I live on?"

"My money would keep you until you could get established at something. You might teach music, for instance. I'm sure Jerd would be willing for you to take the Spinnet. My brother would be the first to enroll his young daughters."

Sudie's eyes were burning. "I couldn't possibly make my own livin'! I ain't strong enough, and I wasn't brought up to work!"

"You wouldn't even have to work, Sudie. There's a Mrs. Dyer in St. Louis, Nettie Dyer. She has a lovely home. If I send a letter with you, she'll give you a room and your meals, and you can live with her a long while on the amount of money I have. She'd make you a splendid chaperon. She knows all the best families, and she'd see that you met them and went to their parties. Four of her daughters have made good marriages, and the last one is engaged to a well-to-do young man."

"What are you hintin' at, ma'am?"

"I'm only being practical, Sudie. The natural thing for a young and lovely widow like yourself is a second marriage. There are several eligible and quite wealthy men in St. Louis. Men who would jump at the chance to marry a beautiful girl like you, who would love you deeply and give you every luxury you could dream up."

"Now you're tryin' to sell me off!"

"Trying to help you find a good life, Sudie."

"Same thing!"

"I should think living in the village, going to parties, having new clothes and friends . . ."

"No!"

". . . would appeal to you more than living in a cabin, this one for instance, rarely seeing even your neighbors, and doing your own work."

"Well, it don't!"

"Why doesn't it, Sudie?"

"Because!"

Devora studied the pretty, defiant face, trying to understand the girl's rejection of an easy life in the village. Could it be love of Jerd, she wondered, then discarded the thought. Sudie loved no one but herself, now that her twin was gone.

"I won't do any of your silly things," Sudie taunted. "What do you say to that?"

"Only that you'll want a life of your own."

"Pooh!"

"I know you're in a bad position, Sudie. But consider my suggestions. Think about them carefully. I truly believe that the next time Piepmeier comes, which will be as soon as he learns about . . . Frank, you'll want him to take you to St. Louis, to Nettie Dyer."

Sudie looked vaguely frightened. "Why, I don't know what to think of you, ma'am," she said. "What ails you? I thought you were kind and sweet. I thought you liked me!"

"I recognize your . . . appeal, Sudie."

"I thought you were willin' for me to stay here, to live with you, and help raise my very own twin's very own . . . 'specially now, 'cause there's only Lill, and she's same's my own! I thought—"

"You were wrong."

"But why, ma'am, why? Don't I help, don't I work, don't I earn my—"

"No cabin is big enough for two mistresses, Sudie. No wife is willing to share her husband with another woman."

Sudie jumped to her feet. "I'll tell Jerd on you!" she cried. "Talkin' to me so sweet and sneakin'! I'll tell him how you're treatin' me, his own wife's twin!" She stood glaring at Devora. Suddenly she caught her breath, her eyes cooled, and she said, deliberately, "Yes, indeed. I'll tell him, and if that don't work, we'll see. You big country woman, you, we'll see."

She started for the door, and when she was halfway across the room, it swung open and Jerd entered, carrying an armload of wood. She came to a full stop, and burst into tears. He regarded her, went to the wood box, and dumped his wood.

She followed him, weeping aloud.

He turned and looked at her, absently brushing at the front of his coat. He moved his eyes to Devora, who met them in silence, then to Sudie again and asked, "What's going on here?"

"Oh, Jerd!" Sudie wept, her voice shaking. "She wants to get rid of me!"

"Who does?"

She whirled, pointed at Devora, whirled back.

"You've made a mistake," he said.

"She's goin' to turn me out!"

"Devora ain't like that."

"She says I've got to marry Juney, and I'd rather d-die! Or else I've got to do some other awful thing, and if I d-don't, she's goin' to turn me out!"

She dropped her face into her hands and stood before him, swept by tears, small and lost and defenseless. Her weeping was the only sound, soft and choking and pretty, like everything about her was pretty.

Jerd stared at Devora.

Devora waited.

Sudie spun, ran to the door, still crying aloud, tugged it open, and was gone. Her weeping was still faintly audible until Jerd closed the door.

He returned to the hearth and stood in front of Devora. "What happened between you two?" he asked.

"Won't you at least take off your coat before we talk, Jerd?"

Silently he removed his wraps and hung them up, silently lowered himself into his chair, which Sudie had so recently occupied. "Now," he said, "tell me."

"We've all known," Devora said carefully, "that since the day Piepmeier brought her here, Sudie has been in an uncomfortable position."

Jerd nodded.

"She's a widow, penniless, and with no one to turn to, apparently, except us."

"I reckon that's right."

"Yet she must have a life of her own, a secure future."

"Yes . . . yes, she must."

"I've been thinking about it a great deal, and I came up with three possible courses of action. I'd just suggested them to her when you walked in."

"Piepmeier was one?"

"Yes."

"She don't want him."

"She appeared to like him at first."

"I won't try to push her into no marrying," Jerd said. "She's got to love a man first. Besides, it's too soon after she's a widow."

"It wasn't too soon for her to come out here with the intention of marrying you."

"Like you just said, she had to turn to somebody, and I was her sister's man. The babes was like her own. Could be the man one twin'd marry, the other one might too, just natural like."

"Next, when she wouldn't even discuss Piepmeier, I offered to send her back to North Carolina with that money my father left me."

"She's scared of going back there."

"Why?"

"I don't know. But she shows her fright the same way Sarie done when she'd be scared of something, and that's how I can tell."

"Then I offered to pay her keep in St. Louis until she could support herself, perhaps teaching music."

"You ain't obliged to use your money, Devora."

"It's fair enough that I should. She came here and found me in what she thought was to be her place. She's welcome to the money."

"About her supporting herself—she ain't real strong."

"Last, I explained she could live with Nettie Dyer in St. Louis a long time on this money. She'd meet people, and go to parties; she'd be married in no time."

Jerd leaned forward, incredulous. "You want her out of here, don't you?" he asked.

"Wouldn't any woman?"

"How long did you live in your brother's home?"

"From the time he established one, and before that."

"Did his wife ever try to get you out?"

"Of course not."

"What was your position?"

"Sister . . . aunt."

"Ain't that what Sudie is here?"

"Oh, Jerd!" Devora cried. "I was sister to the husband, not the dead wife, the twin-wife!"

"Did you tell Sudie you'd put her out if she don't do what you say?"

"No. I told her— Oh, I suppose I did virtually say that."

He stared at her, and she could see hurt come into his dark eyes, spread and grow. He said, "That would be turning a helpless girl—Devora, for God's sake, what woman are you?"

She felt desperate anger take her, heard herself flinging words into his pulsing hurt. "That's what I asked you once: 'What man are you?' Remember, Jerd? It was right after I'd killed the Osage, or you'd killed him, or we'd done it together. Not that it mattered—we had to do it to save our lives. Now, with Sudie a living ghost between us, we've got to save our marriage. What do you want her here for anyhow—a third wife?"

His eyes were cold. He rose heavily from his chair. "She's got nowhere to go, no person to turn to," he said. "What can she do but stay? Stay until she can make up her mind, and leave of her own will. It wouldn't be right to drive a stray dog off like you want to do her."

She met his eyes fiercely. "This is the same," she said, "as the Indian."

He took his wraps and his rifle, went to the door. "I'm going hunting," he said, "and I don't know when I'll be back," and was gone.

~ _Chapter Twenty-One_ ~

Devora sat alone all evening, tending the fire. The food left from noon still hung in cookpots; Jerd's place at table was the only one laid. Big Tom dozed on the hearth, his whiskers twitching.

Sudie had not reappeared for food, nor had Devora offered her a tray. Disturbed over Jerd, she herself had eaten nothing. It was him she was concerned about, stalking through the dark timber with only his rifle for protection and his dog for company, driven from his home by the women in it.

She glanced once more at the clock, and the hour was ten. Perhaps he had already returned, and was even now sleeping in the barn, his great body thrust warmly into the clean, loose hay. Or was he lying somewhere in the forest, an arrow in his heart, his scalped head in a puddle of freezing blood?

She went onto the dogtrot and stood, anxiously looking and listening. The night was starred and cold and empty. She shivered, turned into the kitchen, and was about to close the door when she heard a quick, shrill bark not too far away, and recognized it as Spot's homecoming signal.

She hurried back outside, her breath short. The dog barked again, a fast, happy staccato, ending in an excited yip. He came at her from the direction of the timber, a hurtling white splotch, and suddenly he was upon her, jumping and yipping and whining and beating his tail. She laughed, squatted, put her arms around him and hugged his wriggling body, turning her face aside to protect her mouth from his warm, eager tongue.

She sensed Jerd's approach even though she couldn't hear his moccasined feet, and was standing erect, one hand resting on Spot's head, when he stepped onto the dogtrot. She said, her heart going fast with the knowledge that he was safe, "Welcome home. Your supper's ready."

He passed her without reply and went inside. She followed, meaning to dish up his food at once, but he went on across the kitchen, flung down his pallet, undressed, and settled himself, without speaking.

Devora sank upon the bunk and stared at his back, thinking how wide and solid and forbidding it was. Finally, after the clock struck eleven and Sudie did not appear, she barred the door and went to bed, but not immediately to sleep.

This was the first night since she had refused him that it had been possible for Jerd to come to her. Only, he was unaware that Sudie was not just beyond that open bedroom door. If he knew, or if she were to go to him now, on the pallet, and confess her regret over denying him, would he draw her into his arms and take her as he had taken her before, in need and love and with promise?

She sighed, turned her head wearily on the pillow. She could not seek him in that manner a second time. When he returned to her bed, if ever he did, it must be of his own volition. She moved her head again and wished to weep as she had done before, longed to weep for Frank, lonely on his hilltop, and could not.

She woke early, and after Jerd had gone outside, dressed quickly, feeling rested and confident.

It'll work out, she thought, braiding her hair, watching flames build around the wood Jerd had put on the coals. Sudie will choose St. Louis, I'm sure she will . . . it just isn't possible she'd actually decide against it. She's restless now . . . that will get worse, and she'll be happy to live in a villlage where there are men, lots of them, to flirt with and have a fine time. Which means she'll go of her own accord, and I won't have to quarrel with Jerd over her again.

Jerd, as was usual after a period of solitude, was quite himself at breakfast, which they ate alone before daylight. He spoke of his work plans for the day, and she spoke of hers.

It wasn't until he was ready to leave to run his traps that Sudie was mentioned. He paused at the door, his hand on the latch, and turned.

"About Sudie," he said, "what I said yesterday holds."

He opened the door, closed it, and was gone.

Hands steady, she began to clear the table, leaving Sudie's place set. No matter what quarrel it caused, Sudie must go.

And soon.

She was dressing Lill when the girl came trailing in. Their eyes met and Devora said, "Good morning," but Sudie merely jerked her chin and went about her own affairs. She filled a bowl with mush, poured herself a mug of tea, and sat at the table eating slowly, behaving as if she were alone in the room.

Later, she made a busy stir about washing her bowl, spoon, and mug and putting them away. Afterward she came to Devora's chair, bent toward the baby, and held out her arms, smiling and dimpling.

"Come, darlin', Sudie's precious girl-baby," she cooed. "Come to your very own Sudie, darlin'."

Lill stared, her lips quivered, tucked up into a smile, and she lifted her hands, and Sudie swung her into her arms and danced around the room, laughing aloud.

Presently she established herself in Jerd's fireside chair and looked straight at Devora. "Hand me that shawl, will you, ma'am?" she asked. "The one you just dropped off your lap. I want to keep my baby nice and warmy-warm, so's she won't get sick like her poor little brother."

Devora tossed her the shawl, and took up her darning.

Sudie made a fuss about covering Lill, and began to rock her in her arms and croon one of the gay things she played frequently on the Spinnet. While she sang, she patted Lill's cheek, ran a finger into her curls, kissed her eyebrows, and kept glancing prettily at Devora.

"See?" she asked at last, breaking off her song. "She does so love her Sudie, the precious girl-baby! She'd miss her somethin' fierce if she was to leave her."

Devora's heart began to pound. She wove her needle in and out of a small hole in one of Jerd's stockings, pulled her thread through, wove again.

"Where's Jerd, ma'am?"

"Running his traps."

"Pshaw. That means all day, don't it?"

"Not necessarily."

Devora wove, pulled, wove.

"I aim to apologize for upsettin' him so. I'm goin' to tell him how it was, the conversation you and I had in this room, and all. I want to make him understand why you spoke to me like you did, and made me cry. So's he won't be put out with you, ma'am."

"He understands perfectly."

"But ma'am, how could he? When it's because this poor, innocent baby's a burden to you?"

"Oh Sudie, that's nonsense."

"But she is, ma'am, whether you realize it or not! I've been thinkin' and thinkin', and I know! That's why you sent her off with strangers!"

"Mahala and Prosper are hardly strangers to her."

"Well, anyhow. I'm goin' to explain to Jerd how the whole thing's my fault. And I'm goin' to take all the care of this darlin' baby from this minute on. Then Jerd'll see—you won't be near so cross, ma'am."

Devora let her darning fall into her lap and gazed at Sudie in unwilling admiration. In spite of herself, she smiled briefly.

"See, ma'am?" Sudie cried happily. "Ain't I right, though? Really, you've got to be careful . . . behavin' like you did yesterday! 'Cause if you keep that up, Jerd'll get the notion you're jealous. Of poor little me. He knows how all the girls back in New Bern were jealous of Sarie, and he saw for himself they didn't have any reason to be! She couldn't help it if she was so sweet and darlin' that all the men just worshiped her, could she, ma'am?"

Devora plied her needle again, and though her fingers were unsteady, her voice was quite even. "While you were doing your thinking, Sudie," she said, "did you include dresses and bonnets and pelisses in your thoughts? Did it occur to you how charming—and adorable—you'll look in the various costumes, yours and Sarie's—when you meet all the new, exciting men you'll find when you leave here to go to—St. Louis, for instance?"

Deliberately she lifted her look to Sudie's, which showed fear. She felt her own eyes harden, grow cold and demand; she saw Sudie's lose the fear, blaze, and refuse.

They sat across the hearth from each other, Devora's work neglected in her hands, Lill forgotten in Sudie's arms. The fire snapped, the clock stroked off its seconds, and their eyes fought.

A furious barking set up, a faint hallooing came to them, grew louder, and a clattering of hooves mixed into the other noises. Still their eyes battled.

The hallooing became a shouting.

Devora laid aside her darning, walked to the door and out, looked toward the barnlot, called a welcome, returned to the kitchen.

"It's Piepmeier," she said. "You'll have only to say the word, and he'll do anything you want, whether he wants it or not. I'll see to it that you have the opportunity to say it."

Sudie put her shoulder toward Devora, held Lill closer and went on singing again, as if nothing had taken place. Devora, her legs suddenly weak, began to mix a double batch of corn bread to help fill the perpetually hungry Piepmeier.

It's starting, she thought, moving her hands with deliberation to avoid spilling the meal and salt and milk. This is it, the time of decision. It's possible she'll go. If only Jerd gets back after dark, if only she decides to go at once, and has her clothes packed before he gets here. If . . . if . . .

Glancing at Sudie's yellow head bent so tenderly over the drowsy baby, her ears filled with the pretty singing, she wondered at herself. Why, she thought, I'm wicked, really wicked. I've killed a man, and now I'm plotting against Sudie, who is afraid of some unexplained thing. Yet I won't stop, can't stop.

She felt cold air and looked up. Piepmeier was coming in, eyes on Sudie. After the door thudded to, he kept standing, uncertain.

"How is she?" he asked at last. "I would of broke my neck to be here with her, but I was way yonder ahunting. When I heer'd about the little feller, I rid all night, got here fast as I could. Didn't stop but at the Pikes', where I et breakfast."

"Take off your things," Devora said. "Sit at the fire with Sudie and thaw out. You've had a long, cold ride."

He nodded, gulped, swallowed, still watching Sudie's back. In noisy silence he removed his wraps, hung them up, and sat down in Devora's fireside chair, joints popping.

Sudie glanced at him coolly, still crooning to the baby, her cheek against the small head. Piepmeier cleared his throat, tried to speak, failed, and sat tensely in the big chair, his knees spread, his moccasined feet sprawled on their sides.

Devora began to make a deliberate clatter at her work. Presently she could hear them talking, Sudie in plaintive murmurs, Piepmeier in a comforting, low rumble. What they were saying, she could not hear, nor did she want to, not until the moment Sudie announced her impending departure.

She put her dinner beans on to simmer as Sudie laid Lill in her bed. She buttoned on her pelisse and tied a shawl over her head as Sudie began chattering animatedly to the bemused Piepmeier.

To give them privacy, she headed for the barnlot, where she puttered at unnecessary chores to fill her time. She scattered grain for the hens, carried water to the already filled troughs, forked hay into mangers, searched for eggs, and found none.

When she could think of nothing more to do, she sat on a three-legged stool Jerd used for milking, and waited. She breathed the clean hay and cow smells of the barn. After a while her toes grew cold, and then her fingers, but she didn't move.

She must allow Sudie all the time she needed in which to handle Piepmeier.

And if she doesn't make him take her to St. Louis? she asked herself bluntly. If Jerd is right, and she's terribly afraid . . . too afraid to go even there . . . what then?

At last, filled with anxiety, she returned to the cabin and pushed open the door. Music flowed over her on the warmth of the kitchen. Sudie was at the Spinnet, playing and singing; Piepmeier, all knees and elbows, sat the edge of his chair, eyes on Sudie, lips hanging apart.

Devora's hopes plunged. Nothing had been settled. Sudie was too busy with her little flirting ways, and Piepmeier too abjectly adoring for anything of importance to have transpired between them.

Quietly, she took off her wraps and began to work. If either of them noticed her as she moved about, there was no indication.

Abruptly Sudie turned away from the Spinnet, slanted her eyes provocatively at Piepmeier, and asked, "Wouldn't you like to take me for a nice walk, Juney?"

"Why, effen it hain't too cold for a little thing like you," he grinned, "it'd pleasure me fierce!"

"Then hold my pelisse for me. No, you silly, that's wrongside out! There . . . that's the way! Now, give me my bonnet . . . careful of the ribbons. Thank you, Juney, you're simply precious!"

She tied the blue ribbons in a bow at one side of her face, dimpled enchantingly, and waited. He grabbed his coat, somehow got the door unlatched, and stood aside. She went dancing out ahead of him.

Devora closed the door, which he left standing open. Her breath trembled. She hurried to the window and looked out. Piepmeier was opening the gate for Sudie, hovering over her in his thin, gangling eagerness, foolish and pitiable and somehow touching. She dropped the curtain, ashamed of spying on him, and wandered aimlessly about the room, caught in the suspense of waiting to learn the outcome of their walk.

She chose a book from the mantel and began to read. At first the phrases held no meaning, but presently they fell into sentences and thoughts, and she filled her time with them, although not once did she forget the two walking under the far-up sun, or what they might or might not be saying.

The wind whipped suddenly around the corner of the cabin; it rattled the shingles, whined at the window. She let her book fall shut, and returned it to its place with the others. She poked up the fire, added wood, tucked in Lill's covers, thinking of Frank, missing him.

Taking her bucket to the dogtrot barrel for water, she found that the wind carried a piercing coldness, and looked in the direction in which Sudie and Piepmeier had gone to see if the change in temperature had started them homeward. They were running toward the cabin, Sudie as light and graceful as a leaf borne on the wind, Piepmeier loping and ungainly.

They burst into the kitchen on a wave of cold, Sudie laughing, Piepmeier happier-faced than Devora had ever seen him. Sick at heart, she set her bucket on the workshelf, and began to fill her kettle from it.

Nothing was decided, for had Sudie convinced Piepmeier that he must take her to St. Louis and leave her there, he would not now be lumbering about the room like a happy colt, taking her pelisse and handling her bonnet as if it were a beribboned egg.

Unless, Devora thought abruptly, she's led him to think she'll marry him when they get there. She searched his face. She couldn't stand by and watch his futile bliss and not try to save him from heartbreak. Yet, study him as she might, she could determine nothing.

To keep occupied, she got out the churn, poured the accumulated cream into it, and began to work the dasher. Sudie and Piepmeier settled into the fireside chairs, the girl holding Lill, being sad and gay by turns, the young man venturing a comforting word or grinning helplessly, according to Sudie's mood.

Jerd got home before noon, and Piepmeier went out to the barnlot with him. Sudie murmured an excuse, and with a sly look at Devora, slipped away to her room.

She can still go, Devora thought. Piepmeier won't leave before morning, at the soonest. There's still a chance.

Sudie did not make her appearance until the food was on the table and the tea poured. Devora had just set the teapot back on its hearth trivet and was crossing to the workshelf, when she saw the door swing inward. Sudie entered softly, closed the door noiselessly and stood, hands clasped at her bosom, her attention on the men, who were talking at the fire and did not see her.

She was dressed all in white, and wore a white ribbon tied around her head in such a manner that it held the array of curls in place. The only color about her, aside from her hair, was the blue of her eyes and the pink of her wistful lips. She looked, Devora thought, like a bride or an angel.

Lingeringly, Sudie ran her gaze around the room, caressing everything it touched until it came to Devora, at which time it grew less soft, slid away, and centered on the table.

As soon as Devora reached the workshelf, Sudie joined her there, making her usual pretty fuss about being a help. She said, loudly enough for the men at the fireplace to hear, "Let me cut that pan of corn bread for you, ma'am, and put it on the table." She went on, in a cold little murmur for Devora's ears alone as she hacked at the hot bread, "I've decided somethin' that'll interest you."

"You have?" Devora asked, instantly hopeful.

"Somethin' about those talks you insisted on havin' . . . talks I didn't want."

"Yes, Sudie?"

"About your plans for me that I didn't like."

"Go on."

"And still don't like."

"But if you've decided—?"

Sudie flashed her an odd little smile. She piled the uneven squares of corn bread on a trencher and lifted it in both hands. "I've thought your plans through since yesterday," she said, "all of 'em. And there's just the one thing left for me to do."

"Yes?"

"You'll know what it is . . . you'll find out pretty soon," Sudie said. "I'm just tellin' you now, ahead of time, that I can take care of myself."

She spun, made for the table, set the bread on it, and began to rearrange things minutely, her hands fluttering gracefully among the trenchers and mugs.

Swept by a premonition of trouble, Devora thought, Careful . . . careful.

"Come to supper," she heard her own voice say on an outpouring of breath, watched the men approach, heard their words, but could not distinguish them, heard Sudie's laugh, sweetly childlike.

She picked up Lill, walked to the table, sat down. She drew a slow breath, another, and another. She spooned mashed potatoes onto her trencher, made a pool of gravy in their center, and began to feed the baby, one small bite at a time.

Her thoughts were going wild with speculation about Sudie. She kept trying to force them into calmness.

Piepmeier guffawed, and she knew that Sudie was exercising her charm. She offered Lill another bit of potato, watched her eager little mouth open for it, listened to the red lips smack.

She became aware that Piepmeier and Sudie were looking at her in a waiting silence, and gazed blankly back. It was Sudie who said, finally, "Didn't you hear me, ma'am? Juney's thought up the sweetest, darlin'est things! He's goin' to take me berryin' in the spring, and boatin' in the summer, and gatherin' nuts in the fall! He's goin' to visit us real often, and see I have fun the year 'round! What do you think of that?"

She sat motionless, unable to say a word. Sudie had made no decision after all, at least not one that would change things. She had simply announced that she was going to stay here, in this cabin, as long as she pleased.

Devora looked first at Piepmeier, who was beaming upon Sudie, sure of his right to court her. She looked at Sudie, whose blue eyes were fixed on her, and while their eyes met, Sudie's lips moved, and slowly, enchantingly, she smiled. The tiny pulse beating in the hollow of her throat was the only sign of her nervousness.

She looked last at Jerd, who had not even put food on his trencher, but had stared unblinkingly at Sudie from the moment he sat down.

"Well, ma'am," asked Sudie, "what's your opinion?"

"Our lives are our own," Devora said numbly, "which gives us all the privilege of living them . . . or trying to . . . any way we choose."

Sudie dimpled, made a little sitting bow. "Thank you, ma'am," she smiled. "Thank you kindly!"

"I sure appreciate it myself," Piepmeier said awkwardly, his face turning red at his own words. "Now that you've give your blessing, so to speak, you'll likely have me underfoot more'n ever."

"Sudie," Jerd said, his quiet word like a blow.

Sudie's eyes slid to his, dropped. The pulse at her throat jerked.

Piepmeier, caught by Jerd's tone, glanced curiously from him to Sudie. The grin that had been splitting his face dropped away.

"Eat, Sudie," Jerd said.

Eyes on her trencher, Sudie broke off a crumb of corn bread and tucked it into her mouth.

"Drink," Jerd said.

He gave her mug a shove, as if to move it closer. The push sent it over, spilling its contents along the table.

"Sorry, Devora," he said, watching Sudie.

Devora tried to smile reassuringly, even though she knew he would not see. She put Lill down and stood, glimpsing the bewilderment on Piepmeier and the fear on Sudie. After she had mopped the table and refilled the mug, Jerd lifted the one from beside her trencher and set it before Sudie.

"Your tea," he said.

Devora put the refilled mug at her own place, and sank into her chair, suddenly trembling. She looked at Jerd, and a pang went through her at the harshness and implacability in the lines of his great body, and on his face. She took Lill on her lap again, and stiffened her jaw to stop its quivering, and waited.

"Drink your tea, Sudie," Jerd said.

Sudie looked everywhere, nowhere. "I . . . really don't care for it," she whispered.

"Why not?"

"I d-don't know."

He reached over, took the mug. "Then I'll drink it."

Sudie's eyes came flying up, and they were wide and blue and wild. The pulse in her throat was pounding visibly, and she screamed, "No . . . no . . . don't drink it, don't drink it!"

"Why not?" Jerd asked, and he still had never moved his merciless, dark stare from her. When she did not answer, he asked, "What was in that little white paper . . . what was it I seen you dump into Devora's tea, Sudie?"

Her hands gripped each other, pressed into her breasts. Her lips went pale, and they said, "Nothing . . . not a thing."

"It was poison . . . wasn't it?"

She cried softly, "Oh, how can you s-say such a thing? Poor Sarie, poor darlin' . . . she's lucky to be dead, to get away from such a m-mean man!"

Piepmeier's eyes were bulging.

Devora's breath was dry and hurting.

She saw Jerd's face change. It took on contempt.

"The same poison you used on your husband," he said flatly. "That you put in his glass of wine."

"You can't prove it, you can't prove it . . . it ain't true!" Sudie screamed.

Jerd set the mug on the table. "This right here is proof for me," he said, "and I reckon it'd be proof for them in Wilmington. Either you get out of this cabin now, today, of your own will, or I'll let them know where you are."

Sudie turned frantically to Piepmeier. "Juney . . . you don't believe him! Do you, Juney . . . do you?"

The confusion on his face gave way to doubt.

"I don't know," he said slowly. "So much so quick. But there's one sure-Gawd way you can show he ain't right."

"How, Juney . . . how? I'll do anything . . . anything!"

He picked up the mug and held it toward her.

"Drink. Even one swaller."

Her face pallid, she flounced off her bench and snatched the mug. Part of the tea sloshed over the table and down the skirt of her dress. Whimpering, she ran to the fireplace, dashed the remaining liquid into the flames, hurled the mug after it, and came running back to Piepmeier, who had risen.

She flung herself against him. "I can't s-stand for you to talk like that," she sobbed, tears sliding down her face. "Love don't need proof, Juney . . . you know that! And I'm goin' to marry you, like you been beggin' for . . . ain't that enough to show we love each other . . . ain't it?"

He stood with his fists hanging at his sides. "It don't smell good to me, not none of it."

"Juney . . . Juney darlin'," Sudie cried, fastening her arms around his neck. "You've got to marry me and take me away from these awful people . . . g-got to!"

Piepmeier loosened her arms, stood her away, and looked over her head at Jerd. There was sadness in his eyes. "I'll ride her to St. Louis effen you want," he said tonelessly.

"Thanks." Jerd stood up. "Go pack, Sudie. You leave in an hour."

She whirled to him in tearful dismay. "I c-couldn't, not possibly! It'd take . . . oh . . . days!"

"Pack what you can," Jerd said. "It's that or go now with nothing."

She stared up at him, and her tears dried away. Her lips trembled so she could barely shape words.

"B-but what'll I do in St. Louis?"

"You'll make out."

"What'll I do for money?"

Devora put Lill down, got to her shaking legs, and started for the chest beside the fireplace. All this seemed to be happening so fast she could not comprehend it.

"I told you I'd give you enough to live on for a while, Sudie," she said unsteadily. "You're still welcome to it."

Jerd stepped forward, laid his hand on her arm, stopped her. She looked into his dark eyes, and they gentled for her, and he said, with a softness touching the rough quiet of his voice, "No. This is my chore."

She stood where she was, in the center of the room, and watched him go to the chest and hunt out his kerchief of money. He untied the corners, removed four dollars, dropped them loose into the chest, retied the kerchief, and put it into Sudie's outstretched hands.

"Sixteen dollars," he told her. Then, to Piepmeier, "I'd be obliged if you'd help with her plunder. Take grub along from the cellar."

Piepmeier nodded, and opened the dogtrot door. Sudie spun about and whisked through it. Piepmeier followed; the door thudded shut.

Devora felt her breath shake.

Jerd picked up Lill, who was toddling dangerously near the fire, and deposited her in bed. He turned to Devora, looked at her deeply, and said, "You was right about Sudie. We never ought to of took her in."

Words were beating in Devora, pushing onto her tongue, but she could only stand, trembling, and witness the miracle.

Jerd's voice continued, low and rough and sure. "No wonder she come running to the wilderness. She'd killed a man, and she was scared and wanted to hide. So, when you tried to make her leave, she felt so pushed she schemed to get you outen her way so she'd be safe." He paused, and when he went on, his voice had hoarsened. "She might of killed you . . . if I hadn't looked up."

"Jerd," Devora said. "Jerd, you needn't—"

"No, I've got this to say, once and for all. I begun to get my eyes open the day Sudie come here. It was seeing her in the same room with you. Her so pretty and even sweetlike when it suited, but spoiled and flirty and certain-sure to get her own way. Then—you. Quiet and proud-standing and a lady, yet so warm and full of being a woman. I knowed afore she come that I loved you . . . that I'd never dreamt what real love was . . . I know it now. But I was took in and sorry for her, the mess went on—"

"Jerd, you needn't tell me these things."

He half-lifted one big hand, and she fell silent.

"The day the babe died."

"Yesterday, Jerd."

Surprised realization showed on his face. "Yesterday," he repeated. "Prosper was in his barn when I took the word. Mahala was in the cabin, and she didn't hear what he told me about . . . her . . . Sarie, that is. Or how he figures he's the pappy of the babes on account of how much Lill takes after him . . . more every day."

"But why, Jerd? Why would Prosper confess a thing like that?"

"It goes hard for a man to lose his only son," Jerd said. "Particular, if he can't never have another one."

"But to tell you—you, of all people! When he must have known you might kill him for it!"

"Oh, the bile come up in me. I hankered to bust his head for him. But Lill does take after him . . . I seen it myself, not knowing. I wasn't surprised, when it come down to it, to find out what kind Sarie was. It hit me, standing in Prosper's barn, how she'd sure liked her men. And there was Sudie . . . likely it was men behind her trouble with her husband. And there was you . . . different from them."

"Mahala will see that resemblance between Lill and Prosper someday,"

Devora said softly. "And when she does, it will break her heart . . . and heal it again."

"We can work it for Lill to stay with them a lot," Jerd said. "We'll be raising our own family, and they can't have no other."

Her heartbeat began to surge, and she could no longer speak, but she smiled upon him, so ugly-handsome with his unruly, faded hair, and her lips were not steady. She sought his eyes, and they were soft with amber lights, and his mouth had lost its harshness.

He smiled back at her, his face younger and rid of care, and though he did not touch her or even move to her, she was wrapped in love. They kept standing with their love and their smiling, and the jabber of the baby, the snap of the fire and the sound of the clock made a kind of music.

Piepmeier shouted from outside, and they went onto the dogtrot together. Piepmeier and Sudie, mounted double on his horse, were riding through the gate. The young man lifted his hand in farewell, but Sudie did not look back.

"He's learnt a lesson," Jerd said grimly, "without getting too bad hurt."

He put his arm around Devora.

They stood, watching.

She could feel the pump of his heart in her shoulder, along her body.

A great sigh shuddered through her. She leaned on him. She looked to the timber, where Piepmeier and Sudie were already passing through the first stripped growth. In the distance between, big, feathery snow was coming thinly down, the flakes touching the ground, brushing Devora's cheeks, coming faster now, onto Jerd's hair, one or two resting on his shoulders. She sighed again and stood with him under the falling snow.